SUBMERGING

BOOK THREE of *THE STARLIGHT CHRONICLES*

C. S. Johnson

1

C. S. JOHNSON

THE STARLIGHT CHRONICLES

Once more, for Sam. I look forward to the day when we truly see each other, face to face and heart to heart. Until then, I write for you as much as I write for myself.

I also want to dedicate this book to Eric. I have never forgotten the moment you, in seeing me lost in sadness and uncertainty, opened your heart to me and gave me comfort. The memory of it always comes to the front of my mind when I wonder if I have made any difference in the world. Thank you for making such a difference in mine.

Finally, I also owe this book in part to Andy. Many thanks for that small moment in the coffeehouse where we discussed sanctification; it gave me the clarity to see the cynicism in my heart was meant to be a precious thorn in my side.

THE STARLIGHT CHRONICLES

THE STARLIGHT CHRONICLES

☼1☼
Expectancy

The smile flew up onto my face the moment I woke up. It was a good day to be me.

Psh. *Every day* is a good day to be me, I thought with a grin.

"Ah." I sighed happily as I sat up in my bed and stretched. I felt happy as a teenager could be. (It was very temporary, I assure you.)

"Ugh … is it morning already?" The changeling dragon on my bed, Elysian—my self-proclaimed supernatural mentor—rolled over onto his scaly back, shielding his eyes from the brightness of the springtime sunlight peeking through my bedroom window. He groaned groggily, and I stifled back a laugh.

"Come on, Ely," I quipped, shooting myself out of bed as I pushed down my brown hair from its bed-head form. "Today's a good day."

"Whoa. Who are you, and what have you done with the real Hamilton Dinger?" Elysian asked, using his bat-like wings to prop himself up.

I glanced over at the scaly dragon on my bed. I knew what he was thinking. Me? In a good mood? It was as rare as petroleum companies going green (meaning it was only done when enough people were ticked off). But there was a good reason I was happy.

The month of April had arrived, and while it came with scholarly benchmarks and horrendous amounts of rain, it also brought a special gift: My birthday.

"My seventeenth birthday is almost here." I grinned as I started getting ready for the day. "That means I get to start harassing my friends for presents, and my parents for money and a party, and maybe a car this year."

"And you'll pester me to start considering you mature, I'll bet." Elysian groaned again, this time with annoyance rather than lethargy. "Ugh, this is terrible."

"Just let it go, would you?"

I lost my grin momentarily as I caught sight of the mess on my desk; I hadn't had a chance to finish my homework from English. *Oh well.*

The homework didn't matter to me anyway. It's not like it was an important class. Really everyone (important) knows English today. Who really cares about books when you have the Internet? And who really cares about school when Mrs. Night is teaching? Her class must've been set up as a charity for capacity-challenged teachers. (I have to stop myself here; if there is one thing that makes me angry, it is incompetency).

There were many, many more important things to think about anyway. I was two years away from graduating high school. I had a great girlfriend, a good, *paid* internship at the Mayor's office, and a college scholarship or two lined up, with at least one full-ride. And even with all of that, there was nothing I wanted more than just *more.*

And I was going to get it. After all, I was also something of a superhero, a Starlight Warrior known to the public as "Wingdinger," and every day I was growing more in strength, power, and speed. A slight bubble of happiness swelled within my heart at the sight of the blood red, four-point star on my wrist—the mark that branded me as a defender of Earth and solidified my calling.

6

Yes, I thought. Change was coming, and along with it, growth, respect, and understanding.

There was nothing I wanted more, and I was finally okay with admitting it to myself.

"Birthdays don't strike me as happy, so much as depressing or pointless," Elysian remarked, drawing me out of my thoughts.

"I'm not surprised you hate birthdays," I replied, wrinkling my nose. "You seem to dislike anything of supreme importance."

"Birthdays are not that important to me," Elysian explained, "because I don't have one. But even a lot of humans don't seem to like birthdays that much. Some people even find them depressing."

"Just the women, I think," I replied. "Either that or the unimportant people."

Elysian rolled his eyes. "What's the point of celebrating the anniversary of your birth? It's not like you did anything to deserve a party. Mothers do all the work."

"It's just a day that celebrates the awesomeness of a person—and since I'm so awesome, my party's going to be awesome. And I want a car, too."

"Yes, how wonderfully mature and humble you are," Elysian muttered sarcastically. "Why do you even want a car, anyway? If you really need to go somewhere, you can ride on my back."

"I can't just ride you to school or take Gwen out on a date on your back," I retorted. I hoped he wouldn't push anymore

7

on the subject. People don't make careers out of being superheroes—not really. What was I going to do when Elysian and I were no longer needed to take down the bad guys in Apollo City?

For good measure, I pretended to ignore the rest of my thoughts on the matter and focused on preparing for the day. "I'm supposed to meet Mikey and Gwen after work today, so I won't be home for a while."

"You have work? It's the weekend."

I rolled my eyes, irritated at Elysian. *He's supposed to be my mentor, but he doesn't even remember my schedule half the time. He's worse than my parents.*

While I'm not one for giving credit, I could at least admit my parents had proper excuses for not paying attention to me, much as it was still inexcusable. My parents, Mark and Cheryl, had their own jobs and my three-year-old brother, Adam, to look after. From what I could tell, Elysian only had to watch the news, slink around the city looking for our enemies, and ... Well, that was about it, actually. And apparently even some of that was not necessary, since more often than not the monsters managed to find me anyway.

"Yes, I have work now. Remember, Cheryl got me that part-time job at the Mayor's office?"

Some part of me figured Elysian just didn't like to recall it. My job with the Mayor's office did not impress him in the slightest; I still got ticked off with him as I thought about his reaction. He was upset that it could interfere with my so-called superhero duties.

I was, even though I'd never admit it to Elysian's face, starting to understand where he was coming from on the issue.

Last fall, a meteorite landed in the middle of my home, Apollo City, smashing up a bunch of buildings and leaving a massive hole in the ground. I considered this an excellent symbol for what its arrival meant for my life.

It wasn't long after the meteorite struck that things started happening. Elysian had shown up, along with my previously-unknown superpowers. Elysian tried to convince me of my destiny to be a fallen Star, something he called an *Astroneshama* (in "Star language," no less), and to use my abilities to fight off the other new arrivals to the city, the villainous Seven Deadly Sinisters, and their leader, Orpheus.

Somehow, I'd gone from all-around all-star high school student, top athlete, and class genius (not to mention charmingly irresistible and good-looking), Hamilton Dinger, to Wingdinger, the superhero of Apollo City, who was half-loved, half-hated, fully determined, and slightly irritated—a fallen Star on a mission to destroy evil and save the world (also still charmingly irresistible and good-looking).

It was a classic case of boy meets destiny. Or something like that, anyway.

Elysian rolled over and nuzzled into my now-empty bed, looking like a scaly dog of sorts as he wriggled around. I was half-tempted to rub his belly as a joke, but before I could, he snarled, "Oh, is that the job where you more or less file stuff for three to four hours a couple of times a week?"

"Shut up." I swatted at him. He dodged my blow and catapulted himself to the window, where he settled down like a huge lizard-cat.

"It's raining today," Elysian murmured as he glanced out the window to see the thunderclouds.

"It'll stop by the time I'm out of work." I shrugged it off easily enough.

"Would be a good day for our enemies to attack, too," Elysian observed.

"Seriously? What stops them from attacking any other day?" *What did rain have to do with anything?* "Wasn't it just once? I could think of tons of different attacks that didn't affect the weather."

"I guess you're right."

Of course I'm right.

"You might as well stop worrying about it." I grabbed the last of my English homework and stuffed it into the small briefcase I used for work. Glorified file boy or not, I was still getting paid good money and gaining good experience in the government sector; I was also largely unsupervised, so getting the rest of my English homework done wouldn't be a problem. "You might jinx us or something."

"I don't believe in jinxes."

"Good for you."

"I believe in being prepared–"

"Yeah, sure. You know, you worry too much."

"I wouldn't worry so much if you were more serious about this."

"I don't have to be serious about this," I argued, pulling on my shoes. "The bad guys have been really slacking off in the last couple of months. Ever since that sword was given to me—"

"Even though you haven't learned to use it properly—"

"—there haven't been that many attacks. Maybe they've given up—"

"Or maybe they're just biding their time—"

"—and have realized that they can't beat us—"

"Us? You mean you're sharing the credit all of a sudden?"

"Huh?" I looked up, a bit surprised. I'd gotten used to the broken, fragmented arguments between Elysian and myself, but it was always jarring to hear a completely different subject thrown into my train of thought (not to mention one I didn't particularly appreciate).

Elysian smirked. "You mean that you did that unintentionally? Goodness, what is the world coming to?" He giggled into his claws.

I frowned. I hated to be mocked—particularly by someone who wasn't supposed to be real. I was just about to say something (something especially vile, no doubt) when Elysian sighed, quickly losing the joking demeanor.

"I suppose," he said, "Starry Knight and SWORD have both helped us quite a bit lately."

Heat flushed through my face and I turned to the side, hiding my gaze at the mention of Starry Knight, my mysterious, most-of-the-time ally. "I don't think it matters that much," I muttered.

I knew I was lying, but there was nothing else I could do. Why Starry Knight was helping us, who she really was, and why did it matter at all were questions I desperately wanted to know the answers to myself; I could empathize with Elysian in this matter. But unlike him, from the small conversations and the time I'd spent with her, I knew it was going to take a lot of work and patience before she trusted me enough to give me answers.

"You never seem to think much at all where Starry Knight is concerned," Elysian huffed. "Why do you think SWORD is helping us?"

SWORD, the Special World Operations and Research Division, was a secret agency, from what I could tell, investigating the world of the paranormal and supernatural, and possibly the extraterrestrial. The reality that such a task force existed would not have bothered me at all if my best friend's estranged, runaway dad didn't happen to be in charge of the case file with my name on it.

"Well, Mikey's dad told us that SWORD came in to more or less gain control of the situation," I recalled, thinking of the one time they had captured me and Starry Knight. "And they've been doing a lot of clean-up work." I wrinkled my nose. "Chatty Patty, that obsessive anchorwoman for the city's cable news network, has less to report lately than I know she'd like."

Patricia Rookwood had her spies popping up closer to the battlefields lately, but SWORD agents had been getting good at turning several away. Ratings for her show have been down lately, too, I recalled. Ever since my last big standoff with Orpheus and the Sinisters, actually. The event had been hailed from the press as a severe "gas leak" that caused "hallucinations" in the central northern district of the city.

Thinking of that battle in particular, I glanced at the small, crystalline orb on my desk. I'd told my parents, and the maids as needed, that it was a paperweight. But that wasn't the full truth; it was actually the remnant of a Sinister, Meropae, I'd sealed away with my own sword a few months ago. (I did use it as a paperweight sometimes, though.)

It was almost proof I was capable of holding off the Sinisters on my own, without anyone else's help.

It was also an irritating memory, because the other Sinister I'd managed to seal away, Alcyonë, had been taken from me. Starry Knight laid claim to it the moment I showed it to her.

Irritation briefly shot through me. While I did want to work with Starry Knight, I was also upset with her on a regular basis. And it was mostly her fault.

"Why is Starry Knight helping us?" Elysian muttered. "That's the question that's been bothering me for a while now."

"What about Starry Knight?" I asked, trying my best to keep my tone neutral.

"I've heard of fallen Stars coming down to Earth before," Elysian said. When he saw the surprised look on my face, he snarled. "What? You didn't think you were the first, did you?"

I frowned. "Dante mentioned it," I admitted, "when I was in the SWORD's black site. But you've never mentioned it."

"It's not supposed to happen very often." Elysian shrugged. "Anyway," he continued, "I'm not surprised SWORD is well-versed in their situations. There are many things in this world not everyone is willing to accept. You can be the prime example in that one, kid."

"Shut up." I threw a pillow at him as he laughed. "Just stop," I muttered. "That's not who I am anymore."

"Definitely," Elysian agreed. There was enough of a pause in his words where solemnity had sneaked in, so I forgave him for his previous slight.

"Why are you so fixated on Starry Knight?" I asked again.

"I'm not the only one," Elysian said defensively. "You've always seemed to have a soft spot for her. I just realized too late that it was a soft skull."

"Are you really still angry I made you let her go at the end of that big battle with Orpheus?" I bristled. "Get over it. I told you I talked with her quite a bit in the prison at the black site, and ... we came to an agreement, and that's really all there is to it."

"I doubt that." Elysian snorted, letting out a small stream of smoke through his dragon nose.

Part of me cringed; he was right. There *was* much more to it, but I couldn't even admit a lot of it to myself. I still hadn't told him about how I kissed her.

Memories of kissing her rushed through me, as if I'd suddenly crossed paths with a waterfall of warmth. My lips tinged with the sudden sensations of spices, prickly and perfect all at once.

I shook my head, trying to clear it. But I knew it was futile on some level, and reluctant on others.

14

"She's hiding something," Elysian declared.

I snorted, glad he'd been so caught up in his own thoughts that he didn't seen mine had been derailed. "That's pretty obvious. Congratulations on your stunning logic."

Elysian narrowed his yellowish-green eyes at me and flicked his tail. "*You* were the one I was meant to find," he said. "So why is she so intent on doing the job you were meant to do?"

"I don't see the big deal about that. I mean, you just said SWORD had helped us, too."

"What's her motivation, though?" He began to pace, which, considering he was a small dragon, was pretty hilarious to watch in my bedroom, but the sense of seriousness involved was unnerving. "It can't be to protect this world. After all, she'd just tried to destroy it to get them captured in her power that time ... "

"My duty was to capture the Sinisters and protect the other people," I asserted. "Maybe hers was just to destroy the Sinisters. That's enough of a difference to make a difference, right?"

"Your mother would congratulate you on your lawyerspeak," Elysian muttered.

It was at that moment my mother, Cheryl, as though she knew we'd mentioned her, called up from downstairs.

"Hamilton! It's time for breakfast. Your turkey dumplings are going to get cold if you don't hurry."

"Ugh, not breakfast."

15

"What's wrong this time?" Elysian asked, more out of duty than desire to know.

"Cheryl's still on her meat-heavy, sugar-less diet," I explained. "I don't think I've actually eaten anything in this house since Helga came to cook for us." A mental image of my mother's heavyset Russian cook flashed across my mind, and I felt scars form instantly at its graze.

I might have liked her better if she didn't remind me so much of Mr. Lockard, my old, idiotic drama teacher. Helga was Lockard's unibrow twin, and that was no simple matter to just overlook. It was enough that it made me wonder if they were related, but I doubted it.

After getting his soul stolen and eaten last semester—the thought of which earned my mind another couple of scars—Lockard had been moved to hospice care, according to the gossip grapevine at the school. Helga, on my mother's pay, could afford better care than that. Some of the Sinisters' other victims had recovered quickly enough, after all.

Personally, I would think all the bloody, fresh meat of my mother's diet would be enough to disgust anyone out of a coma.

Cheryl called out again. "We have to get going soon. Stefano's expecting us at nine."

My stomach grumbled, angry it would be missing another meal. It was distracted along with me, however, when Elysian said, "Ugh, I still can't believe you took that stupid job. It's already getting in the way of our mission."

I gritted my teeth. There was just no end to the parade of irritation and idiots in my life. Between Elysian, the parentals, my brother, or the many minions of evil who want me dead or worse, I was beginning to think life was *supposed* to be hard.

But Cheryl was also right; the mayor, Stefano Mills, was nothing short of inspiring, and I hated the thought of letting him down or looking bad in front of him. And the sooner I got through work, the sooner I could meet with Gwen and Mikey to plan my birthday party. What could be better than getting a few hours in on the government's dollar, and then getting coffee with my girlfriend and my best friend, discussing my upcoming birthday party?

I'd have to argue with Elysian another time; it was no doubt likely to happen anyway. "You're one lucky dragon, Elysian, or I'd make your species extinct. I've got to go." With that remark, I hurried out the door and down the stairs.

"I don't believe in luck either!" Elysian called after me. "Besides," he added, no doubt more for his measure than mine, "there's still my brother that you would have to contend with."

Even though I was briefly intrigued, I shook my head. I let it go. After all, I had more important things to worry about and more interesting things to look forward to.

THE STARLIGHT CHRONICLES

☼<u>2</u>☼
Work

There is something magical about getting paid money for a job you enjoy.

I smirked to myself as I finished the last paragraph for my English class homework. "That's the last I'll have to worry about your selfish monologue, Holden Caulfield," I muttered, not surprised to find out he was just as miserable at the end as he had been in the beginning, and throughout the middle. If *I'd* been the one talking, I wouldn't have worried at all about how to get through life. I would just live through it.

Glancing around, I found myself alone in my small cubicle. I was in charge of filing a lot of memos, court orders, records, and other things. Sometimes I would answer the phone for the city clerk, and once, when they were short, I got to sit in a meeting with Apollo City's Sanitation Department and take notes on the meeting for the mayor. They also had free coffee.

Although, I sighed as I looked at my own half-empty cup, it was nothing compared to Rachel's. I was glad I only had a few more minutes before I could leave. Then I would be able to get some real coffee, I thought to myself, once more cursing the government's poor choice of blend.

In fact, I could probably skip out now, I thought. While I was watching the phone until the city clerk came back, it wasn't like the city didn't have voicemail.

It didn't take me long to convince myself I was right. I dumped the tasteless coffee into the small kitchenette sink, before I picked up my briefcase and started to head out.

"Oh, Hamilton, is that you?"

I didn't have to fake the smile I immediately put on my face, although the reflex was common enough when I thought I was going to get in trouble. "Mr. Mills."

Apollo City's new mayor had taken office at the beginning of the year, and while I was uncertain of working for the man leading the charge against Wingdinger and company, my unease had immediately been put to rest when I first met Stefano Mills.

He was a bit short and a bit round, but always impeccably dressed; I never saw him without a coffee mug in hand, including at press conferences. He had a salt and pepper beard, while his hair, though all still in place, was more black than gray. But what sold me on him was his kindness. He was always talking about helping the poor, getting more funds to the city schools, and raising awareness for those who were society's outcasts. He was even seeking a pay cut to help redistribute some of the funding for the city budget and to help grow a program for at-risk juveniles.

It also helped that he told me in secret he wouldn't get anything done if he wasn't projecting an image completely set against Wingdinger and Starry Knight. I figured out after my "trial by file," as I'd called it in a joke, that he was using a lot of the emergency funding to redistribute wealth in the city economy. I had to admire a man who found such an easy way around bureaucracy.

19

"Hamilton, please. Call me Stefano," he said, adding a little laugh at the end, like we were old chums from Harvard or Oxford or something. "Are you heading out?"

"Uh, almost. I was just doing a walkthrough," I said. I gave him my suck-up smile, still not wanting to get in trouble for heading out early. "I want to work in government one day, and this is a nice building."

That sounded lame, even to me. But sometimes, you have to sound lame. Especially in politics, I reminded myself.

"I know. Your mother has told me you have ambition." Stefano brushed his arm aside, beckoning my attention toward the row of pictures with the past councilmen and Apollo City mayors. "You keep up your good work and you'll get on here one day, too."

"I hope so," I lied.

No, I didn't really hope so. I wanted to move somewhere more important than Apollo City. It was a smaller city by many standards, and while we had some interesting tourist attractions, thanks to the city founder's crazy stargazing superstitions, the main business in town was still shipping off Lake Erie's marina.

"You're able to stay on during the summer months coming up, right?" Stefano asked. "I was thinking of asking you to take on some more responsibilities this summer. You've been doing such a good job with all the filing and managing in the clerk's office, not to mention your help with your mother's case." His warm brown eyes crinkled with what I suspected to be a paternal sort of pride, and I felt a reciprocated

THE STARLIGHT CHRONICLES

appreciation, although it was weird to think of him as a male, Latino version of Cheryl.

"It shouldn't be a problem," I lied again, as I thought of how much Elysian was going to flip.

Stefano leaned forward and whispered, "Between you and me, I think the city clerk's getting concerned with how well you've been doing. He's been stepping up his game since we brought you on last month."

I laughed. "Cecil doesn't have to worry. I have two more years of high school, and then college to worry about first."

We started walking and chatting a bit on this and that while we headed for the exit. As nice as Stefano was, it wasn't long before I hoped he would leave me alone. I wanted to go meet my friends. As easy as government work was for me, it was pretty boring. I wanted stimulation.

Loud, blaring noise broke out as I reached the front of the building. I frowned a bit at first, and then I remembered the protest was going on. *I didn't want* that *kind of stimulation.*

"I can't believe they haven't gone home yet," I muttered.

"Oh, there are some people who will protest anything," Stefano assured me. "I've lost track of their exact demands, but I do hope they go home soon. It looks like the rain, while it stopped for a bit earlier, will start again soon. I wouldn't want them to get sick." He sighed and frowned, his eyes reflecting a true sadness for the people he was in charge of leading.

I decided not to say anything. Stefano was a nice guy, feeling sorry for the people who made his job harder. There had been a bunch of protesters coming up to City Hall's porch trying to advocate for something that had to do with taxes, the media, and government regulation for some time now. I didn't really care. There were between fifty and a hundred people out there, and I still didn't know exactly what they were there for.

Most of them were probably incapable of doing anything but protesting for a better life. On some level, I did think Mayor Mills wasted sympathy on them. They should have just gone out and gotten better jobs.

"You think the rain will come back?" I asked, looking up at the sky.

"Most certainly. I've lived here for a long time," Stefano replied. He gave me a boyish grin and pointed in the direction of the marina. "I got my first job working at the docks in the North District when I was a teenager. Knowing the signs of coming change, especially potentially deadly change, is the mark of a conscientious worker."

Don't I know that. I nodded, but I appreciated the wisdom behind it. After all, change was coming. I could tell that myself. "Well, I'll see you later this week."

"Yes, please come in anytime you can." Stefano flashed another smile in my direction. "It's good to see some of the younger generation getting in on politics. It's not an easy task, you know." He shook my hand, and then said his goodbyes. "Have a good day, Hamilton. I'm actually late for a meeting with your mother at the moment."

"Well, don't keep her waiting. Even talking to me won't get her off your back," I said.

He laughed, and I smiled. Stefano had a full-bellied laugh, something like I would imagine Santa Claus having.

Still, as much as I liked the guy, I waited until he left my sight before I headed out the staff door. I didn't want him to notice I was still cutting out about twenty minutes early from work. Not that I thought he'd have an issue with it anyway. He got along with Cheryl well, so he wouldn't get very far crossing her. That more or less meant my job was safe. Mostly safe.

I managed to poke my way through the crowd of protesters and make it down the street in one piece. None of them really bothered me, but I couldn't help thinking of ungrateful children, too upset to do anything until Mayor Mills, the city's resident fairy godfather, came out to let them swarm around his head as they made incessant, unnecessary demands. Probably in their loudest voices, too, I thought with a smirk.

"You look happy. What are you thinking about?"

"Huh?" I looked up to see Gwen Kessler smiling over at me. She was sitting on a bench by the bus stop, relaxed and cheery, her auburn hair twisting in the small springtime breeze. "Oh, hi, Gwen. I almost didn't see you there," I said with a slight apology. Seeing the disappointed look on her face, I instantly added, "I was too busy thinking about you."

"You were too busy thinking about me to notice me?" Gwen asked, a small smile playing on her lips.

THE STARLIGHT CHRONICLES

I was just relieved she didn't seem insulted anymore. "Yeah, you know it." I laughed. "I'm looking forward to my party. You and Mikey have any good news for me today?"

"Rachel's is our last stop," she promised. "She's good on the food, but we still need to order the cake."

"I'm sure she'll have something special for that. Jason mentioned she was looking to expand on her catering services."

"That's true," Gwen agreed. "And I guess that makes sense. I heard Jason talking about trying to help her."

"You mean helping to bake my cake?" I felt just a bit slightly horrified at the thought.

After a small giggle, as much at my expression as my expense, Gwen leaned over and gave me a quick kiss on the cheek. "I wouldn't worry about it," she said. "I'm not sure, really." Then she reached her hand out and took mine as we headed up the street.

I gave her a smile and squeezed her hand, thinking about how great Gwen was. She was kind, and she was smart, and she really cared about me.

I glanced over at her and took the sight in. Her dress, with the pretty flowers and bold colors, clashed charmingly with her hair, and while she wore some makeup, the growing heat of the oncoming summertime had smudged some of it off. I liked her like this. She was real.

She was real, she didn't yell at me for being incompetent, and she didn't think I was a glory-hog or a show-off or insecure or selfish. And she didn't kiss me passionately in one moment and then break it off in the next, leaving me to wonder for weeks on end if she liked it or even remembered it.

That was why I liked Gwen.

I was about to compliment her again when a voice called out to us. "Hey guys!"

We looked over to see Mikey Salyards closing in on us from the other side of the block. Instantly, a sense of dread and anticipation drippled through me, but I squashed it down guilt as much as I could.

"Mikey!"

Mikey had been my best friend for a long time. He wasn't just any friend, or one I had for more political than personal reasons. He was like a brother to me. Mikey even knew I was Wingdinger, and I didn't feel the need to worry about him knowing.

That made me feel all the worse when it came to his dad. A few months ago, Mikey mentioned to me, very briefly and very tersely, that he knew his dad was back in town. And normally, that wouldn't have bothered me at all. But since finding out in the most inconvenient way possible that his dad, Dante, was working with SWORD to track down me, Starry Knight, and the other Sinisters, I had refrained from letting Mikey know of just *what* had drawn his dad back to Apollo City.

THE STARLIGHT CHRONICLES

Thankfully, SWORD didn't seem to want Dante to connect with Mikey anyway. But I still felt weird about not telling Mikey.

Mikey joined us at last. "You guys are not going to believe it, but—"

My stomach clenched. There's a good reason I don't like surprises.

"—I got Kyle Lancaster's band to sign up for live entertainment."

I felt a long sigh of relief expel itself from my lungs as Mikey went on talking about the details, and Gwen interrupted him every so often, gushing about their music and asking about specific songs.

Even I had to admit, that was pretty cool. Kyle and his band, Caution: Hot Contents, had played a couple of the middle school dances and some of the seniors' parties. How could I not like a band whose name was inspired by coffee cup warnings?

"So as long as they can play outside, I think we'll be good to go." Mikey turned to me. "Do you think it'll be okay to have them outside, Dinger?"

"Uh, yeah. Shouldn't be a problem," I heard myself mutter. I squeezed Gwen's hand again, recalling something important. "But they need to be out by ten," I reminded him. "Everyone's got to leave by ten o'clock."

Mikey rolled his eyes. "Your mother's curfew is ridiculous," he grumbled.

"Yeah, it sucks, man," I agreed, even though Cheryl didn't have a problem with the party running later.

The truth was, I—or should I say Wingdinger—had somewhere else to be that night. And Elysian wouldn't let me miss that particular meeting for the world. Even though I secretly, desperately wanted to be there, too.

"Well," Gwen spoke up, "at least your mom didn't tell you when the party had to start. We can just get the party started earlier to make sure there's enough time for everyone."

I grinned. "There's a reason I like you, Gwen Kessler," I schmoozed. "And it's for that smart, sexy brain of yours."

Out of the corner of my eye, I saw Mikey roll his eyes again. I let the matter go, especially since Gwen blushed, but also because we'd reached our intended destination.

Rachel's Café was the small coffeehouse and bar I'd adopted as my main source of caffeine and my only consistent source of comfort. It was a small place, but it harbored a huge talent in Rachel Cole, the owner, manager, and main barista of the café.

She was working as we came in, and I could tell from the bright pink-and-white striped apron she had on that she had been baking recently. I could feel the anticipation inside of me start to bubble up like an opposite of heartburn. "Hi, Rachel!"

27

Rachel's long red hair was braided back, and it whipped around as she turned toward us. "Oh, hey you guys! Go grab a seat. I know we've got a meeting."

Mikey, Gwen, and I all headed over to a booth, one of our usual locations, and sat down.

While Gwen and Mikey began talking about their math class homework, I did a cursory glance around the room. A moment later, I relaxed. There was no sign of any of Rachel's crazy family members who, in their own ways, just made me feel uncomfortable. There was Grandpa Odd, Rachel's senile-and-a-half grandfather, her male-bashing but desperately dating mother, Leticia-called-Letty, and her cousin Raiya, who was in my class and determined to make me mad every chance she had. It spoke volumes of my love for Rachel's cooking and coffee that I still came anyway. All of them just made me cringe too much.

"Sorry to keep you waiting." Rachel popped out of the kitchen with a tray in her hands. As she came around to our table, my anticipation turned into satisfaction. I could see she was bringing us cookies and cake samples.

"Now," she began, "I understand you'd like a cake for your birthday, Hamilton." She gestured toward the tray full of samples and a small plate of cookies. "Go ahead and see what you like best."

"I'd eat anything if you made it, Rachel," I assured her as I made a grab for the cookies, while Gwen and Mikey went for the slices of cake. While I was interested in the samples, it wasn't often Rachel made the gingerbread chocolate chip cookies I liked. Ever since Christmas, I'd been hoping for another batch of them.

THE STARLIGHT CHRONICLES

Rachel went through the various cake samples she'd made, as Mikey, Gwen, and I all sampled them. Rachel was prepared for the presentation, I noticed. From watching her, I thought it seemed like she'd taken a lot of time to prepare.

She introduced each flavor of cake with pomp and downplayed affection, more like they were her children than her baked goods. She told us what was in each of them, and I almost laughed at her several times, despite her care. I personally didn't care if something was non-GMO, or organic, or homegrown. That was something my crazy, diet-obsessed mother might like, but not me. I just cared about taste. I was almost glad when some customers came in and Rachel had to go take care of them.

"So, Dinger, what do you think?" Mikey asked a while later as we were going through another round of cake slices.

"I like the strawberry best," Gwen offered. "Especially with the chocolate icing."

"Sounds good," I agreed. "But since there are—how many people coming now, Mike?"

"About fifty," he said, wiping some peanut butter icing off his face.

"Well, since there are a bunch of people coming, maybe we should do something a bit safer? Something more agreeable?"

"So you think the chocolate?" Gwen asked.

"I think everyone would probably prefer the chocolate. I would like the strawberry," I said with an apologetic sigh.

"But with so many people coming, I wouldn't want to have them disappointed."

"But it's your birthday," Gwen argued. "If you really want it, get it."

"Yeah, I'm sure no one will really mind," Mikey offered. "After all, all of these taste great."

"Still ... I don't know. It doesn't seem fair. I mean, they're bringing me all the presents and everything."

"Why don't you just tell them your favorite is the chocolate one?" a new voice asked from behind me.

I groaned under my breath. I didn't even have to turn around to know Raiya had made her appearance. I steeled myself before facing her. "What makes you think I like the chocolate one best?"

I didn't exactly know what it was about Raiya that made me dislike her. She was slightly shorter than me and seemed a bit scrawny for sixteen or seventeen. I didn't think she was particularly attractive. She seemed rather plain.

I was willing to bet I didn't like her because she disagreed with me on a lot of points, and she was good at making a case for her claims, too. Maybe she reminded me too much of my mother.

She arched an eyebrow at me from behind the curtain of her long bangs. "You order mocha practically every time you come in here, and you've had two samples of the chocolate, but only one of the others. It seems logical you'd like the chocolate cake with the mocha icing best."

"That's mocha-flavored?" Mikey asked. "I thought it was a weird sort of milk chocolate."

"The crumble on top is made from espresso beans," Raiya told him, as he looked on the cake with renewed interest.

"I happen to agree with Gwen," I muttered defiantly. "I like the cherry best."

"Strawberry," Gwen muttered.

"Strawberry," I corrected.

"If you really did," Raiya said with a saccharine smile, "then you wouldn't mind inconveniencing the people at your party with it."

"What's that supposed to mean?" I asked darkly.

"It means you usually do what you want, regardless of what other people think."

"I don't *always* do what I want," I argued back.

"Oh, you mean like losing to me in gym class the other day?" Raiya gave me another syrupy smile; I swore I was going to get Diabetes talking to her.

"Wait, what happened?" Mikey started laughing as he saw my face. "I gotta hear this."

Gwen spoke up. "We had an archery contest for gym class, since we're starting on track this week. Raiya ended up beating his score."

"By *two* points," I stressed.

It was a make-up exam for me, since the previous week I had to cut out of class due to "illness" (another supernatural attack). Coming out of the locker room, I'd been all too pleased to see my favorite *Raiya sunshine* heading to join us, knowing I could easily beat her. After all, from all the time I spent watching Starry Knight with her bow and arrow, I'd learned a few tricks and I had easily risen to the top of my own gym class.

As Gwen was repeating the story to Mikey and Raiya was filling in some comments here and there, I felt my humiliation fume.

Finally, I couldn't take anymore. "I only lost because I was too shocked to see you wearing something other than your old, ugly Rosemont school uniform," I huffed indignantly. "That alone would've given anyone a heart attack."

Raiya, Gwen, and even Mikey all quieted immediately. I knew at that moment I probably didn't say quite the right thing.

Rachel came back at just the right moment. "So, Hamilton, what's the verdict?"

"I'll have a strawberry cake," I said, glaring at Raiya, who made me even angrier by just standing there, looking amused. "With the chocolate icing."

Raiya shrugged and moved away, while Rachel smiled. "Great!" she exclaimed. "I'll put it in. Jason's coming in soon, and I'll see if he wants to help me make it."

"Okay," I said, the steely smile briefly resurrecting itself as Rachel skipped off to the kitchen, her golden eyes gleaming. I sat down again and grabbed another ginger cookie. "Well, that's taken care of."

"You know, if you want, we can ask Rachel to make two cakes," Gwen offered. "If you really liked the chocolate cake."

"No, no, it's cool, Gwen." I put my arm around her and shifted closer to her. "I liked the strawberry best. Really."

Gwen stiffened underneath my touch, and I pulled back under the guise of checking my phone. Mikey also looked at his phone as the moment passed in awkward silence, before glancing at me from over his phone.

I decided to bribe them out of their mood. "So, uh, what do you guys want? My treat, since you've been planning my party."

"If you're treating them, I want in on it, too." Jason Harbor, another one of my best friends, came up to our table and sat down in Rachel's empty chair.

"I'm already doing you a favor." I snorted. "You're helping Rachel with her baking."

"You can tell she's excited about the opportunity to expand her business, can't you?" Jason smiled. "She's been thinking about getting into the higher end of catering for a long time now. Remember my party last year, the one that ended with the meteorite smashing through the city? That was the one that gave her the idea for it. Your birthday's going to be a trial run."

He turned to look at Rachel as she came out of the kitchen with another full tray, this time for some other table. She grinned and waved his way, and Jason, who had a tragic crush on her, helplessly grinned back.

"Still waiting for her to dump Lee, I see," Gwen said. "Even though the wedding's this summer."

"Yep, he sure is," I agreed.

"He really should just let it go," Mikey murmured. "It's getting creepy."

"Says the person in love with a superhero," I countered smoothly. "I guess it takes a hopeless guy to know one."

Mikey frowned, while Gwen laughed. "Are you really still mooning over Starry Knight?" she asked.

"Shut up," he muttered. "Dinger, I'll take the dinner special, if you're buying."

Classic Mikey, I thought. He's learned well from me. Change the subject if uncomfortable. "Sure. How about you, Gwen? What can I get for you?"

A spark of pain flared around the mark on my wrist, sending through me a sensation of mixed irritation and, to my surprise, a bit of relief. While it was pinching and painful at times, it was the warning I received when the Sinisters and their minions were causing trouble. The supernatural enemy was at work, and it was time for Wingdinger to step up.

"I filled up on cake, but I'll take a drink," Gwen said, interrupting my train of pain.

"Ugh ... sure, no problem. Let me, uh, go talk to Rachel."

Jason spoke up. "I can put the orders in for you. You don't have to worry Rachel about it."

"Oh. Cool. Thanks, man." *Ugh. How am I going to get out of here now?*

"I'll go get it started," Jason remarked, as he stood up and headed toward the kitchen.

"Great. Sounds great." The spark surged into a flare. I gritted my teeth together in slight discomfort. The mark on my wrist, a blood-red diamond star, was tingling in response to something wicked.

I waited until Jason was gone before I said anything else. Gwen wasn't really talking, and I was pretty sure the discussion of Mikey's crushed aspirations for a relationship with Starry Knight had silenced him for a bit. I glanced down at my phone. Maybe pretend there was an emergency? That Cheryl needed me? Or maybe the mayor's office? Or my brother had an accident? Which excuses hadn't I used recently?

Somewhere inside my mind, I was disappointed with myself. I couldn't think of *anything* remotely likely in a moment of pressure.

Mikey met my gaze again, and I glanced down at my phone, trying to signal him to text me. When he just looked at me with a confused, quizzical look on his face, I sighed. *It's not like I asked him a math question.* "I have to go," I mouthed silently to him.

Thankfully, Mikey caught on. "Oh, shoot!" he said. "Ugh, Gwen, can you excuse me and Dinger for a moment? We have to talk to Jason about our next game night. It's his turn to host again, and we forgot to tell him."

"Okay," Gwen agreed, shifting in her seat so I could get out. "Are you allowed back in Rachel's kitchen?" she asked, as we headed over.

"Yes, totally," Mikey assured her.

I don't think Gwen bought that; I certainly didn't. We scurried around back too quickly for it to be convincing. I peeked around to see the kitchen was empty for the moment.

"Thanks, Mikey," I said. "I appreciate it. I'll slip out the back. Just wait here, and tell Gwen Jason needed my help with something from Mrs. Smithe's class. Martha's class is hard, she'll buy that."

"No, I want to come with you," Mikey insisted. "I need more info for my blog."

"Come on, please? Just stay here and keep her distracted. Tell her about stuff. Tell her about how your dad's back in town and you don't want to see him."

"Really, Dinger?" Mikey scowled. "That's what I should talk to her about?"

"Sorry," I muttered, instantly recognizing I'd overstepped a line. "I'm sorry."

Another change, I noticed. I was more apt to apologize, since I'd accepted my calling.

But I didn't have the time to wonder at it; I had to get Mikey to help me out here. And talking about his dad was just brilliant. It was exactly the kind of thing Gwen would get wrapped up in and barely even notice I was gone. "Come on, I don't want to have to apologize to Gwen for cutting out early again. Do you know how many times I've had to do it in recent weeks?"

"Yeah. You usually ask me to watch her for you while you go off and fight the bad guys, remember?"

"Then you should know how much I hate doing that."

"Actually," Mikey said, "I think you kind of like it."

"What?" I groaned. "Ugh, never mind. I don't have time for this argument now. Please, just distract her. I'll be back as soon as this demon is taken care of."

"Yeah, well, then you really owe me now."

"Okay. Give me your phone. I'll take pictures and a video while I'm gone. Whatever you want for your blog. Here, you take my phone. I'll text you when I'm coming back."

"Fine." Mikey handed me his phone. "See if Starry Knight will take a picture with you."

"Ugh, really? Come on, you know I don't like her." Mikey's hardened look said it all. "Okay, fine. But we're even after this. And if she says no, there's nothing I can do about that."

"Fine. Now go before Jason and Rachel get back," Mikey hissed.

I gave him a grateful smile and skipped out the back door. Taking a quick assessment of my surroundings, I headed through the back alleyways, pressing into the mark on my wrist as it continued to echo a cautioned pain throughout me. Power blazed out from the mark, wrapping me up in a flame of power, as my ordinary high school student identity burned away, and only my fallen Star self, Wingdinger, was left behind.

Reaching out into the air, I summoned up my sword; it appeared at my will, like fire and light coming out of nothing, and my fingers gripped it with a certainty in full accordance with my heart. I was tempted to take a moment, to sit back and marvel once more at the workmanship of the Sealing Sword, my own weapon, given to me to wield. There was nothing in the world like knowing power, and having the chance to change your life.

"Time to get to work," I said with a grin.

38

As much as I didn't want to admit it to Mikey, there was a certain excitement to getting to save the world. I didn't see the point in telling him. He would just be jealous, and after the last time I had to worry about that, I didn't want to make him jealous in the least. I didn't really like leaving Gwen behind either, but she seemed to be okay with it. Honestly, I dreaded the day when she wouldn't believe my excuses anymore. But I could count on Mike to keep her busy during my absence. That's what friends were for, right?

The burning twinge in my arm began to glow, and as I pushed a wayward feather from my renowned wingdings out of my face, I caught sight of a growing aura just a few blocks away. I grinned; I'd found the battlefield. I couldn't tell what sort of demon monster it was just yet, but I was close enough to know it wouldn't be a terribly long battle. There was something about the power that seemed to be subdued already.

Hopefully, I thought, that means Elysian is already there, taking care of it. That *was* part of his job, whether he did it or not.

Starry Knight could be there, too.

I faltered only slightly at the thought, and more because I didn't want to look bad in front of her than anything else. If there was someone I would die trying to impress, it was Starry Knight.

☼3☼
More Work

An odd mix of confusion and disappointment surged through me as I came upon the center of the wicked aura. "Huh?" The confusion became more pronounced as I looked around.

Starry Knight wasn't anywhere to be seen. Elysian hadn't arrived yet, either. There was no sign of some demonic spirit or shadow monster wailing around.

I was starting to wonder if something had gone wrong when a cry thundered out from behind me.

"Stop! Please stop," a man was calling out as he ran in my direction. "I already gave you my wallet, and I told you I don't have anything else for you."

Okay, I thought. "Here we go." Stress crept up through my body, and my fingers gripped ever more tightly around the hilt of my sword.

Before I could say anything, another man came running out. I was taken aback; the man *looked* normal, but there was a toxic shadow clinging to his body.

"I still need your Soulfire." The man's voice reverberated in a discordant way, like he was talking, but there was someone—or something—talking through him.

Creepy, I thought.

"Come on, man, this isn't funny. I'm sorry I laughed at you earlier." The first man tripped and fell, then he scrambled to get further away from the demon-man. Shaking myself free of my initial shock, I hurried over.

A blazing arrow of light shot out from behind me and landed between the demonic man and his prey. I glanced around briefly, and my heart soared in both appreciation and excitement. I could see the familiar outline of my co-defender as she stood on a building top behind me. Her white wings gleamed in the small amount of sunshine left from the rainclouds, and her hair, pulled up in its half-bun, shifted with the wind of her own power. I gave her a small smile while she took out another arrow.

I saw the demonic man was focused on her, so I didn't miss my chance; I reached down, grabbed the fallen man, and pulled him up. Starry Knight could deal with the demoniac. "Come on," I told him. "Let's get you somewhere safe."

"Thank you! Oh, thank you so much." The guy was breathing hard and fast, and his hands were shaking. "He just starting attacking me for no real reason."

"How do you know him?" I asked, as he hobbled over me. He was a full-grown man, in his mid-forties or early fifties, and it was hard to keep my own balance while he grabbed at me. I knew he was afraid, so I couldn't fault him. But I still wish he'd been just a bit more aware of how he wasn't helping me help him, either.

"He works with me. I know he's been acting weird lately— but still, I never thought he'd attack *me*; I mean, management, maybe, but we've been colleagues for a year now."

41

Dealing with people, I thought, is difficult. Especially when it comes to difficult people.

I supposed I'd have to get used to it, if I wanted to work in politics. As he rambled on, I thought about how Mayor Mills might deal with such a person. He'd empathize, then he'd get practical. I decided that was a good way to do it.

"That's definitely a tough situation, sir," I said. "Starry Knight and I are going to see if we can stop him. You need to stay out of the way." I let go of him, even though he didn't let go of me. I sighed quietly. "I'll need you to step back so I can help your friend."

"Oh. Oh, okay. Sorry. Never been in this kind of situation before … do you think it would be okay if I smoked?" he asked.

"Ugh … " Never thought I'd be asked that question. He seemed to answer it himself as he pulled out a cigarette and began to try to light it with shaking hands. I couldn't resist watching him as he burned himself a few times before managing to get it lit. "Okay, then. Just be safe. Stay out of sight. If you move, go somewhere safe."

He mumbled and bumbled around a bit, and I finally decided, at the sound of a loud crashing noise and seeing Elysian's shadow hurling toward the scene, it was time to go.

"Elysian!" I shouted, as I moved out toward the street.

"Kid!" he called back, swooping down to meet me. Starry Knight was holding her own against the possessed man. "We'd better get this taken care of soon," he told me in a soft tone; no easy feat for his deep big-dragon voice. "There is a

42

crowd watching from a lot of the buildings. Police are on their way."

"Can you give us some cloud cover?" I asked. "That guy told me that the demon monster is a friend of his." At Elysian's frown, I added, "Not like a real demon, but maybe there's one inside of him? Like there was with Mikey a couple of months ago?"

"That would explain it. Go find out. I'll give you the cover you need," Elysian replied. "Watch yourself."

I was already heading out as Elysian rose into the sky. I didn't see much, but there was a lot of smoke starting to cloud the outside of my vision field. "Starry Knight!" I called out.

She looked back at the sound of my voice. I was about to tell her to try to get the man subdued when he grabbed at her from behind. "Watch out!"

The demonic man gripped her throat and choked her in a headlock. I came running into him, just as Starry Knight managed to swivel out of his grasp.

I hit the man at an impressive speed. The guy and I both flew into the ground, and I swear I felt the road crack under the pressure. Still, I looked up at my partner with a sheepish grin. "Didn't mean to let him get an opening. You okay?"

"I'll live," she assured me. I didn't even mind the bite in her tone, or how her strikingly violet eyes narrowed at my arrival. If she was well enough to give me a hard time, I knew she was fine. And I was glad for that.

43

She checked the man on the road beside me. "He's out cold."

"Good," I said. "I didn't want to have to use my sword."

Starry Knight indicated the clouds starting to form around us. "What's Elysian doing?"

"He's giving us a cloud cover," I said. "The other guy—"

"Is he safe?" Starry Knight interrupted.

I'd known Starry Knight long enough to know she was concerned about the people, despite what Elysian might have thought about her. I nodded my head in response and said, "He told me that this guy works with him. Can you hold him down? I'm going to try to see if I can … "

My words trailed off as I realized I didn't even really know what it was I did to help people like this. Cure him? Set him free from the demonic hold he had on his heart? I didn't really know to describe it the first time I did it, and I still didn't really know. A lot of the ways I found myself explaining it sounded insane, even inside my own head.

Fortunately, Starry Knight seemed to know me pretty well, too. She held down the man's shoulders and nodded. "That's fine. If you need me, I'll be here."

I was surprised by the remark; there wasn't much Starry Knight could do, if you asked me. Not when the guy was like this. Unless she meant actually ending his life. Hopefully she didn't mean that. But as I looked at her and met her gaze, I realized she was trying to support me. I celebrated a small

THE STARLIGHT CHRONICLES

victory as I turned my gaze from her. While she had stipulated, very clearly, that we were only going to be allies, I had a feeling we were slowly slipping into friends.

I almost laughed at the thought; I'd never been so happy to be friend-zoned.

Putting that aside for later, I grabbed the wrist of the man and pressed in with my power, just as I learned to do with my own mark.

Instantly, the swirling emotions of his body flushed up, and after applying more pressure, I was able to transport myself into the Realm of the Heart, which was my name for the place between the inner and outer reality.

The heart is an interesting place, I thought as my eyes settled onto a new landscape. It had a reality all its own inside a person.

In this case, the reality in question was something out of a horror film mixed in with my own cubicle at City Hall.

It was a small heart, I guess, because I found the man's inner self pretty quickly. The man was working at a desk, and there was a demon swirling around and around him, sinking himself into his heart and trapping him, speaking for him. Making a puppet out of him.

It was much like this when I'd been in Mikey's heart, I recalled. A demon pulling the strings while the man was caught in a web of lies.

"Sir?" I asked, just a bit hesitantly. The man didn't seem to be old enough for "Sir." He did not seem to be much older than I was, actually. His blackish hair was short and neat, allowing me to see the youthful qualities of his face.

The man didn't look up from his work. The demon shadow turned his attention to me.

After several months on the job of demon hunting and Sinister-slaying, I'd sharpened my assessment skills. It wasn't a demon type I was familiar with; an *eela* had more of a personality, and they tended to create their own bodies with their powers. A *tenwaleisk* kept to a lot of technology, but it did have a human-like side, too; was it possible this was one of them? I knew it wasn't a *bakreel*, a type of monster who usually used animals or plant life for a vessel. Maybe it was a more powerful form of a *bakreel*.

And I knew for certain it wasn't one of the Seven Deadly Sinisters. None of them would deign to use a man's body— and a lowly pencil-pusher at that—to try to gain power. Confusion set in. How was I going to defeat this monster when I didn't recognize its species?

"What are you doing in here?" the demon shadow asked.

"I've come to set this man free," I said, deciding to treat this like some kind of video game experience so it didn't feel quite so surreal. I pulled out my sword, ready to do battle if the man himself wouldn't help me.

"You don't need this soul," the demon told me. "He's been depressed for so long. He feels his job is nothing special, but it's the only thing he has in life. He works long hours. His

THE STARLIGHT CHRONICLES

brother is getting married, and he has no one else. Nothing but an empty job and a hollow life."

"That doesn't matter," I said. "He still has the right to choose a better one. I won't let you take that away from him."

"I see." The demon frowned. "I suppose you belong to *him* then."

"Him?"

"The Prince of Stars," he responded.

"Oh, him." I straightened. "I mean, yes. I am one of his Starlight Warriors."

"I am surprised you are not bitter," the demon spoke. "It is not unusual for a fallen Star to hate the Prince."

"What are you talking about?" I asked. "Why would I be bitter?"

The demon's eye gleamed with renewed interest. "Oh, I see; you don't know, do you? Oh, this is priceless!" He began to laugh, and not only was it a terrible laugh, but I hated how much superiority I could hear in it.

My sword faltered. "What don't I know?"

"All the fallen Stars living on Earth were sent here as a result of the Prince's ruling on the matter. It is a punishment."

The word "punishment" stopped me as nothing else could have. "What do you mean?" I asked slowly. "I have a purpose for being here. It wasn't to be punished … "

Was it?

I mean, sure, some days it felt like it. But it wasn't really a direct punishment. It couldn't be.

This is a demon monster. He is your enemy. He wouldn't tell you the truth. Unless the truth is worse than lying to you. I shook my head, trying to clear my thoughts and find some source of truth to break me away from the demon's words.

There was a small push behind my own heart, and I grappled onto its warmth. The Prince would not betray me, I thought. He was supposed to be the good one in all of this. After all, Adonaias had specifically told me that I'd been forgiven.

But forgiven doesn't necessarily mean "unpunished," my lawyer side reminded me.

One thing at a time, I decided. First, cut down the demon. Then ask the uncomfortable questions.

Before I could make my move, the demon suddenly lashed out and curled around me, cutting me off from movement. I struggled against him, but his power held me back. "What are you doing?" I asked through clenched teeth.

"Why, trying to take your power, of course." The demon offered me a creepy, distorted grin. "As a fallen Star, your heart and soul are much more powerful than that of a human.

THE STARLIGHT CHRONICLES

All I need to do is find a weakness … " He laughed again, and in that instant I began to worry. There wasn't anything I knew of that would let Starry Knight or Elysian follow me into this realm. I was completely by myself.

A shadow of a hand formed from the demon's aura and, before I could say anything else, it cut through my armor and my tunic and strangled itself around the core of my being.

"Ack!" I choked out with a hiss, as a burning pain began to surge throughout my body. I felt a sense of unconsciousness slipping around me as my soul began to separate itself from my form.

Seconds later, the demon slid back and began to cry out in pain. "Augh!"

Through half-open eyes, I watched as my energy burst free from my skin, showing a glimpse of the mold from which my heart had rested, cradled in its light like a flame in a larger fire. As I watched, power reached out and grabbed the demon's shadow, and burned through it with a blood-red flame.

I felt my body begin to move again as the demon burned up, the blood flame dissolving it into nothing but fire residue.

"Ah," I muttered, my hand flying to my chest. The red flame of my soul slipped back inside of me. I felt it brush against my fingers as it oozed past, returning to its home. "How did I do that?"

The demon holding the man hostage was gone. I looked up to see a college-age student before me, with dark eyes and darker hair—normal, once more.

49

"Thank you," he said.

I watched as the tiny, cramped cubicle blew over, and a bright morning sky filled with twinkling lights settled around him.

"You're welcome," I said back. "Um, are you okay now?"

"I'm having a hard time," he admitted. There was an air of loneliness and uncertainty around him still, I noticed. I was about ask what was bothering him when he continued, "But I'm not ready to give up, like that thing wanted me to. I have people counting on me."

Oh, well that was good then. I guess I shouldn't really be asking people I've never met personal questions. "Are you ready to go home?" I asked.

"Yes."

And with that, we faded back into the real world, where I found my body kneeling over his, and his still unconscious.

I looked up and blinked, finding the real world a lot brighter than the realm of the guy's heart. I felt his wrist fall out of my hand, and I slouched back onto my legs.

"Did you get to him?" Starry Knight's voice came to me like a voice from the other side of the water.

I heard myself answer, "Yes. He's free."

"Are you okay?"

I looked up at Starry Knight, and her beauty was especially striking to me. I found myself falling forward, my hands wrapping themselves around her. As I broke through the surface, I found myself saying, "Yes. I am."

☼4☼
Aletheia

Still jolted by the demon's attempt to take control of me, I felt my heart swell as I held onto Starry Knight. Without meaning to, I could feel her emotions singing out to me. One of the talents I possessed as a fallen Star, an *Astroneshama*, was the ability to read other people's emotions. I figured it went well with the ability to walk into the Realm of the Heart, too. As I held onto Starry Knight, there was surprise, hesitation, irritation ... and fear, buried under so much of everything else.

Starry Knight, after a long moment of indecision, pushed me back. I knew when she was going to do it. There was a strong resolve about her, and for small second I envied her for it. She was capable of resisting so much, I realized. That demon inside of the man wouldn't have caught her by surprise, and wouldn't have been able to take her heart. Assuming she had one, I thought bitterly as she let me go.

But as I straightened and caught sight of her eyes, I began to pity her. She wasn't suffering like I was, and surprisingly, or maybe not surprisingly, I thought she was worse off for it.

I cleared my throat. "Sorry about that. Transition overload."

"Got it," she muttered, standing up and turning away. "Elysian!"

The dragon arrived by our side a moment later. There was a silent settlement between Starry Knight and myself. One

THE STARLIGHT CHRONICLES

where we agreed not to talk about anything involving her or me.

Anger, unforgiving anger, surged through me as I looked at Starry Knight. Something was wrong with this, I decided. Maybe something was wrong with her. But there was no reason she had to play stupid with our relationship.

"Wait." I said the word without really meaning to, and at her sharp gaze, one with a staggering amount of simultaneous antipathy and annoyance, I pointed to the man on the ground. "Can you check him? You know, for injuries and stuff?"

There were plenty of traits about Starry Knight I'd often considered desirable, but of all of them her healing ability was the one I envied the most. With just a push of her power, she could heal the body of its pain. After all the battles we'd fought together, I had yet to see its limit.

Her resolve broke at the mention of the victim. "Okay." She moved over and picked up the arm I had dropped.

After she removed her glove, I watched as she let her own healing power leech into his body. I felt like I should ask her something. And Mikey's photo op just seemed like too shallow of a reason to ask her to stay with me.

"You did a good job." A new voice behind us made both of us turn around in surprise.

My breath sucked in. I looked around to see it was the lady who had only a few months ago given me the Sealing Sword to capture the Sinisters and destroy their minions. "It's you!"

53

"Hello, Aletheia," Starry Knight murmured. She put the man's arm down. I could see a faint, glowing aura around the man as she finished healing him.

"It's nice to see you again, too, Starry Knight," the newcomer said. "I thought we agreed last time that you would call me Aleia now."

I glanced from Starry Knight to Aletheia—Aleia—and asked, "You've talked to her before?"

When Starry Knight said nothing, Aleia answered for me. "Certainly." Aleia giggled. "We're all friends."

At her words, I stared at her, just a bit incredulously. *Friends?* I didn't think that was quite possible. But as I looked from her, with her long, dark blonde hair and crystalline green eyes, to Starry Knight, and then to Elysian, I thought there was a sense of familiarity and happiness Aleia had in seeing us that none of us seemed to share. And that was comforting. Maybe we were all friends with her separately? *That* made more sense, I decided.

Starry Knight straightened. "I have to go now."

Aleia nodded. "I understand, but you might want to stick around while I'm here."

"The cloud cover is dissipating," Starry Knight said. "I'd rather get going before it's gone." She reached down and picked up the man on the ground. "I'll take care of this guy."

"What will you do with him?" I asked. I thought of Mark, my dad, and how the hospital where he worked was close by.

"Are you going to take him to the emergency room at the hospital?"

"No, I'll just take him back to work," Starry Knight told me. "It's not too far from here." She turned and jumped, her wings plucking her from the ground and carrying her away from me.

"Okay." I watched as she disappeared through the clouds and smoke. Suddenly, the strangeness of her statement hit me. "Wait, how do you know where he—?"

Elysian nudged my hand. "Do you want me to follow her?"

"Elysian," Aleia said, "I would like it if you would stay with us for the moment." She ducked down her head briefly, as she began to search through her long, white robes.

"I guess that's a 'no,'" I told Elysian with a half-hearted shrug. But I pet his nose nicely, as a way of thanking him for his small show of loyalty.

I don't think he heard me, as he was staring at Aleia with a new sense of wonder. "Did you come down from the Celestial Kingdom?" he asked.

"Yes," Aleia answered. There was a smile on her face that seemed quick and easy, and, just as before when I'd briefly met her, I had a feeling I would like her. "I am the Guardian Star of Memory." She pulled out an orb, similar to the ones in which Alcyonë and Meropae were sealed, only bigger. It reminded me of a crystal ball.

"I thought you looked familiar," Elysian muttered. "Yes, we are friends."

"I am surprised you remembered that much," Aleia said. "This side of Time, going through the River Veil can really mess up your memory, especially if you were not supposed to fall."

Fall? Her words triggered my memory, and I thought of the demon inside the man, who said I'd become a fallen Star because of a punishment.

"So my falling ... wasn't intentional?" I asked.

"That's not an easy question to answer, and the answer is complicated, Hamilton."

There was an uneasy feeling in my gut as she said that. I decided to change the subject. Part of me didn't want to know anyway. "How do you know my name?" I asked. "They call me Wingdinger here."

Aleia's eyes twinkled. "Do you really think we are not without our resources?"

"We?" I assumed she was talking about Adonaias, the Prince of Stars, when she said that. I thought about how, on the times I met with him, there had been a strong and settled peace about him that differed from the world's comfort, much as eternal truth differed from the world's truth. "I suppose that would be silly of me," I conceded.

THE STARLIGHT CHRONICLES

The orb between her hands glowed fiercely white and bright. Power surged from its center, and a moment later there was a glass-like, transparent bubble surrounding us.

I looked around in awe; I noticed Elysian had a similar look on his face. "It's a barrier of time," he said, obviously fascinated and slightly terrified at the same time.

Laughing a little, I said, "I guess I don't know enough to be scared of *that*."

"There's nothing to fear," Aleia promised me. "The cloud cover is dispersing, so I thought I would take a moment of our time."

"And hold onto it?" I laughed again.

She smiled at my word play. "I guess so."

Elysian flew around the bubble, eventually coming to a stop near the top. "Everyone else has frozen in time."

I hurried over to the edge and put my hand on it. It felt like a solid kind of soap bubble. My fingers left a trickle of color, despite the transparency. "Wow." Looking past the bubble, I could see that there was indeed no movement beyond the border.

"I have taken this moment out for us," Aleia explained, "so I could remind you of our prior arrangement this week."

I pulled off one of my half-gloves to show her the glittering gold script, still inscribed on my palm:

THE STARLIGHT CHRONICLES

Sailing on the Stars

Meallán

St. Brendan the Navigator

April 23rd, Earth Time 11:00 PM

Dock 42, Apollo City Marina

"I'm not likely to forget." Especially after worrying so much other people would see it and ask about it, I added silently.

"St. Brendan and I will be waiting for you at the marina," she said. "The *Meallán* will be ready to disembark at eleven sharp. Since this is a sort-of impromptu landing on his part, please try not to keep him waiting."

I was just about to ask if I was going on some kind of cruise, when Elysian whooshed down and interrupted me.

"Do you have the powers of Time, then?" Elysian eyed Aleia intently.

She nodded. "My sister and I control the elements of time, but her power is on the universal side, while mine is focused on the personal."

"What does that mean?" I asked.

Elysian glared at me; no doubt I'd interrupted his line of questioning.

THE STARLIGHT CHRONICLES

"It means I work with individual experiences of time, while my sister controls all of it at once." She came closer to me and looked at me closely. "In your human form, don't you see time through your own experience?" She didn't wait for an answer. "Time operates beyond you and through you. You experience it, but it still goes at its own pace."

"You mean like when I'm stuck in English class and it's been five minutes but it feels like an hour?"

"That's the present-tense version of it," Aleia agreed. She grinned again briefly, before adding, "But you see it most when you reflect on your past. Time distances you from pain, but memory also works to help heal your hurts."

I thought about my past, and in particular my pain. As I gazed into the orb Aleia held in her hands, the orb's dark center glowed. I saw my younger self as I was shuffled from babysitter to babysitter, daycare to daycare, struggling to get my parents' attention, celebrating the rare moments when I did, and how it made me forget the pains of their ambivalence.

I thought about the quiet hours in the night and morning, when I couldn't sleep, and how I'd longed for something or someone I could not name, something I later grew to fear. I thought about being overlooked in elementary school by my peers if I was not strong enough, fast enough, smart enough, or attractive enough, even as I studied and worked hard to achieve those things, and succeeded in achieving them, all the while silently wondering if anybody would ever love me for me.

I saw myself on the summer nights when I would get sick, and I would gaze at the moonlight and wonder what was missing in my life.

I gazed downward. *That isn't who I am.* Turning back to Aleia, I brushed it off. "I don't think time manages to heal all wounds," I said.

"No, it doesn't," Aleia agreed quietly. "But our memory of time does shape who we are." She gazed over at Elysian. "And that is why I have come."

"I guess the Prince got my messages about your lack of quality mentorship, Elysian," I teased, trying to add some levity to the group. Elysian's eyes had glassed over, and it made me wonder if he'd seen some of his own unpleasant past in the tiny orb. He didn't seem to notice my remark, either.

Aleia cleared her throat. Elysian and I both turned our attention to her. "Do you have any questions about the appointment?" she asked.

"Nope. Not really."

"I'll be around if you do need me," she said. "I am staying here on Earth with you, until I am called back."

"Oh. Well, that's good." I didn't really know what to say to that. "So you'll help us fight the demons while you're here?"

She put the orb back in her cloak and pulled out a pair of deadly-looking daggers, one in each hand. "It is the duty of a Star to protect," she asserted, twirling them around with a languid grace. "Each one is trained for combat, for this world and for this lifetime."

"Sounds good to me," I muttered, impressed with the elegant features of her weapons. I grinned and held out my hand. "Good to have you on the team."

Aleia shook my hand with a fierce pride and strength. It made me like her all over again. Time resumed as her bubble of power popped. "I'll see you again soon." Then she laughed a bit as she added, "Wingdinger." And just like that, she was gone.

"Well, she seems more agreeable than Starry Knight," I said.

"She's here to take my place." Elysian slumped over. "Have I really been a terrible teacher?"

Yes. I wanted to say it, but I decided not to. I shrugged. "You can't say it's not a good thing that we're getting more help fighting the Sinisters. We still have five to seal away, and Orpheus, too."

"Four," Elysian said.

"Four?" I repeated, surprised. "No, we only managed to get Meropae and Alcyonë. That's only two of the seven."

"Didn't SWORD seal one away as well?"

"Ugh ... " I briefly recalled they'd managed to capture Taygetay, the Sinister of Rage, during our last big battle. "Oh, yeah. I guess so. Do you really think they managed to seal her away, though? She seemed pretty powerful."

Elysian and I exchanged an uncomfortable glance. There were no easy ways to answer that question.

"Hey, hold still a moment."

"What? Is there something on my belly?" Elysian looked down, his long dragon face squashing itself into his neck area. "Or on my tail?"

I laughed as I pulled out Mikey's camera and took a few quick shots. "There," I said. "That should satisfy him."

"Aw, what did you do that for?" Elysian grumbled as I jumped on his back. He took off and I grabbed on.

"Mikey wanted some pictures and a video," I explained. "He asked me for Starry Knight's picture, but I forgot."

Elysian grumbled. "I know you like your friend, but I have to say you both need to be careful about taking pictures. Not to mention posting stuff online."

"We will. He's the one who's keeping Gwen out of our hair," I said. "This is the least I can do in return. Besides, I'm sure other people have gotten some good pictures of you. Even at Rachel's, there was a painting with a dragon in it that looked like you a couple of weeks ago."

"You shouldn't have to do this for Mikey," Elysian argued. "It seems like you're trying to buy his silence or something."

"I don't think it's that." I hesitated. "Okay, fine. Yeah, I think it's stupid, but Mikey's dad is a part of SWORD, if you'll recall, so I'm sure he'll be fine."

"Either that or he'll be seen as an unnecessary complication."

I hadn't thought of that. "Look, let's just get back to Rachel's, okay? I don't want to keep Gwen waiting, and we'll figure out all this other stuff later."

"There's always later for you, isn't there?" Elysian rolled his eyes in disapproval.

I tried not to let it bother me. But as I slipped back into Rachel's Café, I knew it wasn't something I could ignore forever.

As I was peeking around the corner from the front entrance, Mikey waved at me from the otherwise-empty booth.

"Hey," I said slowly. "I guess Gwen … is in the bathroom?" I finished uncertainly.

Mikey grinned. "Not quite. She got a text from Laura and needed to go help her with something for the cheerleading squad."

"What? Why?" I asked. "Gwen's not even on the squad anymore. And they have a ban or something on talking to me, don't they?"

"Come on." Mikey grinned. "We *both* dated Via Delorosa. We know how twisted her sadistic mind can be. Since you didn't get much of a social backlash after you dumped and humiliated her—"

"I'd hardly call it 'humiliating.' I just stopped dating her," I muttered. "*And* I was nice about it. It could've been a lot worse."

"She was probably hoping you'd at least make one big scene with her about it, in public or school," Mikey observed. "You know she likes attention."

"Too much, and only if it's on her own terms."

"Agreed," Mikey said. "That was part of the reason I didn't like her."

"Why did you date her then?" I asked, leaning around the table to see if Rachel was nearby. I wanted a new mocha. And to see if she had any more cookies. "And then why did you let *her* dump *you*? You could've dumped her first, if you really didn't like her."

"We were in middle school, Dinger," Mikey said with a laugh. "Who *doesn't* do something they are for sure going to regret at that age? And as for letting her dump me, well, I didn't really care. Remember? I even told you to let her do the dumping, because she would be better about it."

"I gave her some time," I said fairly, before deciding to change the subject. "So what did Via need Gwen for?"

"Well, considering Gwen was a cheerleader last year, Via has to make it seem like it was her idea to allow you to get together. So she dragged Laura into it."

"And Laura's not going to turn Via down," I finished. Laura Nelson was one of Gwen's best friends, and I knew she was angling to get a promotion to vice-captain next year. She wouldn't object to any scheme of Via's. Not until she grew a backbone of her own, and that was not going to happen as long as Via was in charge of Central's Falcons. "Oh well. There's a reason I don't date cheerleaders anymore."

"Me too," Mikey readily agreed. "I'm looking more in the way of archers these days. Speaking of which ... "

Anger spurted inside of me. "No, she didn't want to get her picture taken." I lied, conveniently not mentioning I didn't even ask. "You'll have to ask her in person, yourself. You know she doesn't like to do me any favors."

Mikey sighed. "Okay. But I am definitely coming with you next time."

"Fine," I snapped. "You can think of an excuse to get us out of whatever we're doing at the time."

"That's easy enough," Mikey asserted, obviously ticked at my tone but unwilling to play on my anger. "I'll just tell Gwen my dad wants to meet with me. And when we get back we'll say we were stood up."

If only that would work, I thought, wondering if Dante Salyards would ever show up on my battlefields again.

"What?" Mikey asked. "You're looking at me funny."

"I thought you didn't want to talk about your dad," I said, using the moment to recover from the direction my own thoughts on the matter had taken.

Mikey shrugged. "So? He's not around now, even if he's back in town. Why not make him useful?" He slouched back a moment and added, "It's not like I'm *really* going to talk to him, anyway."

Unspoken words settled on me quickly enough. We both knew we weren't going to talk about it anymore.

He coughed awkwardly. "You know, you were lucky Gwen got called away by Laura and Via. You've been dumping her on me a lot the last few weeks."

"Do you think she's getting suspicious?" I asked, this time bitterly. "Or are you tired of helping me out?"

"What? No, man. Of course not. I like Gwen," he assured me. "I just thought it was a lucky break today is all."

"And that I'm ignoring her, apparently."

"Well—"

"Save it," I retorted. "I'm going home. Here's your phone." I tossed him the phone and stood up. I started to leave, and then changed my mind. "Why don't you just get over Starry Knight? It's one thing for you to criticize me, but it's another for you to do it while obsessing over some … temperamental harpy." That was a good description of Starry Knight, I decided, recalling how she'd pushed me away earlier.

Mikey didn't answer me. He avoided my gaze, focusing on his phone.

I decided to let it go. For the moment. There are some people who insist on being helpless, I thought, recalling the protesters at the mayor's office earlier. And you can't help them until they are ready to help themselves. I turned and walked away.

"Wait," Mikey called, "You forgot to pay!"

I didn't even care as I headed out and headed home. I'd call Rachel and settle the bill later, I promised to myself. But now I just wanted to go home and be by myself.

THE STARLIGHT CHRONICLES

☼<u>5</u>☼
School

It took me a few days to calm down enough to *want* to talk to Mikey again. It wasn't that I was mad at him, really. But I still decided it was better not to talk to him until I absolutely *had* to.

I mean, I rightfully pitied him. I'm sure my parents' congenial inattention to me was much better than Mikey's dad full-on leaving his mother. And not to mention dealing with his mother's resulting alcoholism and depression, and having his grandmother take them in. I get it; that was hard. And with everything going on, I felt like I had to protect him from finding out his dad was on the side of the "Let's take over the world" crazies, who also happened to be very well informed and very well paid off. That's pretty hard, too.

But to see him place all his hopes and dreams on Starry Knight just put him past my pity limit. It was one thing to have things happen to you; it was another to be blatantly, intentionally stupid about it.

Not to mention, Starry Knight had already told him he "wasn't the one" she was meant for. Sure, she was nice about it, and yeah, it was unlikely any sensible girl would take Mikey up on a date after just meeting him for the first time. But did she really have to be that nice to him? And just who was she "meant for" anyway?

"Dinger? Answer the question, please."

I don't know the answer to that question. I blinked and looked up to see Mrs. Smithe, my AP History teacher, looking down her thick-framed glasses at my face, and I recalled I was in the middle of class, trying to get through a round of review.

"Ugh, what was the question?" I asked.

"What's the oldest city in the United States?" Raiya muttered from behind me.

"St. Augustine," I replied, just as Mrs. Smithe began to ask the question once more.

Mrs. Smithe was by far my favorite teacher, and for good reason: Martha didn't take any crap from people. Except from me and my friends, a lot of the time. "Yes, that's right. Please pay attention," she remarked in a terse voice, after shooting me a glare.

I smiled brightly, charmingly. "Of course, Mrs. Smithe," I assured her. "I always want to make sure—"

"That's enough for now, Dinger," she barked. "Next question's for Raiya."

Jason and Evan von Ponce, both my friends in class, sniggered softly around me as Mrs. Smithe went on with her review questions in her usual relentless fashion. I glanced over at Gwen with a grin, but she just shrugged.

I hope she's not mad at me. Even though Gwen had reassured me she should have been the one to apologize for running out on our date over the weekend, I didn't feel like she was really okay with it. I thought about how great it would have been to take a class on something useful in life, such as how to tell what girls were thinking, when people were really telling the truth, or how to get them to tell you the truth.

I thought about my ability to read someone's emotions. It helped, that was for sure, but there were a million and one reasons Gwen might be feeling sad or frustrated when I was around. I watched her as she answered her own review question ("Explain isolationism vs. imperialism") with a rote precision our old drama teacher, Mr. Lockard, would have appreciated.

Eventually, review for the final exam died down and we had a few moments to settle down and relax.

"I'm slightly disappointed in you, Dinger," Jason said as we discussed my upcoming celebration. "I was so sure you'd want a surprise party."

"Nah. Parties have been scarce enough this year," I reminded him. "No need to try to make it special."

"Is it true that Kyle's band will be playing?" Poncey asked.

"Yeah, Gwen and Mike just told me about that a couple of days ago," I confirmed.

"Cool!" My other friend, Drew McGill, chimed into the conversation with a cheer. "Caution: Hot Contents is huge with the seniors and juniors right now. I wouldn't be surprised if you get some party crashers."

"It's no trouble," I assured him. "Cheryl and Mark know how to hire a good maid service." We laughed, as my parents were a sort-of running joke between all of us.

THE STARLIGHT CHRONICLES

"Between the band and Rachel's catering, you'll need it," Jason agreed.

It was nice to see my friends so excited over my birthday. "Yeah," I agreed again. "This is going to be the party of the year," I sneered as I turned around to face Raiya, who sat directly behind me, much to both of our dismay. "How's Rachel coming along with my cake?" I asked.

"I don't know," Raiya muttered into her paper. She was copying the notes on the board. "I'm not her keeper."

"Do you think it'll be a fun party?" I asked her, deliberately trying to bait her.

She gave me a smirk back. "I doubt my opinion on the matter has ever bothered you."

"That's not an answer," I countered.

"Well, I wouldn't have any way of verifying my answer, would I?" She leaned down and grabbed her books as the bell rang. "I'm not invited."

"Oh, I forgot you weren't." I shrugged. "Oh well."

"Yes," Raiya said. "So it would really be a waste of time to ask me, wouldn't it?" And then she flipped the loose tresses of her hair over her shoulder and left.

"You didn't invite her?" Gwen asked from behind me.

"Gwen, I don't need to argue with her all throughout my own party. You want me to enjoy it, don't you?"

THE STARLIGHT CHRONICLES

"Yes. But I think you like to argue enough that it wouldn't matter."

"There's no winning with her," I muttered darkly as Raiya walked out of the classroom. For once, she didn't turn around and smirk at me like she usually did when she managed to get the last word in our arguments.

"I won't argue with you about it," Gwen replied with a sigh. "I've got a test in math today. I'll see you later."

"Do you want me to walk you to class?" I asked.

"No, I just said I have a test," Gwen repeated. "I've got to hurry."

"We can hurry together."

"You like to stop and talk with all your friends. Don't worry about it."

"Hey, some of them are your friends, too," I reminded her. "Ever since Via took credit for our relationship, more people are okay with talking to me for some reason."

Gwen ignored my comments. She gave me another smile and said, "See you later, Hammy," then headed out.

"Good luck with your test." I don't think she heard me.

"I don't think she heard you," Mrs. Smithe said from her desk.

I smiled. "Oh well. Thanks for the review today, Martha."

"It's Mrs. Smithe till you graduate, Dinger." The quick rebuke was sharp, but it came with a small smile. "So, how's it going, working for Stefano?"

"You know Mayor Mills?" I asked. I didn't know why I was surprised. Martha was an active participant in politics, at the local and federal levels.

"Sort of," Mrs. Smithe admitted. "We were in the same graduating class during high school. He was always a bit slick. I'm not surprised he's in politics."

"He seems like a nice guy."

Mrs. Smithe snorted. "Everyone in politics *seems* nice, Dinger."

"I suppose," I conceded. "But he does seem like he really wants to help. He cares about the people."

"It's easy to care about people you largely imagine to be a certain way, rather than they actually are," Mrs. Smithe muttered. "You need to skedaddle to your next class."

"All right," I said with an exaggerated groan. "Will do, Martha."

"Mrs. Smithe, Dinger."

I grinned and then faltered. It was far from the first time she'd mentioned the rules of her name to me. She mentioned it a while ago, in the hospital, when she'd been injured in a demon attack that happened in the school. Which made me think ... "Can I ask you a question, Mrs. Smithe?"

"If you hurry. Your next class is not going to wait for you."

"They might; it is Latin, after all," I joked. "But, when you were in the hospital during the winter, did you have anyone come visit you?"

"Is this a power play of some kind?" Mrs. Smithe narrowed her gaze. "You came, of course, and Raiya, though she was there anyway. There were a few from my other classes, and one of the subs who said you guys were too hard on her. But that was it. You talked to me the most, if that's what you're wondering about."

"It's not that." I hesitated. "I just thought maybe one of us had to do with your quick recovery. Or maybe someone else?"

"You came to see me after the worst of it," Mrs. Smithe assured me. "So if you are wondering if you're a favorite kind of student, you can stop now. Teachers are not allowed to have favorites. Now, you really should get to class."

"Okay."

"Hamilton."

I nearly jumped at the sound of my first name. It was very rarely she called me that (especially without the last name attached), and when she did, it was usually to let me know I was in trouble. I turned to face her, just a bit bewildered.

Before I could say anything, she said, in very calculated tone, "Don't ask too many questions like that." And then she stood up and began to push me toward the door. Her tone resumed its natural sharpness as she added, "I don't really want to think about my time in the hospital."

THE STARLIGHT CHRONICLES

"But—"

The door slammed in my face.

Okay, that was weird. Very weird. I decided not to say anything for the moment. After all, if Mrs. Smithe said something that seriously or that creepily, I should probably listen to her.

"Psst. Kid."

"Ugh!" I muttered at the familiar sound of my dragon's voice. "Where are you?" I hissed.

"Over here."

That doesn't help at all! I mentally screamed in frustration. Finally, I must have looked bewildered enough for Elysian to take pity on me, because I could feel his small, slimy claws tugging their way up my shirtsleeve.

"I found him."

"Who's 'him?'" I asked impatiently and quietly as I made my way through the hall (I still had to get to class, after all). Sudden terror laced through me. *Was it the person Starry Knight was looking for?*

Terror was instantly buried by forced apathy. *I will ... do absolutely nothing because it* doesn't *matter.*

"The guy who was attacked a few days ago."

Relief, sweet relief, welcomed me. "Oh. Who is he?"

"His name is Logan Reynolds. He works at the city college in an astronomy and physics lab. He's back at work this week and seems to be doing fine."

"That's pretty good," I said. "After the demon inside of him tried to grab *my* soul, or whatever, I guess I can empathize much more."

"What?!" Elysian reeled. He blew up to one of his larger forms and began racing at me. "The demon tried to overcome you, too? You didn't tell me that part!"

"Well, I didn't think it was that important." I was flustered momentarily, surprised Elysian was so upset by it. "I was still able to defeat him."

"Ugh, you make me so mad sometimes. Don't even know what's important or not." Elysian eased up on his scrutiny of me as he went into deep thought. "Hmm … that must have been a *fenfleal* demon."

"What's a fen-feal demon?" I asked.

"*Fenfleal.*" Elysian sighed. "It's more of a rogue demon. Very powerful. They like to act of their own accord. There would be no Sinister manipulation."

"So … it's still bad, but is it more good-bad or worse-bad?" I asked.

"Probably worse," Elysian mused. "The Sinisters and their leader, despite not being very active, are starting to encourage bolder activity, even if it is not under their direction."

THE STARLIGHT CHRONICLES

"You're probably right then. Let's call it worse." I heard the bell ring in the distance. "Great, now you've made me late for my class. Did you really have to find me now? I need to teach you to text."

"Why can't you just give up school?" Elysian argued back. "Or go to a homeschool group, or an online school, where you don't have to worry about showing up?"

I halted outside of my classroom door. "It's the principle of the thing, Ely. And my friends are here." I took out my phone and looked like I was calling someone. "Did you have anything else for me?"

"Oh, yes. I almost forgot. Logan Reynolds works at the Apollo City College in the astronomy—"

"You told me that already." *Give me a break here; I'm already late for class. This can't take forever.*

"It wouldn't hurt to go and see him," Elysian said. "He might be able to tell us something."

"Like what?"

"Like maybe how Starry Knight knows him, for one thing."

I took a sudden interest in the classroom before me, deliberately avoiding Elysian's direct gaze. "All right," I said, trying to make it sound reluctant. "Let's just try to make it seem inauspicious though, okay? I'm still not happy with Mikey. I don't want him to go with us. He doesn't need another interview for his blog or anything."

"It's not like I go around talking with your friends." Elysian snorted. "When do you want to go?"

"I can go after school," I replied quickly. "Well, I can if Gwen's okay with picking up Adam and watching him." I was supposed to help with babysitting my brother from time to time, according to the almighty parental rulers. But Gwen was doing just fine with it. "Maybe I can get her to wait for me at Rachel's."

"She might not like that. Why not take her with you?"

Because I didn't want to deal with Gwen while I was only thinking about Starry Knight, I thought to myself. "This guy's already been housing demons. What if more come back? I might need to transform."

"Fine. But she might need some convincing." Elysian gave me one of his irritating smirks. "You've been running off on her a lot lately."

"For all you don't talk to Mikey, you're starting to sound like him." I roll my eyes, brushing him off my shirt before walking into the classroom. But an active, persistent pleasure stayed constant inside of me, even as I informed my teacher one of my relatives had a devastating health-related concern, as I thought about finding out more about my mysterious and aggravating co-defender.

☼6☼
Inquiry

"I'm just so sorry; I can't believe I completely forgot."

After all this time, I could almost see Gwen smiling through the phone as I talked with her. "It's all right, Hammy. I know you're busy."

"Yeah, but that's no excuse," I said. "I was looking forward to walking you home today."

"You might still be able to, if you think Adam can last the whole time you're at the mayor's office," Gwen suggested.

"True," I said, hoping it didn't sound like I was choking. I didn't really want to put a time limit on my visit. Just in case it got interesting.

But then, I didn't want my girlfriend to think I wasn't interested in being with her, either.

"Hammy, I am here for you. I know your job is important to you, and I don't mind hanging out with Adam," she promised. She said it so reassuringly that I felt another tidal wave of guilt wash down with my gulp.

"Thanks," I sputtered. "Sorry."

Elysian, hanging over my shoulder, just sniggered into his claws. I was close to tying him into my own personal bow tie.

"You okay?" Gwen's voice was one of concern on the other side of the line.

"Yeah. Speaking of okay, how did your test from earlier go?"

I didn't really listen as Gwen talked about how math was hard and blah-blah-blah something something something. I just turned down the street when I heard someone call my name.

"Hey, Dinger!"

Instantly, I was relieved; it was just Jason, and I could deal with Jason. "Hey!" I waved back.

"What?" Gwen's voice had a spark of anger in it.

"Oh, sorry, I was just yelling at a car," I lied. "I gotta go before I get run over. You're too distracting, Gwen." I laughed.

"Fine. I'll talk to you later." She hung up on me, and I wasn't sure if she was appeased or not. Couldn't hurt to try to get her a gift or something soon, I thought.

"Bye," I muttered.

"Lady troubles?" Jason asked.

"What? No, never. Gwen and I are just fine," I said. "In fact, that's just what we were talking about. We're fine. Just fine."

"Okay," Jason said with a smile. He had no reason to assume I was lying or anything. "Where are you going?"

"Uh, just the mayor's office. But I have to pick up something from the college campus for him first."

THE STARLIGHT CHRONICLES

"Wow, that job or internship thing sounds terrible," Jason said. "I'm glad I work for Rachel." He got the typical dopey grin on his face at her name.

"Yeah, how long till her wedding again?" I asked.

"You'll get your invitation," Jason spat back. "Don't worry about it."

"You mean I'm invited?" That was surprising, I thought.

"Yeah. Rachel's grown really fond of you, although I wouldn't put it past her to see this as a chance for you to invite Gwen and seem like a good boyfriend. You know how she believes in true love." Jason paused. "And if nothing else, she invited you since I'm going to be there, helping with her cake and some of the desserts and stuff." He grinned. "She sees the wedding as a good opportunity to advertise."

"Might as well." I couldn't argue with that economic sense. "So, where are you going?" I asked.

"I'm going to see my dad. He's got a part-time job with the college campus now."

"I thought he'd been working at the docks since he lost his job last summer."

"Ugh, well, yeah," Jason awkwardly agreed. "Lee and his family have been really good about helping him with getting work. Dad says it's his engineering degree he's using there. The astrophysics degree, he's using at the college."

"Oh. How's he like it?" I sighed to myself. My fake-interest in this conversation was going to wane really quickly. I could only hope we would get to the college soon.

My wish came true. When we arrived, I marveled that I should have been worried at all. Jason and I were both part of the football team, and while Jason didn't do the swim team like I did in the winter, he was part of the current track season (I *would* have done track, if the mayor's office hadn't been so determined to poach me) so we made good time getting there.

"Apollo City College is pretty spread out. Do you know where you're going?" Jason asked.

"I'm headed to the astronomy lab," I said.

"What's the mayor want from there?" Jason laughed. "He's not checking in after the meteorite again, is he?"

What? "Ugh, I don't think so. Just picking up an envelope."

"Oh." Jason looked up at the sky with a frown. "I'd heard there was some rumor going around that the mayor was worried about the meteor, especially after all the problems getting it moved from the crater it created, and then that power outage a few weeks ago … "

"Power outage?" I asked, amazed I was actually interested now, and irritated I had to hide it.

"Yeah. There was a small outage in one of the inner city districts. It wasn't too far from Rachel's. There was some speculation it was from the meteor."

I remembered the power outage quite clearly, and I knew the meteorite had nothing to do with it. Starry Knight had blown a generator when she used her power to help trap a demon using the communication lines and satellites. "I don't see what the meteorite has to do with anything," I said. "After all, it's just a rock."

Jason laughed. "I know. I can't believe my dad even listens to some of the gossip about it."

"There's actual gossip about it? What are people saying? That it's haunted?" I laughed. "Cursed?"

"Well, all the monsters started coming shortly after it hit the city," Jason reminded me. "Dad says there's a pattern, especially in the radiation output of the thing."

"Huh." I didn't know what to say to that. It still sounded kind of sketchy to me, and that was at best.

"I'm going to go find my dad," he said, smiling as he waved. "I'll see you soon, Dinger."

I waved back. "Thanks. I'll keep an eye out for you," I lied. As he turned the corner, Elysian shuffled out of the folds of my backpack. "Lying about this stuff is getting both easier and harder, Elysian."

He shrugged. "That's probably a good thing."

"I don't think you know what you're talking about." I sighed. "No wonder Aleia came down here; you're a terrible detective." I began walking forward, hoping my familiar-face radar would go off at the sight of what's-his-name. Logan.

"At least I'm *trying*," Elysian shot back. "You're 'too busy.'"

"Impressive that a dragon can do air-quotes," I muttered. "But it doesn't help your case. You still don't have a lot of answers. I bet I have more answers than you, and like you just said, I'm not even trying."

Elysian started to reply, but as we turned the corner I saw the sign for the astronomy department. Walking inside, I immediately felt the surrounding walls press in. I'd seen bigger closets.

In the corner of the room—or half-room—I saw a small shadow digging underneath the only real desk in the room.

"Uh, hello?" I said, not sure if I was in the right place all of a sudden.

There was a small bang as the figure under the desk jumped, hit his head, and let out an impressively loud, "Ouch!"

As he pulled himself out from the crawl space, I saw the person in question was none other than Logan himself.

He was taller and lankier than I remembered. He seemed like he would be just a few years older than me, and, remembering we were at a college, I figured that was probably a safe assumption. He seemed even younger than me, wearing a kind smile as he looked my way. "Can I help you?"

No "kid" or "sir," I noticed. "Hi, I was looking for someone named Logan … "

"That's me," he said, nodding, even as I knew he was sizing me up. "Are you one of the high school newspaper writers who emailed me this week?"

"Uh … " That was a good cover story, but one look at Logan and I decided against it. "Not really," I admitted. "I'm just taking a look around, and I have an interest in astronomy, so I thought I'd see what the lab looks like." It wasn't a *complete* lie.

"Oh, well, this is my office," Logan said, pride in his voice even as it was a hole in the wall. "I'm the leading graduate for my PhD in cosmology, and as such, this is more or less my office. I'm in charge of organizing it and making the reports."

"Would I be able to see the lab?" I asked.

"We've actually downsized a bit in recent years," Logan told me. "But we've been lucky. We actually just finished renovations at Lakeview Observatory. That's where the new lab is for the school."

"Lakeview Observatory?" I asked.

"Yes. The Skarmastad Foundation has provided us room in their facility." Logan squirmed a bit. "It really was very generous of them. The astronomy program offered by the college was nearly shut down until they stepped in. Now enrollment is up a hundred percent."

"So there's twenty people instead of ten?" I asked jokingly, surprised to see Logan nod seriously.

"That's about right," he said. "We've had a lot of interest pour in from the local government lately."

"Why's that?" I asked, moving around to play with one of the many telescopes on the table. It helped make my interest in astronomy seem more genuine than convenient.

"Because of the meteorite," he explained. "I was just about to go see it, actually. It's been in Lakeview for about a month now. I gotta start closing down everything here and get there."

"I see," I said. "What's so big about the meteorite? Did they find any aliens in it?"

"No." Logan laughed a bit. "No, but it's an interesting piece of rock, that's for sure."

"What's so interesting about it?" I asked.

"That's a dangerous question to ask a grad student. There's just so much to tell. Come down to Lakeview sometime and I'll show you," he promised. "What did you say your name was again?"

"Oh, I'm Hamilton. Does the meteorite have to do with those two superheroes running around?" I asked him, meeting his gaze very carefully.

Logan brightened. "I don't know about that. But they're definitely amazing. I was rescued by them this past week; that's why I am getting a lot of interview calls, and I've given this speech a few hundred times this week."

"Sounds cool."

"Some people say they are problematic, but I can tell you, whoever they are, or even whatever they are, I owe them a lot. I don't know what they did, but ever since I was rescued, I've been feeling a lot better."

"Almost like you've been exorcised?" I asked with a misleading laugh.

"That's a good way to put it, I guess," he said, "even though I've never been possessed."

That you know of, anyway. "Well, I will have to go to Lakeview Observatory one of these days. I'm getting ready to apply to college."

"Are you a junior?"

"Next year."

"You can start with some of the dual enrollment classes here, and get college credit for it. Have you heard of that? It's similar to AP course credit."

"I'll have to look into it," I said. "But that's a great idea. Thank you for letting me know about it."

We chatted a bit, and I casually glanced around the office, trying to look at some more of the files (I'd learned the power of files from the Mayor's office, and I wasn't going to forget about it). I backed up toward the door. "Well, I'll let you get back to work," I said. "I'm sure after being saved by Starry Knight, you've got a lot of work to do."

There was no change in his face at all at Starry Knight's name, nor was there any change in his voice. "Agreed."

"Right."

I shut the door and looked down at Elysian. I was glad to see he hadn't done anything stupid, like slithering into the room after I left, trying to look for other clues.

So Logan didn't know me, he didn't know me as Wingdinger, and he didn't seem to know Starry Knight as a real person.

So Starry Knight knew him, I thought. But he didn't know Starry Knight. Or at least, he didn't know her in her supernatural form.

He was in the same boat as me, Elysian, and Mikey, I grumbled silently. He was probably half in love with her, too. That was a bummer.

"Well, what do you think?" I asked.

"We didn't get much."

"Duh. No kidding." I pulled out my phone to see what time it was. "I guess we'll have to check in at the Lakeview Observatory. I don't think getting in there will be too bad; Jason's dad works there now, and we have a standing appointment with Logan, you heard him."

"Let's just go now," Elysian said. "Maybe we can find something else out about all this."

"Come on, no. Not tonight. If we head out now, I can go see Gwen and get Adam before heading home."

"Is that all you think about? Yourself?" Elysian huffed.

"You know, I don't want to have to worry about Cheryl wondering if I am taking care of Adam," I countered. "That's one less thing we need to worry about ourselves."

"Fine. But you do seem to do it a lot, you know. Think of just yourself."

I sighed, resigned, as we headed out the door. "Thinking about myself is easy, Elysian. And it's not confusing. Thinking about Wingdinger, and destiny, and even Starry Knight, and all the questions I don't know the answers to, the ones about Orpheus and the Seven Deadly Sinisters, and their mission to … to what? Take over the world or something? That's confusing. It's easy to think about myself; it's hard to think about things that matter, and even harder to do something about them."

There was a moment of silence. I actually thought Elysian was going to make fun of me for sounding weak.

But he managed to surprise me. "Well, let's try to get it all sorted out as much as we can, then," Elysian said. "Aleia's around now; she'll be able to answer some things for us. And we've got that appointment with her this weekend. Why don't we try to draw up some questions?"

The sunlight of spring hit me as we headed up the block toward Rachel's, making our plans. With every step, my mind seemed more at ease and more clear, like I'd taken allergy medicine and it was finally kicking in.

Elysian talked me through some of his questions. He wanted to know about Orpheus in particular, because he had some awareness of Starry Knight's past, and it did seem unusual, he said, that Asteropy would allow herself to be under someone's guidance.

"Pride is intrinsically competitive, kid," he told me when I asked him about it. "If she's okay with it, I want to know why. And if she's really not, she must be bidding her time."

I thought about Orpheus and our last battle with him. The one-eyed, gray-skinned, foul-smelling leader of the Sinisters was no prize, that was for sure, unless it was a contest straight out of the bowels of the earth.

The rainbow-colored sisters who made up the Seven Deadly Sinisters, though now it was four or five, I recalled, were more or less at odds with him in many things. But Elysian was right; they all united when faced with Starry Knight, whom they had referred to as their "sister."

And Starry Knight had confirmed that, of course. Making it all the more terribly confusing.

How can someone turn against their sister? I thought. Or their brother? I thought about Adam, and tried to imagine fighting him. His three-year-old, gap-toothed grin would undo me in a heartbeat, even though he was a pain to deal with.

I must have voiced this question aloud, because Elysian sneered. "That's not too hard to imagine," he said with an indignant snort.

"What do you mean?" I asked.

"The people you love are almost always the easiest to hate," he said in a disgusted tone. "You know a person well enough,

90

and then, when power comes along, it is easy to see nothing good left."

"I guess so." I didn't want to think about it. Was that why Starry Knight didn't like me? Because I'd been corrupted by power?

I knew from Adonaias I'd been forgiven for the brief respite I'd taken from my superhero gig a few months ago, and I was on the side of good, even if I wasn't completely "good" myself. I could still feel the truth of my condition in many ways.

If I let myself.

Thankfully, I got a text from Gwen telling me she was at Rachel's with Adam. I grinned momentarily; real life was calling.

But my pace remained steady, and I focused once more on Elysian. "We have to find out more," I said.

"Agreed," Elysian said with a small nod of his dragon head. "We have to find out all we can about the Sinisters, and their specific plans, and their roles, if we are to defeat them."

"I used to think defeating them wouldn't be that hard," I admitted. "But there are somethings that just aren't adding up."

"Like what?" Elysian asked. "I mean, other than the obvious parts."

I stuck my tongue out at him. "Like the Soulfire," I said, "for one. There are some victims, like Mikey and Logan, who

THE STARLIGHT CHRONICLES

are up and running again. But there are others, like Samantha Carter and Mr. Lockard, who aren't. Don't you think that's weird?"

Elysian giggled. "Oh, to hear yourself! The great Hamilton Dinger, asking a celestial dragon if something is weird, after several months of avoiding the very foundational ideas to that very weirdness."

"Shut up."

Elysian choked down the rest of his laughter. "All things aside, I do agree with you. The question of Soulfire is a valid concern," he remarked. "Hopefully, we will be able to get some answers soon."

Part of me lightened up at the notion, and part of me dreaded what I would find. The demon who'd been inside of Logan's heart still haunted me with his words. *"It is a punishment."* Was it really a punishment for a star to be sent to Earth? I wondered.

"I think we will." I smiled at my reflection in Rachel's café windows. I saw how normal I looked—attractiveness aside— and I knew instinctively inside of me that the hardest question had already been answered, which was the question of my dedication.

I had a feeling the rest of the pieces would come together eventually. Probably not as smoothly or as quickly as I would have liked, but that had been unlikely anyway.

☼7☼
Concern

It was the best kind of luck, I decided, to have my birthday come on a Saturday. There were just so many good things that happened on Saturday, no other day of the week came close to matching.

For one, I didn't smell cooking meat or hear the *whirr* of my mother's blender. That meant Helga had the day off, and I didn't have to worry about her choking a chicken in my backyard as the band played. *That* in itself was a nice birthday gift.

"Why are you up so early?" Elysian half-rose from his curled up position at the end of my bed.

I almost laughed, seeing him with the dragon version of bedhead.

"You'd think of all days to sleep in, it would be your birthday." He rolled over and stuffed his own face back into the covers.

"I have a couple of hours of work this morning," I explained, pulling on one of my nice shirts and looking for my nicer pair of shoes.

"Ugh, really?"

I smiled; while I did have to work a bit at the mayor's office, filing away some police reports, I didn't mind. Having a job made me feel like an adult, and I was seventeen years old. I wasn't a child, and I knew it was time to put more childish things aside now. The feeling of maturity, coupled with respectable responsibility, was another one of those nice birthday gifts from the universe.

Years later, I would think about that and realize I was still an idiot, seventeen years old or not.

Fortunately, there were plenty of good things that did cushion my ego throughout the day.

I was going to stop by Rachel's on my way home from City Hall, though more out of habit than anything else. Gwen and Mikey were going to come over to my house while I was at work and begin setting up for the party. Jason and Rachel were going to come later with the cake. Drew, Poncey, and another one of my friends, Simon Gangel, were going to bring their extra gaming systems and help Kyle and his crew set up the stage for their performance.

"Tonight's my party," I reminded Elysian. "We're going to have a super-fantabulous time, with good friends, loud music, sweets, and treats from Rachel's."

Elysian perked up at the mention of sweets (his weakness) and then narrowed his gaze. "We have that meeting tonight with Aleia, too. Don't forget."

"Please. I wouldn't forget that." Although it might get pushed back some with the party stuff, I acknowledged to myself. "You don't need to worry. I have everyone leaving at ten. That gives us an hour to get down to the marina, and that will keep the neighbors from calling in the police if the party gets too loud."

Neighbors. That reminded me.

THE STARLIGHT CHRONICLES

I pulled back the curtain and smooshed my face against the window, trying to get a look at the house a few doors down.

"What are you looking at?" Elysian asked.

"Dante's house is just down the street, remember?" When he got that look on his face, the one with one part outrage and the other murderous frustration, I buckled down. "I specifically recall telling you about that months ago. We were at Rachel's and we saw him walk by."

"Yeah, well, the importance of it was lost on me at the time."

Recalling how fascinated with Rachel's new muffins Elysian had been, I wisely hid a smirk. "I'm more worried for Mikey than anything else tonight."

"Are you crazy?"

"No, idiot. But come on, SWORD doesn't seem to be camping out in his backyard, and they haven't bothered us since that time they—"

"Captured you and Starry Knight." Elysian rolled his eyes. "Did you forget how they'd poisoned your friend when he was in monster form? How they tortured you, more or less admitting they are in it for nothing but power? That's not something we 'don't need to be worried about,' kid."

"They sent out some agents afterward. They always help with clean up, nothing more."

"Evil is much better at hiding and waiting than you think." Elysian's somber tone struck me hard. "They might not need to interfere just yet. We don't know what they want, other than power."

"Dante wanted me to protect Mikey," I argued. "That's something."

"Isn't he also the guy who ran out on his family some time ago?"

Elysian had a point, but my argumentative skills were competitive.

"Maybe he was blackmailed," I offered. "Or tricked. Or bribed. Maybe he didn't want to go." Despite my love of debate, I hated defending the man Mikey and I had grown up hating together.

"There's no room to be working with 'what-ifs' here." Elysian was up now, fully alert as he joined me at the window. "Besides, I doubt that would be a nice blanket way of dealing with SWORD. One man's weakness in a company like that won't matter."

I checked the time. "I have to go," I said. "Look, I know we're trying to figure more stuff out. Maybe I can see if there's something in the mayor's office or the police reports."

"Like what?" Elysian huffed.

"I don't know," I shot back. "Couldn't hurt though, right? I mean, the mayor's the one who is bringing the charges against Wingdinger and Starry Knight. Maybe he knows something we don't."

"That pudgy man with the beard?" Elysian asked. "Who always wears a suit?"

"I suppose that's how you'd see him."

"I doubt he knows anything. Politicians only worry about two things. Themselves and their careers."

"You're awfully cynical for only being here for what now, six months? How often are you watching the news?"

"I haven't been lying around doing nothing!" Elysian objected. "I've been looking after you."

Before I could make a mean retort of how that was why he needed a replacement, Cheryl interrupted us. "Hamilton! I'm headed out for the office. Stefano's expecting you at nine sharp today. Don't make me look bad."

Elysian and I exchanged looks, and we silently, mutually agreed to continue the argument later. We would have to worry about things as they came along.

"Happy birthday," Elysian muttered as I left.

I ignored him for the most part, and only felt a little bad about it when I walked outside and looked around.

The morning of my birthday was beautiful. The early morning sunshine was warm, but not oppressive, and there was enough of a breeze to make the wind seem playful.

I sighed, noticing the contrast. Outside, everything was simple and elegant. Inside of me, it was a storm of complications.

I was glad Elysian and I were able to talk more without arguing quite so much; generally, it was more informative than when we fought. I suppose I had more of an appreciation for him after what happened a few months earlier, when I briefly broke ties with my supernatural self.

But I didn't want to think about that. I thought about our plans for the night instead.

From all my friends' homework and test prep practices, I knew very well it was never efficient to be reactive. But Elysian and I were largely unable to plan things when it came to the Sinisters, because what we did know was based only on our observations and experiences. And, until recently, I hadn't wanted the extra stress.

Throbbing pain suddenly lit up my nerve system, as my wrist burned.

"Augh!" I screamed, immediately regretting the outburst. I clenched my teeth together, trying to get myself under control, even as the ache on my arm fluctuated wildly. "Ouch."

The underside of my wrist glowed as my stress levels involuntarily slid up the supernatural spectrum.

"Not now," I grumbled. "Ugh, I have work!"

But I knew, even as I said it, I would be late. I desperately hoped Cheryl didn't find out.

After ducking into an alleyway for cover, I pressed into the four-point star and felt a lightning strike of power swirl around me as my clothes were transformed into armor, my black wings sliced out of my back, and my sword appeared in a scabbard at my side.

It never felt the same, but even at seventeen years old I knew it wasn't any different, either. Transforming would always be an adventure with which I never had to worry about growing bored.

Elysian suddenly appeared at my side again, his own metamorphosis from tiny lizard to fire-breathing sky dragon complete. "Let's go!" he roared, scooping me up.

I cheered a bit and allowed myself a moment of enthusiasm; there was nothing like riding a dragon's back, facing into the wind.

I leaned close, looking for the aura.

"It's a Sinister," Elysian said. "I can tell. It's a powerful one, too. We have to get to her before the harvest."

Not sure how I feel about a Sinister's attack being referred to as a "harvest," but okay, I mused. "I'm looking for it."

"It's close," Elysian agreed. "Look carefully. Remember? Evil is powerful, and better at hiding than good."

I rolled my eyes. I was getting tired of the good and evil stuff. It was so common everyone knew about it. But then again, I suppose that's why not everyone knew about all of it.

Sighing to myself, I briefly glanced over at City Hall as we came up to it. If this hadn't happened, I would be there by now, I thought.

THE STARLIGHT CHRONICLES

It was the strange, orange-colored fuzz around the building that made me falter in my self-gloom. "Elysian," I said. "There's something at the mayor's office."

"Yes. I see it now, too," Elysian agreed. "It seems to be inside."

"Oh, no." I groaned. "It figures. We need to make sure we don't do any damage. The mayor can't have any distractions at the moment."

"I'm not sure that's going to work," Elysian told me. "Be realistic about it." But even as he said it, he began his descent, heading toward the back of the building.

"Hey!"

"You there. Stop!"

There were policemen around as we flew over them. Elysian swung around the corner swiftly, and I could hear them start to follow.

"What are you doing, Elysian?" I yelled up to him. "Trying to get everyone's attention?"

"It might help keep them safe."

"Huh?" I looked over to see Aleia had arrived and was waiting for me, already garbed for battle in a white tunic of her own. Unlike Starry Knight and myself, she did not have any wings. There was a circlet made of silver chains and starlight that held back her dark blonde hair. Her twin daggers were bound at her left side, and a pure white battle dress covered with body armor similar to my own hid all but the toes of her protective boots. A lady warrior, I thought. "You're here."

"Of course," Aleia said with a smile. "I told you I would help. Have you seen the aura?"

"Yes."

"Can you find the heart of it? The strongest point will be where the demon's power resides; that would be its heart." She looked up at Elysian. "We might need you a bit smaller for this one, Elysian."

"All right," he agreed, and I felt a budding resentment at him being so willing to follow her directions. He was never that submissive to me.

"Where's Starry Knight?" I asked, looking around.

Aleia pulled out her orb, filled it with her power, and searched through the power of time to find our mutual ally. "She's coming," she said quietly. "It seems like she had a harder time getting away than you did."

"You can see her? Can you tell me … ?" My voice trailed off as she shook her head.

"Hey, you! You need to stop." The police officers were back.

"Let's just go," I said.

Aleia nodded. "Elysian, lead these guys and the others away from here. No teasing," she warned as Elysian smirked. "Wingdinger," she said, turning to me, "I'd like it if you led the way to the demon. It's a powerful one, and its Sinister is here as well."

We started running, breaking away from Elysian and the police. Thanks to my job, I knew the layout of City Hall pretty well. Aleia and I headed up into a side stairwell, as I punched forward toward the heart of darkness.

"If the Sinister is here," I suggested, "I think we should just go get her. You know, like the killing the snake by cutting off its head philosophy."

"I can see they are close," Aleia said. "We'll have to fight together when we get there."

"All right." I wasn't going to argue with her on that. I spurred ahead of her and charged through the door.

And ran straight into Starry Knight.

In the split second I saw her before we crashed, I could see her eyes grew wide in surprise, and then sharpen as I launched into her.

Even as we collided, my arms were lacing around her and I pulled her close; for the longest, shortest second of my life, it was like we were dancing rather than falling. We toppled together, tangled up; I hit the floor hard on my shoulder, then squeezed her closer, protecting her.

When I looked up a second later, her eyes were blazing their violet gaze into mine, and even as I could tell she was reprimanding me for running into her, my gaze was transfixed by her mouth rather than her words.

Does she remember? I wondered again, for the millionth time, whether she remembered that moment where we were trapped inside her starlight, bound between the heavens and the earth, when I kissed her and she willingly kissed me back.

I wish it didn't bother me so much. But I didn't just remember the kiss itself; I remembered the feeling of home and longing, the simultaneous pain and pleasure, something unparalleled in all my life. And it ate at me, how she pushed me away, how she didn't feel the same way, how she didn't dream of it so vividly when she woke up that she could still taste the remnants of the warmth blazing between us . . .

Reality brought me back with sound waves, and I started hearing her words.

"—need to watch where you're going!" She pushed me off and I relented. "We've got to hurry."

"Yes," Aleia agreed, moving alongside me and pulling me up by the arm.

"It was an accident," I heard myself say. I brushed some imaginary dirt off my tunic, making a show to get a moment to reorient myself. "Let's get going again. It's up here."

"Do you know which Sinister it is?" Aleia asked Starry Knight.

We pushed through the door. "It's Elektra," I said, causing the Sinister before us to turn around and sneer at us.

Her skin was slightly orange, a weird color that made me think of burnt pumpkins. Her black hair was long and pulled back at the neck. A small jewel-like shard glimmered at the top of her arm, marking her as one of the Seven Deadly Sinisters. I noticed quickly she had a glowing confection of pure energy in her palms, and I suddenly wondered how many people she'd managed to steal souls from.

"Well, isn't it nice to see you again?" Her voice was silky smooth, even though it grated against my nerves. "I guess that's my cue to leave."

"You're not going anywhere," Starry Knight spoke up. She pulled out her bow, and Aleia stood ready for battle.

I have to admire the ladies I work with, I thought, watching them out of the corner of my eye. They were real warriors, serious about this. Next to them, I felt like a stage extra for a fight scene in a low-budget film production. I wouldn't be surprised to learn they had trained for years to develop their skills.

Elektra moved quickly, shifting back from our blows, dodging the arrow by the merest of millimeters. Aleia shot a dagger through the air; it sliced into the wall directly behind Elektra as she laughed and took to the skies.

She turned and licked up the power still residing in her hand. I grimaced as she swallowed it whole. I could see her throat expand as it went down. *Did they really have to do that? That's an appetite killer.* I worried my birthday cake was going to be force fed to me later. "Tasty," she purred, pleased with herself.

"You'll pay for that," Starry Knight vowed, bringing her bow to the front.

THE STARLIGHT CHRONICLES

"I doubt that," Elektra said, laughing still. "You know, Sister, while I might have once been happy to share with you, I cannot tell you how nice it is to have all this power."

"It is not yours."

"That did not stop me from making it my own." Elektra cackled to herself.

"That was wrong."

"Well." Elektra alighted down onto the floor once more, obviously teasing us. "We both know what it is doing wrong, don't we?"

"Some of us refuse to enjoy it," Starry Knight sparred, slashing out with her weapon.

Her bow crashed into Elektra, who used her power to keep it from cutting through her.

"You always were a stickler for rules," Elektra teased, obviously trying to bait her.

"Here!" Aleia stepped in. I watched in wonder as Starry Knight and Aleia ambushed her from the front. I circled around, waiting for my opening.

A strange force wrapped itself around me before I could move. I suddenly gasped, coughing as an invisible hand reached around my throat and choked me.

Starry Knight glanced back. "What's wrong?"

Her moment cost her. Elektra's power smashed her. I could see the moment of surprise and blatant pain play out in slow motion, before Starry Knight tumbled down to the floor.

"No!" I breathed, more determined to break free. I grappled with the invisible monster at my throat. I could hear a sort of chuckle from him as I fought.

"One down, two to go!" Elektra cried. She ducked low and tripped Aleia, who stumbled into a railing. Elektra reached out and pushed her hard, sending her flying backward.

My breath caught back into my throat as Aleia fell. I didn't have the strength to protest this time. A strange straggle escaped me as I thrashed around on the floor.

"Krono, don't kill him," Elektra warned. "I need him alive."

Instantly, the force holding me still released me. I doubled over and sucked in air like a reverse-engineered balloon. I clutched at my chest and fell to my knees, still captured but able to breathe normally. I peeked up to see Starry Knight's hand twitch.

Help me, help me, please. I found myself more than slightly uncomfortable, to say the least. "What was that for?" I asked, my voice scraggly, and still unable to move very well.

"Orpheus wants you dead," she explained. "And I want to know why." Her power slid around me like a string of orange lightning, paralyzing me, and lifting me up to meet her gaze. "It's strange. Normally, he would want your power, which is considerable, I see."

Elektra reached out and put her hand over my heart, and I squirmed. A bright flame, bursting out from inside me, shot out at her. She only laughed.

"Yes, you have powerful heart," she said. "How about I take a closer look?" Her eyes, dark and sharp, narrowed as she reached into me.

This time, I didn't just choke. I felt my blood surge. Power lashed out at her, but she continued to press. I could feel it as she reached around and latched onto my heart and soul. My physical body was raked with pain, and, despite the invisible restraint, I cried out.

Elektra just smiled. "Yes. Orpheus was a fool," she muttered. "Your power is too great to just let it die. I must have it for myself."

My eyes blurred over and my body went limp as my own power, the power of my heart, the burning life force inside of me, began pouring out. I would have recognized it anywhere, even if I had never seen it before.

From the beginning, I had wondered what my soul looked like, I vaguely recalled. Most of the ones I'd seen looked like glowing candlelight, burning with different patterns and colors, or small, brightly shining stars.

My Soulfire was a blazing ball of energy; not just a flame but burning with life, time, and tears, all wrapped up in blood-colored Soulfire.

"Yes … " Elektra's eyes reflected my power, lighting up her obsession.

It was the last thing I saw as I closed my eyes. Or at least, it was the last thing my eyes saw.

☼8☼
More Concern

"Am I dead?" My voice echoed all around me. I don't think anyone heard me. I was alone with my thoughts, but not alone.

Before I could get my answer, Elektra screamed. I felt her power release me.

Time had not stilled, but we were still in the middle of a battle. My vision, suddenly able to see all around me, caught sight of her as an arrow sliced through her arm and into her chest.

Aleia suddenly landed beside me. "I'll get her," Aleia shouted, indicating Elektra. "You get him."

"I'm fine now," I said. But as I watched Starry Knight drop to her knees to pick up me up, I realized what was wrong. My self—my Soulfire, my heart, and my consciousness—was outside of my body.

Even so, I still felt the warmth of Starry Knight's embrace as she whisked me off to an alcove in the hall, away from Elektra and Aleia as they continued to square off. It contrasted with the hard, cold cement of the floor of City Hall.

"What's going on?" I asked, as Starry Knight began to check my vitals.

A moment passed before I could see her visibly relax. "Oh, thank goodness," Starry Knight muttered. "She didn't get all of your Soulfire out of your body."

"What are you talking about?" I asked. "Ugh, I can't believe you can't hear me."

I saw Starry Knight take off a glove and place her bare hand over my heart. Her emotions leaped off her, brightly colored flashes and feelings. I could read them as if they had labels: Anger, regret, but most of all, a terrifying amount of fear. I focused on her eyes as they glassed over and her power flowed from her into me.

Another spurt of fire, close to her face, blinked at me. I saw it was the feather in her hair; I was entranced at the dancing light, amused to feel as though it was calling out to me.

Turning back to her emotions, I watched as they changed slightly; there was something more there. I pressed in, working to get closer to her.

As if Starry Knight sensed me, she leaned in. "Come back to me," she whispered, her voice shaky and strong at the same time.

Was it my imagination, or were there tears in her eyes? I felt myself leaning in to look, worming my way back into my flesh, pushing past weariness and reluctance, until my eyes all of a sudden opened and locked on hers.

I felt her joy, rapturous and strong, wash away her dread and push back her fear. A small smirk appeared on her face as she glanced down, a mask of inconsequence hiding her real reaction.

THE STARLIGHT CHRONICLES

"Well," she said, "I guess it's a good thing Aleia and I were here to—*umph*."

Starry Knight's words stopped short as I reached up, pulled her close, and kissed her.

My lips fumbled against hers, desperate and determined, reveling in the feeling of rightness. A surge of power burst through me as she reeled with delight and longing. I was surprised I managed to hold on as I felt my own heart reply in kind.

She might have forgotten our last kiss, I thought, but I was determined to make her remember this one. That was my last coherent thought before the sweet, hot fire of her response swept the rest of them away.

I could feel her fingers tentatively cling to me, keeping me close. My hands held onto her, cradling her face as if offering up a prayer, petitioning this moment to be peeled out of time and spun into an ongoing, separate entity of eternity. Seconds passed as I reached up and found her hair and twisted my hands in its enduring softness; it was intoxicating to the touch, and I ran my hands through it, brushing up against the long red feather in her hair—

When all of a sudden, it burst into open flame. "Augh!" I jumped back at the small fire. "Sorry, I didn't mean to—"

The spark dissolved back into its feather form as quickly as it had lit itself once I stopped touching it. Starry Knight reached up and steadied it, briefly, and I was about to ask her about it when we were further interrupted.

A loud *crash!* from the room over jolted us apart, and I briefly remembered there was a battle outside; one of good versus evil, power against love, and protection over destruction.

I only had seconds, I realized, if I was going to say or do anything. I looked up at Starry Knight, who wore what I imagined was a similar look to the one on my own face—one of confusion and anxiety, the standstill between saying something and wondering if any words would mean condemning the moment.

"Elektra's getting away!" Aleia called out, further ruining the mood. "Are you able to help, guys?"

Still breathless, Starry Knight suddenly backed away as if she had been scalded.

The tangy cinnamon flavor of her was still partially clouding my senses as I sat up.

"Coming, Aleia," she called back as she watched me.

I grumbled, sore as I began to move. "Starry Knight."

She narrowed her eyes. Even from here, I could see her joy switch back into wariness.

I hesitated before saying, "We need to talk."

Starry Knight shook her head. "No."

"Why not?" I asked through gritted teeth.

"I can't."

"Can't or won't?"

"Both," she bit back. "You don't understand."

"Are you guys coming or not?" Aleia asked. "I need your help."

Starry Knight and I exchanged glances, both of us torn between our duties and desire. As another *bang* and *smash* rang out, necessity broke through.

But before we left the alcove, I caught her arm. "I'm not giving up on this," I warned her.

"Like I said, you just don't get it." Starry Knight shook her head and brushed my hand away. "It's better if you just let it go."

"I don't believe that for a second."

"I'm not surprised. You never seem to do the smart thing the first time."

The jag was meant to hurt me, and it did. And it would have hurt a lot more if I hadn't seen the fleeting, flickering look of regret on her face, and I stopped in my tracks as confusion overtook me.

Seeing no choice at that moment, I allowed myself a moment to tuck away the memory of her melting against me, of her lips meeting mine with a matching fierceness. A renewed determination sparked inside of me, and I vowed I would get her to talk to me.

I smiled, despite everything. There was no question now of whether or not she knew of our kiss. "Thanks for the birthday present, fate," I said with a small snicker. It was my favorite gift.

Glass shattered. I hurried to meet up with Aleia and Starry Knight. Aleia, winded and slightly disheveled, was pointing to the window, which had a nice-sized hole shattered through it.

"Where did Elektra go?" I asked. "And where is her minion? You know, the one who was strangling me?"

"Krono is up there." Aleia pointed to one of her daggers, which was stuck in a nearby wall. I studied it for a moment before I saw a haze form around an invisible, humanlike shape. Elektra's power swarmed around him in a static pattern, but there was no other movement.

"Nice work," I said. "I'm surprised he's not moving."

"I sealed him with blood," Aleia explained, showing us a cut on her arm.

Starry Knight balked. "You really shouldn't do that. It's dangerous."

"It's also effective." Aleia turned to me, no doubt noting the flabbergasted look on my face. "Stars have power here on Earth, even fallen Stars. Our blood carries a large portion of that power, and in its purest form. Part of it is because we are born outside of Time's power, and part of it is because we take on elements required to live inside of time while we are here."

"Oh sure," I agreed, more worried about hiding my disgust. There was a good reason I could never follow in Mark's footprints, and it largely had to do with all the blood and

114

bodily fluids he had to deal with at the hospital. I was glad when Starry Knight reached out and pressed her healing powers into Aleia's cut. "Let me jot that down in my notes."

"Kid, the least you could do is pretend to take things seriously." Elysian appeared outside the window. He flew inside and came to rest (uncomfortably) on my shoulder.

"Well, I am seriously trying not to vomit at the moment," I muttered back.

"Where's Elektra?" Starry Knight interrupted.

"She requires more power to be sealed," Aleia explained. "I couldn't get her. She made her exit in dramatic fashion, as you can see."

As I looked out the window again, I began to hear the stomping of several pairs of feet. Peering over the side of the balcony railing, I groaned. "Police … SWAT members, coming up."

"Destroy Krono, and we'll get out of here," Aleia told me. "Use the Sealing Sword."

"No problem," I assured her, pulling out my sword. The gilded wings on the hilt fluttered as I freed it from my scabbard. "I will enjoy this," I said, recalling how the monster had nearly choked me to death.

One powerful slash later, the wall was busted up a bit more, but the demon was gone.

Aleia pulled her dagger out of the wall. "Good work. Let's head out. If you would be so kind, Elysian?"

THE STARLIGHT CHRONICLES

Elysian smiled at Aleia. For all he was upset he'd been more or less replaced, he seemed to like her. I didn't blame him; I liked her too. I already thought she was more informative than Starry Knight, and I'd only fought alongside Aleia once. And she was a pretty decent fighter, I thought. I could already see the fading outline of Elektra's power from where Krono was sealed away into nothingness.

Thinking of that, I recalled I wanted some answers.

As Aleia climbed up on Elysian's back, I turned to Starry Knight and grabbed her arm, then pulled her away. "Come with me for a moment."

She sputtered, obviously upset. But I'd caught her by surprise, and while I knew the SWAT team making its way upstairs didn't give me much time, I was going to take every second I got.

I pulled her away, dragging her through another set of doors, and even though he would have been helpful, I hoped Elysian didn't decide to follow us.

"What are you doing?" Starry Knight finally managed to break free. We'd made it into another stairwell, and that was fine with me.

"I want to talk for a moment."

"No. I've already said no."

"I need to know what happened out there, if nothing else," I said. "We're allies now. You promised."

This is where being the son of the city's top lawyer really came in handy. Lull her in, and then get her to give me the answers I wanted. She sighed, giving in. "Fine."

"Why did Elektra try to ... I don't even really know what she was doing."

"Idiot. She was trying to take your Soulfire."

"Why would she want it? There are plenty of humans who have more power than I do," I said. "Elysian told me once that humans have more power than Stars because they can make choices or something."

"They do," Starry Knight agreed. The crisp tone told me she wasn't happy about talking with me, but she would comply. I think it was some form of a compromise for her.

"So what's so special about our Soulfire then? Or mine?"

A short moment passed before she answered. I could see her weighing out her answers, dividing the small amount she was going to give me from the whole truth. "Every human has a spirit, a will, a mind, and a heart—the last three making up the soul," Starry Knight explained. "The spirit is separate from the soul in humans. In a Star, they are not. When a Sinister tries to take Soulfire inside of a Star, they take both the spirit and the soul. Together, they are known as Starsoul."

"Why is it better to just have the soul then?"

"The spirit is either dead or alive, while the soul is eternal," Starry Knight explained. "Dead spirits are dead; their fate is decided. Living spirits have a special power that protects them from corruption. But souls can still provide power."

117

THE STARLIGHT CHRONICLES

"How?"

"I don't know how to explain it, exactly." Starry Knight sighed. "Any emotions a person feels can provide power. Lost dreams, ambitions. Lost love." She looked at me. "Regret."

"So Elektra was trying to take my Soulfire out of my body."

"Yes."

"And then you brought me back."

"Yes."

I was just about to ask her about the kiss when she added, "And it's a good thing, too. If Orpheus wants your Soulfire, we have to be very careful."

"But he doesn't. He wants me dead, according to what Elektra said."

"We have to go," Starry Knight interrupted. "I can hear the police coming this way."

"I want more answers," I insisted. "This can help me."

"You shouldn't even be fighting." The words had a sharper tone to them, and I didn't hold back, either.

"Look, I *want* to get better. I *have* gotten better!" I protested. "I'd be even better off if you were more willing to help me out."

"Just stop."

THE STARLIGHT CHRONICLES

"No, we're not going back to the beginning of all of our arguments. I promised you I would fight, and I'm going to do it."

Starry Knight shook her head quickly. "I know you want to, and there's nothing I can do about it. But I'd rather you stay out of it. The Sinisters are my responsibility. I'll think of something. You don't need to worry about them."

"Why?" I demanded. "Or can't you talk about that, either?"

"We have to go."

"No, we have to settle this."

She sighed. "Look … just trust me on this. You have to trust me."

"Why should I?" I retorted

"Just … just trust me."

I got angry with her when her eyes went soft, and the violet misted over just slightly enough for my breath to catch.

"Please."

She'd pulled me in without my approval. And I hated her for that. "Oh, my pleasure," I retorted sarcastically. "You—"

The doors a floor below us opened, and pairs of armored officers started coming up the stairs.

It really was the most inconvenient time for this, I thought bitterly.

THE STARLIGHT CHRONICLES

"Stop where you are! Hands up!" one of the SWAT team officers called out.

Starry Knight grabbed me this time, and she led the way back to where Elysian and Aleia had taken off. Squeezing my hand, she leapt up and carried me with her through the broken window.

My own fingers tightened around hers. It was at that moment I secretly began to fear she had just as tight a grip on my heart as she did my hand.

I was so concerned with the idea of just that, I barely noticed Dante Salyards watching us, standing just outside the shadows of the Apollo City Time Tower. I might have said something, if I hadn't caught sight of the time.

One look at the clock and I knew I had been right earlier. I was going to be late for work. In fact, my shift was over before I arrived to start it.

☼9☼
Questions

"So, what was that all about?"

I groaned. *It's not fair. I don't feel like answering Elysian's pesky questions right now.*

"Come on, tell me." Elysian was back down to his "travel size" form, looking more like an awkward lizard than a dragon. I ignored him until his claws sliced into me as he climbed up beside my ear.

"Hey! Watch it," I snapped. "I don't need to go to my party with my shirt full of holes. I have enough problems as it is."

"So, I guess Starry Knight made you mad," Elysian observed.

"What makes you think that?" I asked through gritted teeth.

"What else do you have to be mad about?"

"Uh, I don't know. Maybe getting my soul ripped out of my body for one, or maybe because I missed work for another!"

"Do you know how ridiculous that sounds?"

"Shut up." I raked my fingers through my hair, more frustrated than anything else at the moment. "I'll have to tell Cheryl and Mayor Mills something. I hope it will be enough so I don't get fired."

"City Hall was under attack today. I'm sure they aren't going to punish you."

"That is the *only* thing that comforts me at the moment," I said with a huff. "Well, that and the fact that I don't have to see Cheryl until later tonight. She's working all day at her downtown offices, and even she doesn't have the gall to embarrass me on my birthday at my own party. I hope."

"You're not going to go see her?" Elysian seemed surprised. "You might want to call her then."

"Why?" I asked.

"To make sure she is safe."

"Like I said, she was at her offices this morning. And it is a Saturday. Only a few people were in the building."

"I wonder what caused Elektra to be there then."

"Who knows? That other Sinister, Alcyonë, targeted Mikey for no real reason, it seems, other than he was convenient."

"Is that what Mikey told you?"

I faltered in my steps. "Uh, well, we don't really talk about it too much. I mean, of course he was jealous of me, and I can't blame him for that—"

"I sure can," Elysian muttered.

"—but I never did ask him how he'd managed to get sucked in by a Sinister."

"Maybe you should ask him."

"Maybe I will," I agreed. "I don't think anything Starry Knight told me is going to help me answer any of my questions."

"What did she tell you?"

"Basically, Elektra was after my Soulfire, which I knew, and how it's different from a human's because of the spirit or something."

"Hmm." Elysian frowned. "Your spirit must be alive."

"What?" I gaped. "Of course it's alive. *I'm* alive."

"No, that's not what I meant." Elysian sighed. "Look, there's a very specific function the Star spirit has, and that is access to the Celestial Kingdom. You can communicate with it directly."

"Fat load of help that is," I sneered. "You'd think they'd be more willing to talk to me."

"You're not really in the way of listening," Elysian reminded me with a snort.

"Would you just go away?" I growled. I was more than glad to see Mikey was hurrying toward us. *Thank goodness. I could use a distraction.* "Hey, Mikey," I called out, waving to my best friend.

"Now?" Elysian studied me for a moment. "Boy, Starry Knight must've *really* made you mad."

"I don't want to talk about it!"

123

THE STARLIGHT CHRONICLES

"Dinger! I'm surprised to see you. We were just talking about your party."

"'We?'"

"Me, and Gwen and Jason and Rachel. They just left for your house. They're going to get all the stuff set up."

"Cool. I am definitely ready to party today," I said with a grin as we turned down another block, heading toward my house.

"So I noticed I missed a good fight scene," Mikey said. "It was on the news."

"Already? Man, the media's been getting better at finding us."

"I wouldn't worry about it," Mikey said. "I was in Rachel's at the time and Grandpa Odd—he says hi by the way, and told me to say 'Happy Bard-day' to you, and, yes, that's the actual pronunciation he used, not sure why—and he said the mayor had been making deals with those protesters who have been hanging around the building lately."

"I saw them plenty of times," I agreed. "Hopefully they'll be gone now. It's a nuisance to have them there."

"That's the whole point of 'peaceful protests,' Dinger," Mikey reminded me.

"I didn't see any today, though," I recalled. "Maybe that was why the Sinister attacked. All those protestors. I'm sure some of them would give up their soul for better pay."

"If the mayor was making deals with them, he probably only had a few people from the crowd," Mikey said. "Some were hanging around when the police saw Elektra smash through the window and you and Starry Knight fly out. That'll have the social media lighting up for a few days. I need to get a blog out on it."

I paused. And then I just said it. "Are you sure you should be doing that?"

"I'm being careful," he assured me. "I'm posting while I'm at school, so the traffic won't identify it as me, personally."

"Okay." I thought about Dante, and I thought about SWORD. Dante knew it was Mikey they'd captured a few months ago when he was possessed. Since then, there was no sign they were going to pick Mikey back up, and I would think they'd have more critical things to do than pick up some random blogger. After all, there were millions of bloggers around Apollo City, and even more blogs.

Maybe Dante was trying to keep Mikey out of it? Maybe he didn't know?

Ah, who knew anyway? I mused. There were a lot of unanswered questions at the moment. Probably built up from me ignoring most of them, I realized with a cringe.

But I looked over at Mikey again, and I decided to get some answers as we walked to my house for my birthday party. "So, Mikey, can I ask you some questions?"

"About what?"

THE STARLIGHT CHRONICLES

"I've been thinking," I started slowly, "that I need to start looking for answers. I was wondering if you could tell me about the Sinister who, uh, you know—"

"Borrowed my soul for a bit?" Mikey offered.

"Sure."

"Well, I was upset when she came to see me, initially. And she offered me my hopes and dreams on a platter, pretty much, and didn't tell me the specifics."

I grinned. "So she was kind of like a car salesman?"

Mikey laughed. "Yeah, kind of." But he frowned and said, "She did a good job, though. It was a slow build up, you know? I didn't realize how far crazy I'd gone until it was too late, and I was about to give up entirely when you showed up."

"I see," I said neutrally.

"I read through some of the psychology behind how I felt afterward," he admitted, catching my attention. I knew if Mikey studied up on something, it was big. He barely did anything for school, let alone research. In the last two years, the only thing I'd ever seen him take seriously was the topic of girls.

" … But it was like an addiction and self-entrapment, all wrapped into one. Some of the articles likened it to an abusive relationship."

"Sounds terrible," I agreed. "And it looked terrible, too, if you don't mind me saying so."

Mikey shook his head. "I don't like to think about it."

"I can't blame you there."

A moment passed between us before Mikey glanced over at me. "So ... you didn't happen to get Starry Knight to agree to come to the party, did you?"

I laughed and immediately changed the subject. Between SWORD, the Sinisters, and Starry Knight, I'd had more than enough supernatural drama for the day.

☼10☼
Celebration

"So, how long have you and Gwen been going out now?"

"What?" I yelled back, unable to hear clearly over the crush of voices, music, and other media forms. I was talking with Via Delorosa, much to my despair, and her forever lackey, Laura, who was also Gwen's best friend.

Laura smiled at me. "Via asked you how long you and Gwen have been dating now," she said, enunciating her words. I might have thought she was teaching me English if I knew she wasn't quite *that* terrible.

"About, uh, two months? Six weeks. Something like that," I said back, almost regretting coming over to one of the small snack tables in my backyard.

Via rolled her eyes. "You never were a thoughtful boyfriend," she said. "You're lucky Gwen is desperately in love with you."

I narrowed my eyes at her for a second, before letting it go. Via and I had dated, tragically, and I didn't regret dumping her. I had a feeling she specifically came to my party to find a way to make people care about that, more than to celebrate my birthday. "Yeah," I agreed, "I'm glad Gwen doesn't mind how inattentive to her I am." It was supposed to be a sarcastic comeback, but guilt twisted through my stomach. It was probably truer than I'd have liked (especially if I was feeling guilty). "Why don't you go see what Poncey's up to?" I asked. "I hear he's looking for a new girlfriend."

Via laughed. Even in the muffled static of sound, my ears could hear her musical peals. "Oh, Dinger, you're hilarious." She patted my hand affectionately and said, "Gwen's a lucky, lucky girl."

Okay, I'm not sure what she means by that. *I need to get out of here.*

"I'm going to go check on the cake," I said. "Excuse me."

I'm instinctually quick-witted, so the cake idea came out of virtually nowhere, and I was glad for it. But it was a good idea, too, so I headed back inside the house to the kitchen.

On my way, I slapped high-fives with friends, waved to Gwen as she was chatting with some of our other classmates, complimented the band, and participated in one round of the Awkward Game, my favorite party pastime (I won). I posed for some photos and remarked on which social media tags to use.

But as I slid through the door, relief cloaked me, and I relaxed enough I noticed it. Was it possible to be uneasy at the idea of being comfortable?

I peeked up the stairs in the direction of my bedroom, wondering how Elysian was doing with all the people around and all the baked goods in the kitchen. I grinned at the thought of him sifting away some of the sweets. I should save him a couple, I decided.

"Hey, Birthday Boy," Rachel greeted me. "Did you know you and William Shakespeare have the same birthday? Grandpa told me that earlier."

"Yeah," I muttered, not caring.

"I'll have to ask you for that band's number. We can have them for another music night down at the coffeehouse. They're wonderful."

"I think so, too. Should be no problem getting them to play for your café," I agreed.

"All in all, it looks like your party is a success," Rachel said with a smile.

I waited for the self-satisfaction to rise within me, but it didn't come like it usually did at parties. *Huh. Weird.*

"Do you feel any different?" Rachel asked, handing me some gingerbread chocolate chip cookies.

I took a cookie and bit into it, wondering if she was reading my thoughts. "What do you mean?"

"Do you feel any different now that you're seventeen?" she asked.

"Oh." I didn't think it was because I was seventeen that I felt different. I thought about my previous parties, how I was the king, no matter who really was having a birthday. I'd talk Tetris and sports and movies and everything else for hours, and people would laugh and cheer for me and with me. It was something that meant a lot.

I suppose I had something that meant a lot more to me. And I liked it. *That* was what was different, I realized. I'd taken a small "vacation" from my supernatural self before, when I hated it. But since then, and since coming back, I'd come to see that, while it was work, it was also worth it. I enjoyed it, and even when I didn't, I looked forward to

THE STARLIGHT CHRONICLES

experiencing it again. My power had always been there, a part of myself, but had become a larger part of me while also part of something much larger. Adonaias had always been there, too, but he had changed from a figure to be feared wrongfully into one to be feared rightfully. And Starry Knight … I had been waiting for her, even without knowing I'd been waiting for her; she was a mystery I'd been waiting my whole life for the chance to solve.

There had been a feeling hanging over me in the past few weeks, a feeling that change was coming. It didn't click until that moment that change had already arrived. I was changing, things were changing, and I was finally okay—in fact, more than okay—with that.

It was flooring, the idea I was looking forward to something more in my life than Tetris and being cheered on by my friends. Those things still mattered, of course, but there was more, and I was enthralled there was more.

I caught sight of the clock, and I mentally counted down the hours until I would get to leave and go meet with Aleia, with my supernatural destiny.

"Hamilton?"

"Huh?" I jumped. "Sorry, what did you ask, Rachel?"

"Are you okay?" she asked.

"Oh, yeah, I'm great." I smiled brightly, turning on the full charm. I might have had some kind of epiphany, but I still had a duty to my party peers. "I was just wondering when the cake was coming, that's all."

THE STARLIGHT CHRONICLES

"They're over there. I just got them out."

"'Them?' As in, plural?" I asked. I looked over to see there were a large, double-layer cake, stacked up and ready to go with my name and candles all over it. And then there was a long sheet cake beside it, with no frills or fun stuff on top. "What's this?"

"Raiya told me to bring you a chocolate cake, with the mocha icing." Rachel looked at me carefully, like she was trying not to come off as offensive.

"You didn't have to listen to her," I scoffed. "I was fine with the cherry."

"Strawberry."

"Whatever. The one Gwen wanted." I sighed. "This has to be some kind of joke to her."

"I don't think so." Rachel turned and shrugged. "But joke or not, there's nothing wrong with it. *I* made it, not like the cookies."

"What do you mean?" I asked. "Who made the cookies?"

"Raiya. Gingerbread's her specialty, remember?" Rachel looked at me quizzically. "I've told you that before." Seeing the no doubt horrified, blank look on my face, she added, "Oh well. You know, you might want to be nicer to her. She's really a good friend once you get to know her."

I don't want to get to know her. Even if her cookies had apparently managed to make me dream of gingerbread and autumn moonlight on a regular basis. "I don't think so, Rachel. We argue too much to be friends."

"Do people have to agree on everything to be friends?" Rachel asked.

"Well, no. But it's … I just, you know, there's just—"

"Just stuff it." The sharp tone surprised me. That was what probably managed to make me stop talking. "The cake will be ready soon, Hamilton," Rachel continued, her smile returning, though it was slightly forced. "I'll bring it out in about ten minutes; I just have to light the candles."

"Okay," I said, slinking out of the kitchen as smoothly as I'd entered. "See you then."

For some reason, the rest of my party just seemed like a bit of a haze to me. Gwen surprised me with football tickets, which I would probably never really use (not a Cleveland fan), and she gave me a kiss as she handed them to me. Some others bought me gifts, too—a planner (probably because of all the things I'd "forgotten" in the last six months), a new movie I had no interest in, a new video game I would probably not actually play for several months after the party, but I would research it enough to make it sound like I did, and some other stuff. I also got some gift cards and money and other stuff I liked.

Cheryl and Mark both came in late with Adam and managed to get some cake before everyone else started leaving. While she was pretending to eat her slice, Cheryl showed me the card Mayor Mills had given to her for me; I could tell she was ecstatic about getting to say, "Stefano's giving you a raise!" I didn't have the heart to tell her I'd missed work earlier. But at least it seemed she didn't know about it.

Fortunately, it wasn't long before it was time for everyone to go.

"Bye, guys!" At the end of the night, I waved to everyone as they left. I watched as Mikey took the bags Gwen was holding. He winked at me.

"Thanks so much. See you Monday!" Mikey called back. He was going to take Gwen home, and then come and meet me at the marina. I felt unsure of telling him about the expedition at first, but it was useful to get his help in getting Gwen home safely.

Once the door was shut, I slumped over in relief. I was free. "Elysian!" I called. "It's time. Let's get going."

THE STARLIGHT CHRONICLES

☼11☼
Sailing

It was amazing to me how much I'd grown in truly appreciating the night. Up on Elysian's back, I could see past the whole distance of Apollo City, all the twinkling yellow lights of office buildings and the scattered skyscrapers, the red and white traffic lanes, the shadowed fields of playgrounds and small forests, and the dark but distinct edge of Lake Erie and its waters. The city was dressed in a low cloud cover, and rising mist from the marina area.

Even though I'd become more of a night person since middle school (largely thanks to online chatting and texting and gaming), I wasn't actually outside a lot. So clinging to Elysian's back while the night winds breathed through my wings was a surprising, deep source of the rarest, truest form of magic.

For me, I knew it also held the unique sense of home that could only be groomed or unexpectedly gifted.

"It's almost eleven," I called up, barely catching sight of the clock tower in the distance through the rolling fog.

"We'll get there, don't worry." I could see the smile on his face as he said it.

Elysian descended and slowed when we reached Dock 42, and I jumped down. The instant my feet touched the wooden landing, I knew we were not alone.

Glancing around, I did not see anyone right away. I could see up the hill to Lakeview Observatory, down to the woods, and up to the other hill where my housing development was located. I could see the shipping districts and the smaller container boats. Even in the well-lit areas, the fog was creating a barrier around us, so it was hard to make out details.

"I'm glad to see you've made it," Aleia called out to me.

I smiled to see her form walk out of the cloudy shadows. "I told you I wouldn't miss this."

"I'm glad to hear it." Aleia smiled. She was back in her warrior gear, with her daggers tucked away on one side. She wore a small pouch on the other side (I respected her too much to make a fanny pack joke), out of which she drew her orb.

"I'm going to place a stasis on our time here," she explained as the orb glowed a dark reddish color, lighting up with her power. "This means when we get back, you will be able to come and resume the timeline of your life, beginning at midnight tonight."

"Okay, great." I was glad; I wouldn't have to skip out on sleep to get some experience in. I even had an extra hour to get home before I usually went to bed. Perfect.

"He's here."

I glanced around, looking for another person to come up behind us, maybe walking out of one of the warehouses.

It was only when I heard the booming splash behind me and felt the remaining moonlight flee that I turned around.

My mouth dropped open of its own accord. A ship's anchor was sinking into the bay area. It was similar to the traditional ones from the history books, tethered to the biggest vessel I had ever seen. I whistled in soft shock. "That's one big boat!"

It was huge, in the form of a nineteenth century clipper ship, though there were some distinct differences. Instead of sails, there were giant wings. Up on the main mast was a lookout's post, encircled by halo lights. The body of the ship itself was dressed in cosmic shades, blending in with the sky even as it stood out. Lightning crashed against the bottom of the boat harmlessly, creating a bobbling effect.

"Yes, that's the *Meallán*, and it's captain, St. Brendan the Navigator." Aleia grinned, no doubt pleased at my reaction. "He's come to give us a lift."

"Where are we going?" I was having trouble concentrating as I saw the grand sight before me.

"To see the Star of Time, my sister, at her home between the roof of the world and the edge of the Celestial Kingdom."

"Ahoy there!" I glanced up to see a man, complete with coal black hair and piercing bright blue eyes, standing on the top deck of the *Meallán* as he heralded us.

"Ready to go, are you? The tide's coming in rough, I'm sure, so we best be setting off soon." The man's voice, complete with an Irish brogue, sang out to us invitingly.

Elysian, taking the initiative, hoisted Aleia and me up onto his back and took off, threading his way through the mist and lightning, and finally landing safely on the deck of the *Meallán*.

137

I looked around, suddenly feeling very conscious of how stupid I no doubt looked. My eyes were wide as I looked around, watching the ship's crew make their way along the deck, climbing the masts and adjusting the wings of the sails.

Everything was pristine and pure, glowing yet not glowing, as though it were completely one and the same, and it was completely normal that there were no shadows or darkness on this floating miracle.

"Whoa," I finally managed. I turned to face the captain, who was still looking down at the marina docks.

I came up behind him just as he called out once more. "My lady! Joining us, are you?"

I ran to the side, only to see Starry Knight's unmistakable form by the shoreline.

She waved back. "Not tonight, St. Brendan."

"You've a way of teasing me, lady."

Starry Knight laughed and blew him a kiss, which shocked me. "Never," she promised.

I decided I should not like St. Brendan too much.

"It's good seeing you." St. Brendan waved back. "You know how to reach me if you need me."

Starry Knight said nothing, but waved back. In the last moment, her gaze turned to me. I felt the sails pulse, as the power of the celestial tide took over, and the power of her gaze slowly receded, along with my reality.

THE STARLIGHT CHRONICLES

"So, you're the one they call Wingdinger? Strange name, if you don't mind my saying so."

I turned and reached out a hand. Pending judgment, no need to be rude, no need to be friendly, I thought. "And you are St. Brendan."

"Nice to be making your acquaintance," he said as he smiled back.

"How do you know her?" I asked, nodding down to the far-off shore of the world.

"Lady Justice? Oh, we've been friends since we met," he said. "Shame she's fallen to Earth. It's not often I get to go past." He looked past me at Aleia. "Fortunately, I've a good way of keeping tabs on everyone, don't I, Aletheia?"

Aleia laughed. "You're such a dashing rogue, St. Brendan."

"Alas, only the sea is meant for me," he said with a wink. He turned back to me. "And the Prince, being kind, has given her to me to tend. So, Wingdinger. Let's get you up to Lady Time, then, shall we?"

"How's the sailing look?" Aleia asked.

"We might have some bumps along the way, but what's a bit of fun without a bit of a risk?"

Elysian frowned as Aleia and St. Brendan chatted like long-lost friends. Which, I reminded myself, they probably were.

Meanwhile, Elysian and I managed to look like the awkward wallflowers I usually made fun of at parties.

Elysian spoke first. "He seems nice."

"I don't like him."

"Of course you wouldn't." Elysian rolled his eyes. "I'm, uh, going to take a look around. Just try and stay out of trouble."

St. Brendan and Aleia continued talking as I watched the endless sea of starlight and space dance by.

The night never seemed so bright, I thought, as we flew by suns and stars, some shining hot, some burning cold. All were different, unique, and seemingly with their own temperaments. I looked past the jib to see we were heading toward a pure white star in the distance.

The closer we got to it, the slower we seemed to go, and the more the stars didn't seem like stars, but people and planets for angelic purposes. Here, home was not just a feeling, it was *alive*.

There were blackened stars, silent and dead, too. The remnants of fallen Stars, I realized. Suddenly I could see them everywhere, like scars on a body's skin.

I wondered where mine had been as a lingering sense of despair clutched at my heart. If I was a fallen Star, as Elysian had said, and had more or less been proven to me in several ways before, what could have made me leave such a place?

The whispers of music began to creep out from the horizon, and a pervasive sunlight, though it was brighter, became not only perfectly bearable, but preferred. I could see other stars change from the burning gas balls of my science class to home to humanlike creatures, where their forms were all different shades of beauty rather than distinctive colors.

I watched as the ship soared through a playful pond of comets, running through them like a pile of glitter. I saw the Milky Way as it transformed from a clouded rainbow across the night skies into a river of life, not running from the heart of the galaxy, but light clouded with darkness falling in on itself.

It was a slow death of something ... something that should have been eternal.

"This is what death looks like?" I asked, more to myself than anyone.

"If you want to save something that can choose to be saved or choose not to be saved, you give it time." St. Brendan came up beside me.

"What? What do you mean?" I asked.

"Stars are not unlike the angels, you know. Stars live between Time and Eternity. But it is only within Time that the Angel of Death resides." He smiled wistfully. "But it is because of Time that change is possible."

I didn't have anything profound to say; I knew most people feared death. Before the change in my own life happened, that was part of the reason I thought life didn't have to matter; but I was beginning to see that was precisely why life *did* matter. And I could understand what St. Brendan was saying. Death was definitely a change, and not one that would be ignored.

THE STARLIGHT CHRONICLES

St. Brendan spoke again, his voice a spoken sort of music with its rhythmic lilt. "Humans have the power of choice on Earth while they live. Yes, Death is, but it is only a way to pull what has lasted into what will always last, and a way for what cannot last to be carried off."

"Uh-huh. I see." I turned back to look at the scenery before us, where black chunks of rock and hardness drifted silently. I was again reminded of what the demon inside of Logan had said: To be a fallen Star was a punishment.

With the eerie scars of fallen Stars around me, I decided I didn't really want to talk about this stuff anymore.

"So, what Star are you?" I asked, trying to be polite.

"I'm not a Star," St. Brendan said with a laugh. "I'm a Reborn."

"A Reborn?" I asked.

"I was a human on Earth," he explained. "And when my body died, my spirit was called, and my soul came home. So here I am now."

"Oh. So, when did you live?"

"Oh, I'd lived many years before you," he said. "I made my life and living with the sea, in search of meaning and lasting treasure. I did not find it on Earth, but I found someone who knew the way."

"To Eternity. Then to here."

"Aye," he agreed. "Once I arrived, I was given my job. I map out the worlds all through Eternity and Time, and to the

THE STARLIGHT CHRONICLES

higher realms as well. I record all I find in my log, and I keep it updated."

"Were you here before I fell?" I asked.

"I was, yes." He turned away from me, looking out at something beyond the endless horizon. "You were the Star of Fire, you know."

"I was?" I asked, suddenly awed. I'd forgotten I didn't like him as I leaned in to hear more of the story.

"Yes. It's what you were named for."

"Wingdinger?"

St. Brendan laughed, slapping me on the back in a congenial manner. "I'd forgotten how forgetful the Milky Way's Veil can make you. Sit for a spell, lad, and enjoy the view. I've got to make my rounds. My crew has their jobs as well as I've got mine." He gave me a kind of salute and walked away.

It was as if he'd known I wanted to hear more, I thought bitterly.

"We should be coming up on Lady Time soon."

I looked over to see Elysian had quietly returned. "Oh, you're back now," I said. "Did you enjoy the sights?"

"There's no need to be short with me, kid," Elysian muttered back. His own sharp tone made me look twice at him.

"Are you okay?" I asked, noticing he had gone quiet and contemplative, something I knew Elysian was not, unless he was thinking of something important.

"If you must know," he bit back, "I was looking for my brother."

"Oh." I briefly recalled that Elysian had mentioned his brother, and even other changeling dragons, before. "Did you find him?"

"No."

There was a large amount of feeling behind the answer; I knew there would be an even larger story. I wisely said nothing.

We stared out into everything for some time before Aleia came up to us. "I haven't been sailing with St. Brendan in a long time," she said. "I've forgotten how fun it can be."

"Uh-huh."

"What's wrong?" Aleia asked. "Are you still wondering about Starry Knight?" When I didn't say anything, Aleia sighed. "You know, you really shouldn't worry about her. She didn't come tonight, even though I know she wanted to."

"Why not?" I asked. "She and St. Brendan seem to get along well enough." There was a bitterness to my tone I didn't really want to explain to Aleia, but there was nothing I could do about it.

"She has her reasons for staying away, even as much as she wanted to come," Aleia explained gently. "She and St. Brendan go a long way back. They've always been friends."

Friends with a charming space captain, but not her co-defender.

I didn't say anything. I just huffed and shrugged my shoulder, trying to look indifferent.

Aleia changed the subject. "We'll be passing through the Field of Lights soon," she said. "It's one of the most beautiful sights in all the realms."

Inside, I debated with myself about commenting. Finally, I decided it was no time to alienate Aleia, who was charged with teaching me. So I figured I would suck up my bad mood and play along with her for now. "What's in the Field of Lights?" I asked.

"It's where human souls are allowed to reside before they are called down to Earth." She tugged on my arm. "Come and see with me."

I followed her to the edge of the deck and leaned over, following her lead. We were sailing into a large, nebulous web of light and power.

"Look at them. They're so beautiful." Aleia pointed to a baby-like figure as it slept inside one of the seemingly infinite gelatinous bubbles blossoming up from the heart of the light. I watched as the baby tucked itself into a ball with a fist in its mouth.

"Reminds me of Adam, when Cheryl was pregnant," I said. "Or pictures of tadpole eggs."

145

"They begin to take form down in here, in the time pods, as their physical bodies are being created. But look over there. You see those figures moving?"

I saw the enlightened flashes of childish figures. Some had long hair, some had short hair, and some were taller or shorter. Some were pudgy, and others were lanky. They were just beings of light, but even from where I was, I could see their smiles, hear their laughter, and see their joy.

"Look at that one. It's about to go into its time pod." Seeing my confused look, she further explained, "The egg-like bubble housing the babies."

The child of light she'd pointed out edged close to a bubble. I could see it was a boy, with a love of climbing and curiosity set deeply inside of him. As I watched, his light slipped inside of the pod, and took the shape of a human baby. At first I didn't see how the light was going to survive inside of it, but then it not only settled in, but I saw it grow brighter. His face turned toward me, and I saw he'd begun to smile and squirm like a human baby, too excited to stay still.

Even though I was not chummy with children like Gwen was, I grinned. "He's going to be a handful for his mother."

Aleia smiled. "They wait in the pod until their bodies are ready. And then, of course, they are inserted completely into time and they are born."

"So the baby in the womb is not a full person until birth?" I asked.

"They are a full soul, with personality, temperament, even preferences," Aleia explained, "and their spirits are knitted

146

THE STARLIGHT CHRONICLES

into their physical bodies, while they are being prepared. Life inside the womb is preparing them for life outside the womb, just as your life on Earth is preparing you for life beyond Earth."

"What do you mean by that?" I sure was asking that a lot tonight, I mused. I hope I didn't come across as stupid.

She grinned at me. "Think about it. Eyes that do not need to see, lungs that have no access to air, and arms and feet with nowhere to yet go. Can you imagine what life is like outside of your body now?"

I thought about Elektra's attempt to take my power, my inner light. My vision had expanded all the way around me, and I was able to see things I never could see with my human eyes. "I guess so. Makes sense," I agreed.

A pair of what looked like sisters playfully danced past us, and I saw another baby leap headfirst into his own time pod.

"What's that one over there doing?" I asked, pointing to a baby in a pod who was, in his baby form, starting to crawl out. "Is he being born on Earth?"

Aleia following my direction. We watched as a being, no doubt some kind of Nanny Star, suddenly appeared beside the boy and took him away.

"Looks like the lad will be staying here," St. Brendan spoke.

I almost jumped at his sudden appearance. "What do you mean?"

"The baby died in the womb, Hamilton," Aleia whispered.

I glanced back, an irreconcilable sadness suddenly piercing my heart. "What's going to happen to him? Will he go into some other pod?"

"No," Aleia said. "Every individual soul is unique. While he did not get a chance to live on Earth, he will still get to reside here. Most of the ones who do not get born remain behind, taking care of the others."

"Will he be a new Star then?" I asked.

"No, those are human souls that play there; while other Stars are created, they reside elsewhere. Though they will often visit here to play," St. Brendan explained. "But don't worry about the babe. He'll hear from Gabe soon."

"Who's Gabe?"

"He delivers messages around here, such as that."

"He will be given a new assignment and purpose," Aleia said. "You know how the Prince is fond of second beginnings."

While I don't think she meant it as an insult, second chances were still a bit of a sore point with me. I didn't like to think about my own learning experience in regard to *that* particular lesson. It was enough to have learned it; I didn't want to be reminded of it anytime soon. "Does everyone have a purpose?" I asked, a little skeptical at this point.

St. Brendan laughed. "That's like asking if everyone has love." His brilliant eyes glittered. "Some are born with it, some find it, some make theirs, and some see it in others. The point is not that we have one, or make one, but that we are all part of a larger movement."

I watched as some creatures approached the Field of Lights. I was surprised to see a winged horse among them, and a pair of cat-like creatures with heads like eagles. It was more than enough to distract me. "Mythological creatures are here, too?"

Elysian coughed behind me. "Ugh, you already knew that, kid."

"Oh. Right." I'd forgotten about Elysian. (Imagine that.)

We passed through the Field of Lights, wandered by heavenly meadows, and sailed through seas bound by no land or gravity. I saw trees with no roots, their circulating branches interlaced with other spirits and creatures; I saw clouds stretching across galaxies, netting together different nebulas as they grasped each other with friendship. I saw wonders too bright and too beautiful; many of them passed through my memory as one sight after another sent a wave of awe and respect through me.

And all of this, I thought, was still within Time's power.

Which did make me wonder. Would I see Adonaias, the Prince of Stars, on this trip?

I felt the swirl of the ship as it began to slow to a stop—at a huge castle in the sky, no less. I was amazed to see it was not flat, like it was on earth, but spherical, built out of gemlike stone. There was a cloudy mist of a moat surrounding the palace, a slim stream of nebulous flotsam making Time's residence look more like a strangely-built Saturn than anything else.

"There's the end of the River Veil," St. Brendan said.

I turned toward him, watching as the ship pulled up closer to the edge of my universe.

"Along with the River Guardian, the Serpent." He pointed to the small ring around the castle, the one I'd thought was a small moat. Stepping back, I saw it; rather than being a river or a stream, the white waves were the discarded, scaly skin of a snake-like creature, bound up in a stasis of time, almost as if it had been crushed between moments and seconds.

Before I could ask, Aleia tugged my arm excitedly. "We're here."

☼12☼
Lady Time

It was hard to say what kind of expectations I had for meeting the person responsible for slowing time down during my English classes.

Knowing her power and knowing her sister created conflicting pictures in my mind's eye. Aleia, from my short interactions with her, I knew to be kind, patient, and friendly. She was beautiful in a way that emphasized her strength and her desire for good. I did not know time on Earth to be so kind or patient, and definitely not user-friendly.

Despite that, Lady Time blew my expectations away.

The instant I saw her waiting for us on a small landing platform, I knew she was a Star of great power. I could also tell she was Aleia's sister.

The same brilliant, piercing green eyes caught my gaze, looking not at me but through me, while the celestial torrents added a graceful wind to her ebony locks. A scepter was in her hand, shaped in a way that reminded me of the hand of a clock. A bit cliché, I decided, but she was entitled.

Elysian grumbled behind me, but I ignored him, more out of spite. What could he be upset about here? I wondered. There was too much to be dazzled by to be grumbling. And it said something that *I* was the one saying that.

"See the clouds above the castle?" St. Brendan pointed to the full, fluffy clouds, pure white in their appearance. They looked like the whipped icing on a cupcake made of glass and light. "That is where Time's power ends and the eternal kingdom begins. This is one of the few places on my map where there is a portal that one can go through either way."

Aleia stepped forward as St. Brendan brought us into safe harbor. I watched as she greeted the other Star, and saw the laughter and joy in their faces as they hugged. There had to be a comfort in having a sister, I thought at the sight of them.

Thinking of Adam, I supposed it helped Aleia to have one so close in age and experience. And interest, too. While Adam was my brother, I had never felt particularly close with him; protective, sure, maybe, but not close.

Elysian still had a disgruntled look on his face. I turned to St. Brendan instead. "So what will you do while I'm here?" I asked.

"My crew and I will sit out a spell, relax in the Gardens of Time here no doubt," he said. "But if you're up for it, when you return, I'll show you how to surf." He smiled. "No point in just coming up here for the learning when there is plenty of fun to be had."

"What about your job?" I asked. "Mapping out the universes and stuff?"

"Work is my pleasure," he agreed. "But pleasure is a pleasure, too." He laughed at his own cleverness, before he added, "All aside, people are the true pleasures in life, and it is good to get to spend time with them, in both work and pleasure."

"Did you used to hang out with Starry Knight?" I asked.

THE STARLIGHT CHRONICLES

"Starry Knight? Oh, you mean Lady Justice. Aye, and even you, before you fell. Which is why I'm thinking you'll get the hang of nebula surfing up here right quick."

"Hamilton, come down here," Aleia called as I disembarked on Elysian's back and felt the lightness in the air of space between time and timelessness. "This is my sister, Alora, the Guardian Star of Time, one of the *Manorayashon*, and a First Light Warrior of the Prince."

"Hello." My tongue was thick in my mouth as I reached out my hand in greeting. After all those special dinners with Cheryl's coworkers and colleagues, I knew how to behave when meeting someone. But I had to admit, I was nervous and impressed for the first time in a long time. Well, since meeting Stefano, anyway.

Alora clasped my hand, and I could feel the power inside of her. Her skin was darker than Aleia's—a warm, golden color that made me smile, thinking of how much she remained in the sunlight of her own star. "Welcome to my home." She indicated the sea of clouds around us. "My sister tells me you have many questions."

"Yes, I do," I said.

She looked at me carefully, and said, "Your heart has been softened since you began fighting the Sinisters on Earth."

"My heart?"

"And your ego," Alora said. "The people who won't learn are those who will volitionally hold on to their own views, and those who think they do not need to learn anything more."

153

"I will agree with you that I wouldn't have wanted this several months ago, maybe wouldn't have cared even a few months ago. Elysian can tell you—" I glanced behind me to see Elysian had returned to St. Brendan on the *Meallán*. He was still staring at the flimsy clouds and scaly snakeskin moat. "Elysian! Are you coming?"

He shook his head. "Not now."

I narrowed my gaze at him. He'd been so excited, I thought. Why was he faltering? I would never understand him. "Okay; suit yourself."

I turned back to Alora as we entered in through an archway. There were gardens of flowers, with some I recognized and others I didn't. There were smooth walkways, and so much purity and goodness about the air I swear the power of it propelled the road itself to leap up and meet my steps. There was a glassy, marble sheen to the place, and I saw Alora's castle was made of a fine, crystalline glass.

"It's gold."

"Huh?" I glanced over at her.

"My home is made of gold," she explained, answering my unspoken question. "While you have gold on Earth, most do not realize that gold, in its purest state, is transparent."

I awed over it, and the next few hundred things I saw, as Alora showed me around her home. She talked with me, chatted with me about the weather (because even up in outer space they have weather, I guess), and about her role as the Timekeeper for Earth and its habitat. I barely heard her, but I more or less could see it for myself. I found out she lived on

THE STARLIGHT CHRONICLES

Polaris, the North Star, and no one on Earth was the wiser. Her world, and the world around mine, was a realm only some could see, and others could experience. Others, she told me, did not want to see it.

"Who would want to miss out on this?" I wondered aloud. I was half-glad when she didn't answer me, but rather turned inside of the heart of her home.

Following her, my eyes met a wide-open atrium, with a large blue bubble floating in the middle of it, like it was center stage in a large auditorium. Looking closer, I saw the big blue spherical pool, which held a projection of Earth. All around it, I saw other sparkles of lights, like little specks of glitter stuck to a computer screen.

"The lights show the different Stars, which surround and protect your world," Alora explained as I asked. "Stars were given a unique job at the beginning of creation. We were to give off light during the night, as rest is good for humans. When evil entered the world through humanity, the Stars who were born after continued to shine, but there were some who were given additional tasks.

"There are a large variety, each differing with personality, power, and purpose. But there are a lot of similarities. Each Star was allowed to choose to do his duty, and each one was granted the right to a wish."

"So wishing on a star is a valid fairy tale?" I asked, immediately wishing I hadn't used the term "fairy tale."

"Possibly," Alora said with a small smirk. "If the Star wishes the same wish as the human who wishes on it. That's one of the things which differ for us and humans."

"I remember meeting a Star last Christmas. She gave me a wish."

Alora shook her head. "Lady Hope, Elpece, has often wandered down to Earth. Especially for that time of year. She loves the holidays." Alora indicated a bright pinprick on the pool. "She's currently in what you know as the Orion Constellation. There's a batch of starlings there that she never fails to go and watch as they play."

"Sounds about right." When I last saw her, she had tons of little starling fairies dancing around her that night.

"But she would not have given you a wish. She would have given you a gift, such as fulfilling one of your wishes."

"What's the difference?"

"A wish is something that you alone can determine, while your gifts are innate." Alora pointed her staff at Orion's constellation. "Lady Hope is able to do many things, but first and foremost, she finds a way to give hope to those who need it."

I thought about how I could see emotions as they fluttered through a person, and how I could enter into the Realm of the Heart if I leaned in. "I'm not sure how being able to discern emotions is going to help me."

"You are the Star of Mercy," Alora told me. "Understanding how someone feels is central to sympathy, empathy, and compassion. Reading emotions might seem inconsequential, but the littlest things can make the biggest differences in the end."

So I was the Star of Mercy, and Starry Knight was the Star of Justice, and we'd been friends, apparently argumentative friends, on the other side of Time before I'd fallen—before we'd fallen.

"I guess you're right." I laughed a bit. "I wish I'd brought a notebook. I'm not going to remember everything you tell me."

"Learning is part of my power, as is healing," Alora said. At my raised eyebrows, she explained, "Yes, very similar to Lady Justice's power; after all, justice can easily bring healing after the cause of pain has been righteously judged and condemned, whereas time can distance a person from the hurt and help them see it in a new perspective."

Silently, I agreed, but I suddenly wondered exactly how much Alora knew of the situation between Starry Knight and myself.

"Love, too, can heal all, of course, but time and justice are different elements involved in the worlds under my care. Of course, you know about that, since your own transformation ..."

Still worrying about feeling awkward about Starry Knight, I tried not to lose focus, looking around at the awesome sights around me, every few minutes I had to talk myself out of thinking this was a dream.

THE STARLIGHT CHRONICLES

"You are not just here to learn, of course, even though that is my primary role in this matter. If you're ready, I would like to ask you some questions."

It was at the idea of questions that I forced myself to pay attention. "Sure. That only seems fair, since I'm going to be asking you a lot of questions, too."

Alora smiled. "I'm not after information so much as a confirmation." The pool behind me glittered, transforming from a celestial sky into a globe of cerulean mist as Alora continued. "Are you committed to the choice you have made, in regards to being a Starlight Warrior of the First Light under the Prince?"

"Yes." *Of course I am. I wouldn't be here otherwise.* "Why so many questions about my commitment?" I wondered if it was a reflection of my past choices.

"On Earth, you'll find people don't need to be taught so often as reminded," Alora explained. "And time will test the endurance of your commitment." Her voice softened. "It is not a question to shame you."

"Okay." I tried to let it go.

"All right. If you are ready, step into the pool behind you."

I turned and saw the swirling, clear blue orb. I was confused, but seeing the look on Alora's face, I shrugged. It wouldn't be the first stupid-looking thing I've done for my duty. "What's this for?"

"It is in this pool where the heart of my power resides," Alora explained. "But it is also a portal to the other side, as

THE STARLIGHT CHRONICLES

St. Brendan might have mentioned to you earlier. You have many questions. It is my duty to give you answers, and here is where you will find the first ones."

"So I'll get some answers?" I half-wondered if they would come up in alphabet soup letters.

"Yes. But I must warn you," Alora said, "You might not like what you find."

"I'm not afraid." I dismissed her warning, having heard it before so many times in different video games and movies. If there was something worse than not knowing, I was more than ready to find it; I was tired of being passive with my supernatural self. My palms pushed against the surface, and, before I could say anything else, I felt myself pulled in by a rush of swirling power.

☼13☼
Submergence

The water pressed into me from all around. I opened my mouth and felt myself attempt to scream. Quickly, I realized that was probably not the best idea, and I briefly wondered if I had come all this way just to drown.

But before I could fight my way back to the edge, the water surrounding me transformed into a staggeringly bright light, no longer pressing into me, but shining through me, filling my heart, my eyes, and every inch of my being. I felt the heartbeat behind the starlight, resonating with the rhythm of my own, and a beat pulsated all around and through me.

I saw Eternity open up before me, and I felt the last remnants of Time fall away; life was in every breath, freedom surrounding every molecule, and goodness permeating the fabric of time and space and all the other dimensions. Gravity had a relative effect on my physical body, almost like I was giving it out, rather than being drawn in.

I felt a spirit of wisdom flutter by and understanding playfully whirl around me.

Faces began to form, light upon light in my bubble, and names came with them. I saw Alora, and Aleia, and even Adonaias, reigning above all. I saw millions of others, some Reborn, like St. Brendan, and starlings and souls and all of the beauty of creation, wearing robes of crimson and silver and gold. White flames of fire burned inside of my hands as the cool warmth washed over me.

THE STARLIGHT CHRONICLES

And then I saw her.

It was my Lady Justice, in all the glories of my pre-fallen memory, as she played her harp, her face undaunted by the shadows I'd come to be familiar with on her fallen form. My heart nearly broke; my first question had been answered.

I was in love with her.

The truth hit me hard. In a world where there was no chance at covering up truth, and there was no bravado and no need to hide from vulnerability, I couldn't hide it or deny my feelings.

It was still a surprise, even as it wasn't a surprise.

I tried calling out to her. But her name was a voiceless whisper on my lips.

I don't remember her name. But why? I wondered.

As I watched, a figure came up to me, one I didn't recognize immediately. He gave me a cup full of water, offering it to me to drink. As I looked on at Lady Justice, my hands seemed to work of their own accord and I drank from the cup.

A wave of burned fuzziness swept through me as the last of my body passed away into fire.

The pristine white flame around me dulled into a red spark, as I felt empty pressure slam against me. Fire turned black and painful, as I was stripped of all my pre-fallen glory. My Starsoul began to dissolve, speck by speck; the skin dressing my inner being hardened as it chipped away, tossed to nothingness in the torrent atmosphere. My Soulfire remained, giving off a dark light.

My memory was washing itself away. I saw Lady Justice fall apart, her music no longer playing. I felt my soul start to collapse inside and I saw her light drawing me in, even as my own heart condensed down to a point of singularity.

"Come back!" I called, trying to push against the invisible darkness of the void. All light dispersed, as every dark speck from inside me was left in its place, and a solid emptiness wrapped itself inside of me, pulling me into a life that stopped at the edge of myself.

All the fire inside of me launched out, calling for love, but to no avail. The void smothered me, leaving me with nothing but the warm remnants of a blood-colored flame.

The emptiness of nothingness consumed me, burning me, leaving me alone in silence with only endless agony, loneliness, and shame. I knew I deserved it, I knew it was over. There was nothing I could do. I collapsed into dust and debris, piled up and crushed beneath the foot of righteousness.

"Let there be light."

The familiar voice called out into the darkness, and I saw my Soulfire, darkened with guilt and pain, reduced to ashes, suddenly blaze with new light. It wasn't my Starsoul that encompassed my soul, and that sheltered me beneath the wings of providence.

Before I could ask, in a split second, I felt the earthiness of my human life formed, and I felt the world form underneath me as I returned to it.

I saw new faces; faces of my childhood, my life, and others. I saw my body formed from gathering the dust of the earth, the power of Eternity pressed into the core of my heart and soul, and the brightness of my origin congealed into my blood. The music faded, the voice of truth faded, and the Starsoul changed, adding in my own life's light, melding into my own soul.

My memory was buried in the dirty world of fallen humanity. I watched it all build up again, from the particles of a Star's remaining nothingness. I felt sadness burrow into me, hopelessness engulf me. Paralyzed, I saw only the emptiness of the universe and creation, as I was stripped of my sight.

Gradually, I began to move again, my soul still crying out for love, even as it was unable to see it guiding my steps.

Somewhere in my heart, I felt that tiny pulsing, reminding me of Adonaias' promise. I'd been forgiven.

A shadow burned against the darkness—a small orb of darkness entrapping the light.

The meteorite.

It burst open, and the Seven Deadly Sinisters poured out, supported only by a fallen Orpheus. When they crystalized over, he wept, but only at the sight of the meteorite.

A spark of fire in the distance beckoned back to me.

THE STARLIGHT CHRONICLES

And then I felt the dreariness, the weariness, the sleepiness, and the slumbering as it began to peel away from me, allowing the music to come through, unhindered and clear; I could hear the awakening in my soul as it answered before it was even asked, calling me back.

All at once, the darkness and images were gone, as only fire came through, the blood-colored flame from my Soulfire bursting free and submerging me once more in perfect light.

And then it was over. I felt the water swirl around me again, and I heard Adonaias say to me, same as it had been before, with more of a question behind it: *"Command me."*

I answered back the same as I had before. "Give me wisdom and courage and the strength to follow where you lead me."

Fear left me and peace descended around me. What I thought were angels of all sorts began surrounding me, and then I slipped away, being pulled back to the pool.

As I opened my eyes, I could hear a spirited, voiceless whisper from inside the black hole of my recreated, resurrected heart:

"Do not be afraid. Here I am."

The water relaxed me, and I felt it release me. Before I knew it, Alora reached out a hand, and I took it, wondering at how solid she felt. I felt myself crawl out of the pool in the heart of the Star of Time, and there was no doubt in my mind aliens were not a strong enough argument.

THE STARLIGHT CHRONICLES

Glimpses of eternity, the ravages of transgression and time, and the burden of humanity—all living inside of me—was too much.

"How do you feel?" Alora asked.

"Like I need a nap," I murmured, still shaken and stilled, all at the same time.

"Then sleep. You have time, here," Alora reminded me kindly. "The consecration is over, and you should rest now."

I must've agreed. My eyes closed, too exhausted to dream.

☼14☼
Draco

I found myself awake, seemingly several hours later, looking up from the floor of the garden, and surrounded by fresh grass, soft but unbreakable, and delicate, vibrantly-colored flowers.

"So you're awake."

My eyes darted over to see Elysian up on his haunches, standing over me. The rest of my body was unwilling to move.

"I'm surprised," Elysian continued.

"Because you're awake before me?" I joked.

"No," Elysian retorted. "I'm surprised because it hasn't been that long. I thought you'd be out longer. Not everyone will come up so soon after a baptism of light like that one."

"Baptism?" I struggled to get up, knowing full well Elysian wouldn't be leaving me alone anytime soon. "I don't know if I'd call it that. It was more like, I don't know, a supernova, I guess. I felt crushed and then fluffed out like a sheet in a washing machine."

"You seem to have benefited from it," Elysian said with a shrug. "You even look different."

"What do you mean?"

THE STARLIGHT CHRONICLES

"Your wings." Elysian nodded in their direction. He plucked a feather and handed it to me. "See? It's changed color, from black to red."

"Awesome," I muttered, still groggy. I rubbed my eyes and squinted at the feather between Elysian's claws. He was right, I saw; the ebony of my wings had been seemingly burned, leaving a fiery red quality to my feathers. "I wonder if this means I'll be able to fly now?"

"We'll add it to the list of questions for Lady Time and Aleia."

"Where are they?" I asked.

"They're around. I saw them walking out by the *Meallán* with St. Brendan a while ago. Alora will be looking for you soon, since you're up now."

"Oh, okay." I rubbed my temples. "Elysian, can you tell me why I fell?"

"It is a punishment," Elysian said, "for stars who rebel against their duty or orders. Or misuse their power."

"Why didn't you tell me that?"

"I did. Way back at the beginning, when I was explaining how the Stars began to fall. Remember? You laughed at me and said it was not 'real,' just some part of a fairy tale." He narrowed his gaze. "I suppose you might not have been listening at the time."

167

I had a feeling he was right. "Why would I fall though?" I asked. "Why would I go to Earth? Adonaias told me I'd been forgiven."

Elysian bristled. "Maybe your punishment was delayed. It's happened before. The Prince of Stars delays confronting the fallen. Or it's possible you chose to fall yourself, wishing yourself on Earth. Some stars have done that after falling in love with a human."

"But I wasn't in love with a human at all," I objected. "I was in love with Starry Knight."

"Well, then I—what?" The rough quality of his voice raised an octave higher. Had it been any other time, any other topic, I might have laughed. But there was nothing funny about this.

"Er, yeah. It was a bit of a surprise to me, too."

There was a beat of silence before he responded. "Was it really that much of a surprise?"

"Yes. No. I mean … I don't know." I shook my head. I didn't want to tell him.

"Are you still in love with her?"

Another moment of silence. "I don't know," I finally said. I turned my gaze away and looked out into the distance.

"Either way, you should let it go," Elysian told me sharply. "Love never makes things simpler. It only complicates them."

THE STARLIGHT CHRONICLES

"What's your problem?" I asked. "You've been acting weird since we got on the boat. You're the one who wanted to come."

Elysian's jaw visibly clenched. "You aren't the only one who has been affected by falling," he said.

"What are you talking about?" Then seeing his face, I realized what he meant. "You mean *you*? Because I thought you came to find me."

"That was part of it. But it was a forced exile."

I stood up and looked down to see uncharacteristic defiance written all over my so-called mentor's face; it was hard to see him as my treat-loving lizard who would bury himself into my bedcovers at night. "I don't understand."

"You are a fallen Star. I am among the fallen, too," Elysian muttered. "I thought coming here, I would be reinstated. But I'm not going to be."

"Someone told you?"

"No. Don't be an idiot." Elysian sighed. "Can't you feel it? Can't you *see* it? We are surrounded by a pure world, caught between Time and Eternity. It is protected, heavily, from corruption. It is a miracle we were even allowed to come aboard the *Meallán*."

"I didn't notice." At least, I thought, not at first. My awareness had gradually sunk in, so gradual I barely noticed that I had noticed it at all. "I must be getting used to the miraculous."

"This world is too good for us, even me," Elysian muttered. "And especially you."

Suddenly, I realized he was angry with me—very angry with me. I was more shocked than scared, but also confused. "If all bad is bad, what makes you think *your* bad is better than mine?"

"It's not fair. It's hard enough to get you to admit there are such things as right things and good things, or bad things and wrong things." Elysian began to pace back and forth, stomping around on the perfect grass. "You're a lazy warrior, and a liar. You can't deny it, either," he snapped, before I could interject. "And yet, the Prince had 'forgiven you.' You, and not me."

"Besides the fact you've overlooked all your flaws, have you asked for his forgiveness?" I asked, curious.

Elysian's head briefly transformed into its bigger, more deadly form, his anger doing damage to his self-control. "Do you think *you* needed to!?" His great voice bellowed out of his snout, blowing a strong but harmless wind all around me. "No, there's no doubt about it in my mind that *you* deserved to fall. But *I* was tricked." He returned to his smaller size, before adding, "I know I was tricked."

"Did I trick you?" At his glare, I placed my hands down in calm frustration. "I don't remember. I still don't even remember my Star name. And I'm confused about a lot of things. St. Brendan told me I was the Star of Fire, and Alora told me I was the Star of Mercy, and I can't remember Starry Knight's name, either, even though I was supposed to be in love with her." I slumped down in front of Elysian. "I'm just asking for the truth, honestly. So tell me. Was I the one who tricked you?"

Elysian was silent for a moment. I could see his eyes fall, his anger cooling. "No," he finally murmured. "My brother did."

"Your brother?" That was a surprise. "But you said he was up here. If he tricked you, wouldn't he have fallen along with you?"

Elysian nodded to the scaly, white flotsam surrounding Time's palace. "He's fallen all right. But not all of him left."

I looked past him, and saw the shed skin of the River Guardian. The closer I looked, the more I realized that it shared a lot of Elysian's traits; it had the same scaly pattern, the distinctive curve of the nostrils, and the similar shape of its horns. "That's ... him?"

"His dragon skin," Elysian said. "When Draco fell, he was defiant to the last. He was cursed, and he shed his skin to stay behind, trapped up here, while he escaped with his memories and power. He went to the Earth like you, to live as a mortal. But because his skin is up here, he will never die as a mortal will." Elysian snarled up at the ghostly moat. "Draco always was a cunning beast. He managed to do quite a bit of damage before falling, and even afterward. Adonaias himself cursed him so severely that even the snake—one of his favorite transformations—remains part of the curse. All the days of his life, the snake will slither along the ground of the earth, and Draco himself will never be able to rise in true power."

"What happened to him? Is he still on Earth?"

"I suppose. He's hard to keep track of." Elysian narrowed his gaze. "But it was said he would meet his end. His death has already begun. Justice will come to him, and it will be his undoing."

"How did he trick you?" I asked.

"Before he left, he managed to convince me to help steal some water from the River of Life."

"What's the River of Life?"

"It's pretty self-explanatory from the name." Elysian rolled his eyes. "The River Veil protects this world from the fallen; the River of Life is the source of all life. It's said to be made of the blood of the Prince himself."

"That's creepy." I tried to add some levity into the conversation.

"It's because of the River's power that he was able to shed his dragon skin and transform into a human-like form," Elysian said. "I was tricked into getting it."

"How did you manage to steal it?"

"Aleia is one of the Stars who watch over it. Lady Time remains here, in the ongoing present, but Memory has to flow somewhere. You'll find all sorts of memories in the River of Life." Elysian hung his head. "I was her friend before we fell. But I betrayed her."

"So that's why you have trust issues," I joked. I didn't want to talk about this anymore. I don't know why, exactly, but it was hard to brush off. I was getting scared.

THE STARLIGHT CHRONICLES

Elysian bristled. "You'd feel different about it if it had been you."

"Probably." I thought about what Alora had said about compassion earlier. But I didn't need to read Elysian's emotions; they were written plainly on his face.

"That's why," Elysian continued, "you need to forget about Starry Knight, whether you love her or not. You'll only end up hurting her, or getting hurt yourself. And that's not going to help us capture the Sinisters again."

I didn't know if I agreed with him or not. He had a point, and it had been a hard lesson he'd learned. I didn't want to diminish that. "I am sorry about what happened to you, Elysian."

He sat down on the ground and crossed his arms. "I thought if I could get you to seal away the Sinisters again, it might help us get back into the Celestial Kingdom." He glared at me. "I guess you don't need that, though, since you've been 'forgiven,' according to Adonaias."

"I might not need to earn forgiveness," I agreed. "But I'm still on Earth. And that should tell you forgiveness is important, but it's not the same as not needing it. It's not the same as perfection."

"It's not on us to earn forgiveness." Elysian and I looked to see St. Brendan standing behind us. He was still in his captain's outfit, but he looked strangely at home in the gardens of Time. He took his hat off in greeting and looked over at me. "You can earn trust, and respect, and even affection. But mercy earned is not mercy."

THE STARLIGHT CHRONICLES

Elysian snorted. "I don't remember inviting you into the conversation."

"Elysian," I muttered. "It's all right. It's not like we were talking in private."

"I was."

St. Brendan smiled. "In terms of invitations, I've come to extend one of my own. Lady Alora has asked that you, now that you've rested, come and see her in the atrium once more."

"Sure." I nodded. "Can you just give us a few moments?"

"Aye, no problem. She'll be waiting for you."

"Thanks." I watched as he exited as quietly as he'd entered, before turning back to Elysian. "Let's talk about this later, okay? I need a break."

"It's always later for you. It's an insult," Elysian insisted, "that you are forgiven, when you have obviously done more wrong than I have."

I could feel my patience snap. "What do you mean, 'obviously?'" I asked, my own temper kindling. "Besides, I don't know why I fell, and you don't seem to know either, and I really don't see how I caused you any grief before we met on Earth. You might wish you were better than me, Elysian, and goodness knows you act like it all the time. But you're not, and you're not going to be. Especially with that kind of thinking." I pointed up at the remainder of his brother above us. "Maybe you'll end up like him if you're not careful."

I stood up and turned around. "I'm going to see Alora. You coming?"

"Pft. No," Elysian snarled.

"Fine." I walked off, wondering if that was really the most honest conversation I'd ever had with Elysian.

☼15☼
Knowing

Alora was waiting for me inside her castle home, back in the atrium, where her star of light pooled brightly in the middle of everything. She nodded in welcome.

"Hello." I waved, just a bit nervously. I didn't recall much about coming out of the pool before, but I had a feeling I didn't look my best, and I didn't want her to think of me as weak. I decided to do my best in improving upon my previous impression. "St. Brendan said you would be here."

"Thank you for coming," she said. "I'm glad to see you are feeling well."

"Much better," I agreed. "So, what's next?" I almost joked about whether or not I would have to face a pit of snakes or a minotaur.

"Your questions." Alora's gaze went solemn. She gestured for me to follow her as she began to walk around the room. "My questions have been answered."

"You mean about my commitment?" I asked.

"Not quite. I was more curious about how you had managed to fall down to Earth to begin with," Alora admitted. "There are very few instances where Stars and beings such as yourself have managed to get through without my approval or compliance. In fact," she murmured, turning back toward the watery pool of light before us, "there has only been one major rip in my power since I was given charge over the Mortal Realm."

"That's a pretty good record," I said, trying to make her feel better about the situation.

Her crystalline green eyes went sharp as she paused in her steps. "You know as well as I do the implications cannot be ignored."

"I know." I shuffled my feet. It had been many months since I felt properly flustered. "Sorry."

"I'm not mad at you," she assured me. "I'm angry at the evil that it has caused. But let us turn our attention to Orpheus and his charges."

"Starry Knight—er, Lady Justice—once called—"

"You should call her Starry Knight," Alora told me. "As of now, she has been able to rebuild an identity from the ruins of her former role. Let us call her what she would have us call her."

"Okay by me." "Lady Justice" was too weird of a name, anyway. It was hard to fit to the fighting figure I'd come to know as we sparred over Sinisters and demon creatures. "She once said that Orpheus had been a Leader in the Celestial Kingdom. What did she mean by that?"

"He was originally in charge of the Seven Starry Virtues, who, incidentally, became the Seven Deadly Sinisters," Alora told me. "He was their Leader Star, who watched over them, worked with them, and cared for them."

"So he was responsible for causing them to fall?" I asked.

177

THE STARLIGHT CHRONICLES

Alora began to move once more. "There are a couple of things I know you do not understand," she began, "and I will try to answer your questions as much I can. But there are some things I cannot tell you, and for reasons I cannot tell you."

For the first time since my arrival, irritation plagued me. It would be too easy to have all the answers, I supposed.

"One thing should be clear: You, and all Stars, make your own choices. Your logic, your emotions, your being, and even your instincts to a high degree—these are all gifts you have at your disposal, along with many more, and you have the choice to use them as you see fit. In a place with no time, there is very little cause for you to believe you have to make such choices or decisions right away."

I nodded, saying nothing.

"Because of this, there are consequences that follow, especially when evil choices are made. Falling is a punishment," Alora explained. "But it is not the only one. The Sinisters chose to follow Orpheus, as he chose to follow his own master, and so they were punished by being trapped in a prison of light—trapped within the heart of a bright star."

A chilling awareness took hold of me. When the meteorite first struck Apollo City, starting this whole adventure and rekindling my dormant supernatural powers, I was caught up in the blast and knocked out. I was sent to the hospital to recover, only to dream a vision—a vision of a bright star; one that called to me in song and light. As I watched it, it exploded.

THE STARLIGHT CHRONICLES

Recognition finally hit me. "Starry Knight's star."

"Yes."

"She was their sister." It was incredulous, I thought. How could Adonaias make Starry Knight imprison her own sisters? That just seemed too cruel to me. But there was another, more-pressing question. "Why didn't she choose to follow Orpheus, when he starting leading the rest away?" I asked. "I mean, she couldn't have been trapped with them, so she refused to go along with Orpheus, right?"

"Yes. She was the only one he really wanted to follow him," Alora explained. "Once she said no, he went after her sisters."

I felt my mouth open in surprise. "That's just—"

"What?" Alora asked, giving me a small, teasing smile. "Evil?"

"Yes!" I sputtered. "That's terrible. Why would he do that?"

"Because he wanted her power," Alora explained. "Power is a strong lure for evil."

I could understand wanting power. Being powerless was not fun; I knew that from high school all too well. "But he already had power," I said. "He was in charge of her."

"Yes, but that doesn't mean he could control her, or that she belonged to him."

It didn't seem to make much difference to me. But then, my mother did have a lifelong appreciation of semantics for good reason. "I suppose." I sighed. "So, I guess he's still after power. That's why he's stealing the Soulfire from humans. He needs their power to do something."

179

"Yes." Alora sighed. "Orpheus wants to rule over the Celestial Kingdom and all the Realms. The key to doing so lies in the Mortal Realm."

"Why? How? Soulfire doesn't seem to do much, other than allow the Sinisters to move around and cause trouble with their minions."

"Soulfire is just part of it. Orpheus needs other things, too."

"Like what?"

"Blood, for one. Blood is a powerful source of life and memory in humans, and in demons it can lend direction." Alora sighed. "There is also Starsoul, and a Star's wish. With these four things—Soulfire, blood, Starsoul, and a Star's wish—he could manage to rip the kingdom from my power."

"Why those things?" I asked.

"Soulfire is the life-giving energy from their origins. Blood helps seal them to the human world. Fire purifies." She looked at me, and I had a sudden thought of Starry Knight's feather. When I touched it before, it erupted into a bright flame. Was that its power? I wondered. To purify evil?

Alora continued, unaware that I'd paused in my listening. "A Star's wish has great power in moving worlds, or even Realms."

I jerked out of my contemplation. "And he has those things now?"

"Not all of them. Soulfire from humans is readily available, and blood can easily be found in sacrifice. A Star's wish—well, there aren't too many in the Mortal Realm who have that power anymore, and of course, Starsoul is only found in Stars, too." Alora sighed.

Recalling how Orpheus wanted to kill me, rather than use my power, I was suddenly confused. Maybe mine wasn't good enough, I recalled, since I had fallen.

I decided to ask another question. "How can that stuff help him gain enough power to take his revenge? I can understand that it's powerful stuff, but how does that affect us here?"

"All of the Realms are intricately connected to the Immortal Realm. Your universe is the only one who has managed to break through my power."

"The rip in Space-Time you mentioned earlier?"

"Yes." She grimaced, and for the first time I could see the power in her hatred. There was a gritty, grim overcast to her expression. It made my toes curl just looking at it.

I would not want her for a foe, I thought. "Why is the rip so important?"

"Because, Orpheus' master seeks to separate the kingdom from its King," Alora explained. "There are two ways to take over a kingdom. One can either dispose of the king in question, or one can take the kingdom."

"So that is why the Prince has come to work with you. He's working to stop him. Who is Orpheus' master?" I asked.

"Alküzor." The name sent a stinging heat into my fingertips. Alora glanced over at her pool. A powerful cloud of green, glowing eyes that were looking up at me appeared in the misty waters.

Recognition once more poured through me. "I've seen those eyes before." I walked up and placed my hand against the waters. My hands were shielded against the wetness. "I saw them when the meteorite came crashing through Apollo

THE STARLIGHT CHRONICLES

City and exploded in the city. I was in the hospital at the time." My fingers tightened against the glassy surface.

"He is trapped in his spirit form, stuck inside the bright fires of the Earth, but he works through his minions."

"Why would Orpheus want to listen to him?" I asked.

Alora smiled. "You should know, from all your time with the humans, why."

I shook my head. "I can't imagine why."

"If there is something you want, something you desperately want, there is a way to get it. That's why it's important to want the right things." Alora stepped into the archways of the atrium and looked out over a balcony. Farther than the eye could see, the growing power and majesty of the universe continually expanded from under my feet. "Orpheus wanted a power that wasn't his. He wasn't able to get it."

"So Alküzor got it for him?" I asked.

"No." Alora shook her head. "Starry Knight refused him."

A new appreciation for Starry Knight's self-control budded inside of me, even though I'd lamented it earlier when we kissed.

I was suddenly proud of her. She did the right thing, and, recalling Orpheus' power, I had no doubt it had been no easy task. "So now Orpheus is determined to get revenge and power. He thinks his master will find a way to give him Starry Knight's power once he has control over this Realm."

"Yes."

"That's a large, complicated plan." I shook my head. "Why doesn't he just get over her rejection and just accept his power's limitations? Seems simpler."

Alora laughed. "I wish that were so," she said. "Some things are not so easy to get over. Maybe Aleia will tell you her story one day."

"Aleia?"

"Yes."

I wondered at it, before I waved it off. "I know her story. Elysian told me. She has fallen because she was tricked into helping Draco."

"She has been forgiven for that," Alora replied softly. "Though there is still a price to be paid."

"Helping me seems like a fitting punishment," I said with a sigh.

Alora chuckled. "I do not see it as a punishment," she remarked, reminding me *she* was supposed to be helping me, too.

"Good to know." I grinned back. Star or not, it never hurt to be charming.

"I do not see it as a chore, either," Aleia interjected, as she stepped out onto the balcony, taking her place by her sister's side.

"Aleia." I nearly jumped. "I wasn't saying anything bad about you."

She laughed. "I'm not worried, I promise. I came to see how you were doing."

"Alora's told me Orpheus is out to kidnap and conquer the universe for his master, so he can have the power he wants over Starry Knight and everyone else," I explained.

"That's a succinct way of putting it," Alora murmured.

"Did you get all your questions answered?" Aleia asked.

"For the most part," I said. "I do have one more question, I guess."

"What is it?"

"Where do I fit in, with all this?" A whisper of helplessness wrecked through me suddenly. I fought hard to keep my confused turmoil out of my voice. "I mean, it's all very well and good that Orpheus needs to be stopped, and Alküzor or whatever his name is should be punished, and all his evil contained. But where do I come in? I know I am a fallen Star, but I didn't even know about it until Elysian came to find me, and even now, I don't remember everything I should."

By the time I was finished, there was a bitter anger that was unleashed with every word. Yes, I had been excited to embrace my supernatural powers. But now, I was up against the most determined egomaniac literature could describe, who had forces beyond what I could even imagine and all the time in the universe to achieve his goal. How could the eighty to a hundred years of my life make any difference?

I glanced back up at the two of them, regretting my outburst, even though I was consumed by the paralyzed fear of an impossible situation.

"You are a fallen Star, called to seal away the Sinisters once more," Aleia said.

"I know that," I scoffed. "Why?"

Alora and Aleia exchanged glances and had a silent conversation between the two of them. They seemed to be weighing out their concerns between them. Finally, Alora turned back to me.

THE STARLIGHT CHRONICLES

"There are lots of reasons why," she explained gently. "But you already know the answer."

I wanted to shout, "No I don't!" But I thought better of it. "Then I don't understand it." (*That* sounded smarter.)

"It could be something you'll figure out later," Aleia said. Her tone was light and, in all fairness, I knew she was only trying to be helpful. But I felt her words were condescending at best and reproachful at worst. "You'll just need to have faith."

That's stupid. I sighed. "Are you saying I shouldn't question anything then?"

It's not that." Alora shook her head. "But it's about making sure you are asking the *right* questions. So many people get stuck in trying to answer questions they don't need to have answered."

"Or they actually don't want to have answered," Aleia added.

"Or if they ask about things that aren't relevant to what they're looking for?" I suggested. "That's a lawyer trick, like circular reasoning or misdirection."

Alora's lips quirked up in a rueful smile. "I see you've been learning quite a bit on Earth." She stepped forward and took my hand. "You have been consecrated for your task. You have learned, and you have my blessing as you continue on to capture the Sinisters and live your life."

"I do want to know," I said, "what I will do when everything is over. You know, when the Sinisters and Orpheus are captured and everything. I've learned about the

185

THE STARLIGHT CHRONICLES

past, and why I am in my own present, but what about the future?"

Alora straightened. "It is not for me to tell you what life will bring to you," she said. "But I can tell you the purpose of your life is not just to seal away the evil you've encountered. There is much more to it—and you get to decide a great deal of it."

"Is it possible I'll be able to retire from the superhero business one day?" I asked. A small swirl of hope fluttered around inside of me at the thought. "I'll be able to become a human? I could wish for that, right?"

A moment passed, and before she said it, I knew it was bad news. "You no longer have a wish," Alora told me in a quiet voice.

I frowned. "But Adonaias said I was forgiven. Wouldn't that mean—"

"No." Alora shook her head again.

I sighed. It had to be enough that I was called, and I had answered, even if I wasn't entirely certain why.

THE STARLIGHT CHRONICLES

☼16☼
Surfing

We embarked on the *Meallán* soon after I left Alora. She sent us off with a flurry of pomp, hugging Aleia and even petting Elysian, who was still seemed pretty grumpy to me.

I decided I liked her, even if I wasn't sure if I liked her answers. Or even some of her information.

She pulled me close in a hug as well before I left, giving me a cloak of friendship and well-wishes. She used the opportunity to warn me.

"I want you to know, there's been another issue with Orpheus," she murmured. "He has been talking with someone I can't see."

"Someone you can't see?" I asked. "Someone outside of Time?"

"Or able to manipulate it." Her breath tickled my ear as she whispered. "There are not many demons and minions of evil who can hide from me; other Stars or beings could be responsible. It could be trouble."

"I'll look into it," I promised. "Though I'm not sure how."

"We might have a traitor in our midst," she cautioned. "So please be discrete." Her eyes went to Elysian and Aleia, before landing on St. Brendan. I wondered if she could even mean her sister, or Elysian. Or was she even worried it could be Starry Knight? I was stricken by the thought, but before I could ask about it, she stepped back from the ship and it was time for us to leave.

"Please be safe."

"That we will, Lady Time." St. Brendan's Irish brogue was complemented with a thick layer of respect and admiration as he gave her his own gallant farewell.

As soon as Alora's star was just a spark on the horizon, he turned and grinned mischievously at me. "Are you ready to go surfing, then?"

I laughed, but it was only several moments later that I realized he was serious. I refused to worry about it. Right then, anyway.

Despite my intentions to keep St. Brendan at bay, I felt a kinship with him growing every time he laughed. And I was giving him plenty to laugh about, apparently, as I clung to the borrowed meteor-like surfboard in my hand. Its energy radiated from the core of the unique material. "Are you sure about this?" I asked, probably for the tenth time.

"You're the one who should be sure," he remarked cheerfully. His hands rested comfortably on the helm of the *Meallán* as he pulled in closer to a small sun. "Have courage, and you'll be fine." He pointed out to the growing surge of a solar flare. "Push off on your stomach and head for the top of the surf using your wings. Once you're there, pull up onto your knees, and eventually onto your feet. Take your time; you've plenty of it."

"I'll be right there with you," Aleia promised, tucking her long skirt into her boots so she could move more easily. "We

THE STARLIGHT CHRONICLES

have done this before, Hamilton," she promised. "And you were great."

"I'm still not sure about doing it now, though," I retorted. "Should I practice some more on the deck?"

"You've practiced enough. Just try it." St. Brendan grinned. "I'll be along to pick you up by the time you finish riding out the wave." He pointed out in the distance, to the left of the ship. "That there's where we're heading."

Squinting past the surging solar flares, I saw it was actually a large tree, one of the circular ones, where the roots were tucked in and around the trunk. A small, bright river of sliver and red water flowed through its heart.

Resignation overcame me. "Alright."

I balanced on the deck's railing with my surfboard and let out a sigh. Chances were, I would not die. It was hard to say if that particular thought was less terrifying than thinking I would wind up looking silly. I'd never actually surfed before. On Earth, anyway.

"Go on now!" St. Brendan banked hard to the starboard side, and I felt the ship rock underneath me, I jumped as I lost balance, and grabbed onto the board's edges tightly.

The celestial winds seem to pick up, allowing me to glide. It was similar to what I imagined riding over the water would be like, and I felt a nervous giggle escape me regardless. I looked forward to the bright sun before me, as a flare lashed out.

It was time to move. I slanted my wings to push myself in the direction toward the "wave" of the sun's power; I shot

189

toward it and, by the time it was close, I had relaxed. Out of the corner of my eye, I could see St. Brendan and some of his crew cheering me on.

I pulled up onto my knees as the pressure increased. I reached out my hands to steady myself, and, saying one last quick prayer, felt my confidence shift along with my balance as I rose to my feet.

"This is amazing!" I felt a strange sense of vertigo as I glanced below me, seeing no water or support; but I knew it was there, even if I couldn't see it. My wings widened, slowing my speed a bit, and my hands flowered open to grab the wind and stardust as my board hit the warm wave of surging sunlight.

"Great job!" St. Brendan called out.

Applause and acclaim from others reached me as I glided along the waves. I tried a couple of tricks out, and was more surprised at how familiar the motion seemed to me.

A jump and a twist and a turnaround later, the flare had passed and my velocity dwindled. As he'd promised, St. Brendan was close by. Using my wings, I channeled the remaining energy to push toward his boat.

"Great going, lad." St. Brendan commended me as he reached out and pulled me back onto the deck. "See? You always had it in you. I told you it wouldn't take you long to enjoy it again."

I slumped over on the deck. "That was awesome," I agreed. "I can't believe I ever forgot how to do that. It felt so natural."

THE STARLIGHT CHRONICLES

"As I've said, the River Veil is a tricky one," St. Brendan assured me. He sat down beside me, checking the board over.

I watched him for a moment. "You said you knew me as the Star of Fire before. How come Lady Time said I was the Star of Mercy?"

The look of concentration lost its focus briefly. "Yes, I did know you, in both forms." He looked over at me. "It is as I said earlier. Mercy is not earned. You were born as the Star of Fire, one of the first ones to be counted among Earth's protectors. Before long, you grew in power, and others noticed, including those who rebelled—the Warriors of the Second Light."

"Did they trick me into joining them?" I asked.

"As I understand it, they wanted to bring down the highest orders of the Stars first and foremost. After all, they were rebelling, not just against the Prince, but all of creation in many ways."

"Elysian told me of their leader before," I suddenly recalled. "Alküzor."

"Aye."

"No one knew exactly why he decided to turn. Is that true?"

"No one can speak for another," St. Brendan agreed. "But there are common traits of those who would separate from the Prince, with power and pride at the center of it all. If I'm allowed to have a gamble on it, I would wager those to be the primary reasons.

191

THE STARLIGHT CHRONICLES

"But as for those who did rebel, they managed to take quite a bit of Stars and Angels along with them. One of them was Orpheus. And he wanted nothing more than to bring down Lady Justice."

Starry Knight. No wonder Orpheus had been so angry to see her on Earth, I recalled. In seeing her for who she truly was, he had to have realized he failed in destroying her.

"He'd been a Leader Star in the Kingdom, in charge of the Seven Starry Virtues, and often known to others as a Star of Courage. Now, the Prince has plans for Stars marrying, just as humans do. And when he met milady, because of their shared love for music, particularly the harp, and many other commonalities, he brought it on himself to ask for the Prince's blessing."

Shock shot through me. Alora hadn't mentioned that the reason Orpheus wanted Starry Knight was because he had been in love with her. Maybe that was the real reason he'd been upset, I mused. He had failed to forget about her. "Let me guess. The Prince said no?"

"Aye, you've the right of it. Orpheus was surprised, to say the least, at the Prince's response. And his confusion, rather than trust the Prince, left his heart open to temptation."

"So he rebelled and got the rest of the Starry Virtues to turn with him, in hopes of getting Starry Knight—I mean, Lady Justice—to fall as well, in revenge?"

"I suspect that is the case." St. Brendan nodded. "He was a fool to do so. He should have known better than anyone how dedicated milady was."

THE STARLIGHT CHRONICLES

I thought of Starry Knight's focus, the quiet, steady relentlessness about her fighting style, and the heights of her ambition. "That's true. But she ended up falling, too."

"Milady had her own weakness," St. Brendan agreed. "She held her sisters, after they turned, in the bright prison of her own star, rather than let them fall to Earth or burn in Time's end. I suspect it was love that caused her downfall."

"Love?" I asked. "How can love be a downfall?"

"Easily enough, when it is misplaced or manipulated."

It took me a moment to agree with him, and a moment more to ask the question I'd asked Alora and Aleia. "What was I doing?" I asked. If I had been in love with Starry Knight as well, maybe that meant something. "How did I know Starry Knight?"

"When some of the Stars rebelled, you joined them. Orpheus was a friend of yours, too, believe it or not as you will. He no doubt poisoned your mind."

I grimaced at the thought. "Maybe he tricked me," I said, "like Elysian's brother did to him."

"It would not be above the Second Light, unfortunately," St. Brendan agreed. "I do not know the details of the event, but you wanted to come back to the Prince's side before too long."

"I wanted to come back?"

"Yes. So, the Prince, being the Prince, offered you mercy. Lady Justice objected, I believe, but the Prince had worked

THE STARLIGHT CHRONICLES

out the terms to where you would be punished, but you would also be forgiven."

So Starry Knight hadn't liked me. Not even really back before we'd fallen. I could see her now, getting along with me, all the while thinking I deserved to be punished more severely. Just like Elysian did.

That would be like her, I thought. "Oh. Why can't he just have forgiven me? It doesn't seem that hard, especially since he is the Prince."

"You've been up here a while now. You can tell this is a different world from your own; and the worlds after this, even more. You cannot come back to perfection with imperfection; they resist each other like oil and water. It is a matter of justice then, and rebirth, recreation. So the Prince provided a way for justice, and then gave you mercy. Then, you were reborn, the first Star to be reborn." St. Brendan looked over at him. "Inside of you, in your own Soulfire, you have been given what the Reborn call the Blood Flame. It burns within you, along with your own fire.

"I don't think it's any coincidence you were the Star of Fire before Mercy. Fire cleanses, and fire gives life and light even as it destroys; and blood—blood covers up the sin and scars of a broken being."

"That's weird." I said it without thinking, and almost regretted it, before St. Brendan laughed.

"Aye, it is 'weird,'" he agreed. "But we take for granted the ideas we have are somehow 'normal.'" He nodded in the direction of another small, nearby sun. "Speaking of normal,

THE STARLIGHT CHRONICLES

how do you feel about another run? It's not every day you get to surf on the waves of sunlight."

I grinned. "Sounds good to me."

Several more rounds of nebula surfing later, I felt strangely different. I loved chatting with St. Brendan; he was a well of information. Not just on my past, but on the stories of Time and the various legends and myths I thought only belonged to Earth.

His perception on the situation I had to deal with was different from what Alora saw, even from Aleia. He *knew* the Stars, not just *knew of* them. It made a world of difference to me, to understand them and their actions.

There was something to knowing, I thought. Understanding the Celestial Kingdom, and the Stars and other souls who lived around it solidified my supernatural identity, much like St. Brendan's board gave me the power to surf on waves of energy and light. With everything I learned, and with all that was impressed upon me, I felt belief and certainty strengthen into the core of my identity.

THE STARLIGHT CHRONICLES

☼17☼
Return

It seemed all too soon before Time's palace in the sky winked at me as the *Meallán*, after smoothly sailing through the stars, dropped us off at the large tree.

"It looks like it is time for me to leave," St. Brendan said. His eyes were on a horizon of his choice, as though he was not just looking at the scene before him, but reading it like a book.

"Why?" I asked.

He chuckled. "Even the Celestial Kingdom has tides."

I held out my hand, and when he grasped it I felt friendship and brotherhood come alive. "Thank you for everything."

"I'll look forward to seeing you again," St. Brendan agreed. He turned to Aleia. "You're sure you've a way back?"

She smiled. "Yes, we'll be okay. We're going the way of the Rabbit Hole."

I watched as his lips pursed together at the name. "Have care, then," he said, "for some of the unliving are around there."

"The unliving?" I asked. "What's that? Zombie stars?"

"Come on," Elysian muttered. "Even I know zombies are the undead, not the unliving."

"It's just confusing," I huffed back.

Aleia ignored me and Elysian. "You know that's always a risk, St. Brendan," she said. "We need not fear them."

He nodded. "Aye, my lady. But take the warning just as well, for my sake." St. Brendan turned and headed back up his ship. "All right! We're pulling out!" he called up to his crew. The wings of his sails broadened as the anchor rolled up, and I could see the other crew members shuffling around as the *Meallán* once more headed out onto the celestial sea.

"St. Brendan!" Aleia called out. "Thanks for the ride."

"You know well it's no trouble for you, my lady," he called back, tipping his head to her. "I'll look for you when you have need of me again. Farewell!"

And then the ship darted across the night, like a flash of lightning.

"I liked him," I said.

"St. Brendan is a favorite around these parts. He passes through every so often, and we are always glad to see him," Aleia replied. "He has been a good ally, too, in keeping tabs on things for Alora."

"So, how are we getting home?" I asked.

"The Rabbit Hole," Aleia said. At my expression, she laughed. "I wasn't making a joke earlier."

"What's the Rabbit Hole?" I asked.

"It's my old home," Aleia said. "It's not too far; it's located in the middle of this place." She glanced around at the wide expanse of the tree, the enormous branches providing a

197

THE STARLIGHT CHRONICLES

unique umbrella-like protection. "If you follow the river, it flows right into the heart of my home. Elysian should be able to take us."

"At your service," Elysian muttered. He knelt down for us, and we climbed on.

"So, did you enjoy yourself?" Aleia asked me, as Elysian headed around the willowing branches of the space tree.

"Yeah, I guess so." I shrugged. "Surfing was great. Alora's time pool was pretty interesting."

"It's more of a symbolic thing," Aleia assured me. "It's a way for you to experience the things words don't always explain."

"I would have preferred the words," I decided.

"You might enjoy my time pool better," Aleia said with a laugh.

"Is that near the Rabbit Hole?" I asked, partway in jest.

"Yes."

I should have known surprises were pretty common, given the time I spent with Aleia. But I soon learned even suspecting surprises was not enough. As Elysian flew, in his silent moping state, we passed around the spherical tree, viewing the surrounding galaxies and light-years of the universe's grandest displays. Any of them could have been worthy of being Aleia's old home.

The purity of the white water flowed down into the heart of the grand tree, setting in a pool of water that ran red. The

Rabbit Hole turned out to be a small island in the middle of a blood-rippled river, where he finally stopped.

"This is it?" I asked.

"Yes."

"Alora's pool was blue at first."

"And mine is red," Aleia replied. "Is it really unusual to you? Even in your own human body, blood is red when it carries oxygen and blue when it does not."

"I don't really want to think about blood," I said. "I can handle it, but there's a reason I want to be a lawyer like Cheryl, rather than a doctor like Mark."

"Yeah, you prefer making people bleed rather than stitching them up. Get a grip," Elysian grumbled.

I decided to ignore him as we landed. From under the humongous tree, I could see so many things. The tree stretched up from under the ground of my feet, and I couldn't see the top. The waterfall was running down inside of the tree to one side, and on the other side there was what looked like a black hole tucked into the small heart of the island.

Something shiny and familiar caught my eye. "What are those?" I asked Aleia.

There were little bundles of bubble-like shapes, full of a pure water-like substance, bunched together. They came tumbling out of the heart of the tree and simmered throughout the water's borders.

THE STARLIGHT CHRONICLES

She was walking over to the edge of the water, trying to grab one. "These are memories," she explained. "Each one is a small orb, similar to my own, that holds a moment in Time. You can hold them and see particular memories. I'm trying to get some so you'll be able to see memories of your past."

"Oh, well, grab as many as you can. Nothing more interesting to talk about than myself, you know."

"Don't I know it," Aleia said with a chuckle, catching my sarcasm.

"What would happen if I drink the water?" I asked, recalling Elysian's story about his wayward brother.

Aleia sighed. "Drinking the bloodwater of the River of Life, without it being offered, only leads to suffering." She looked over at me and Elysian and said, "You can gain immortal life, but as Draco, Elysian's brother, discovered, it is more of a curse than anything else."

"Does it let you make a wish?" I asked. "Or is it just immortality across the board?"

"Unfortunately, or maybe fortunately, it is just immortality," Aleia said. Her voice went soft and her eyes darkened. "But without it offered, it is liquid damnation." She cupped some of the water in her hands and let it drizzle back into the rippled waters. "Those who have drunk it against grace have been cursed in the worst sort of ways. They took it, thinking it would lead to their greatest wish, but immortality is only an attractive offer, shall we say, when it is coupled with mercy."

THE STARLIGHT CHRONICLES

"I can see that," I agreed, again thinking of Elysian's brother, trapped in some kind of human form while his snakeskin was being used to surround Time's palace. Deciding to change the subject, I pointed to the wormhole behind Elysian. "Is that the Rabbit Hole?"

"Yes, that's it. We only have to jump through it, and we'll be able to go back down to Earth. We'll land back in Apollo City, where I had used my power to halt the time on Earth while we were here."

"Are there other portals throughout Time's Realm?" I asked.

Aleia bit her lip. "Only one," she confided. "And it is located where the hole in the space-time continuum occurred."

"Alora mentioned that."

"I know. She has been working to fix it ever since it was torn open."

"Why can't she fix it? Shouldn't take that much work, should it?"

"There are complications with it," Aleia said. "And that's all I even know."

"Oh." I wondered what had happened. Surely it wasn't that hard for Time to figure out? I shook my head. I wouldn't have to worry about it, as long as I had the Sinisters and their leader to deal with. I turned my attention back to more current matters. "So, time travel is as easy as jumping into this hole? Could I get lost?" I asked.

"It's unlikely. Around here, you end up where you need to be or where you should be quite easily. It's very rare that someone will be where they are not meant to be."

A scraggly voice called out to us. "You mean like me, Star Warrior?"

"Auck." I jumped as what I'd assumed to be a dirty rock turned over and looked at me.

"What is that?" Elysian asked, a horrified expression no doubt similar to my own contorting his face.

A wicked smile formed into the wrinkles and scarred gashes.

Aleia pulled out her daggers. "I'd forgotten about you and your sister, Folly."

"I see." The rock-like lady laughed crudely. "We did not know you were coming, or we might have been better prepared."

"Prepared? Prepared for what?" I asked.

"Company," another voice, scraggly and low, piped up. "We're usually the most welcoming of hosts."

"This is not your home, even though you'd tried to make it yours," Aleia snapped. She turned to me. "This is Folly, and her sister demon, Foolishness."

"That's an unfortunate pair of names," I offered.

Aleia wrinkled her nose. "Unfortunate, but accurate."

"Can they harm us?" Elysian asked. He shrunk down to his smaller size and scooted in closer to the fallen figures.

"No," Aleia said. "They are bound to the island by my power. It would take a lot to break it." She turned back to us and explained, "They came here shortly after your brother"— she glanced uneasily at Elysian—"tricked us. I bound them here with my blood, and they've been here ever since."

"Why don't they disappear, the way Krono did?"

"Because Earth is actually a hard place for the unliving to live without constant support," Aleia explained. "Up here, however, surrounded by more of the supernatural, it is easier for them to fight against our powers."

"Alora didn't have any issues."

"Alora has never fallen, either," Aleia murmured, clearly unhappy with the turn of our conversation. "Please, let's just get into the pool so we can return to Earth."

She deftly jumped into the pool, beckoning Elysian and me to follow her.

"Well," Elysian said, "I'll see you back home."

"Great. Don't wait up for me," I muttered back. Elysian had not been good company during this trip; I would not be sorry for a break from him.

"Fine." He huffed out two long strands of smoke from his dragon nostrils and then, swirling around, dove into the wormhole portal.

I hurried to follow after him, when Folly spoke up. "So, you're the Star of Mercy now, huh?"

I knew she was trying to bait me. Reluctantly, she succeeded. "How do you know me?" I asked.

Folly laughed. "You were the one Lady Justice sent to Earth along with her sisters. It was quite amusing, because you had been so very much in love with her at the time."

My body stilled. Even my heart seemed to pause in its beating. "What?"

"You heard her," Foolishness said. Much like her sister, she was a stone figure of a demon, lying in full-bodied form on the ground, crushed by the gravity of her crimes.

"Don't tell me they didn't tell you everything at Lady Time's place," Folly added.

"Then again, they never tell anyone the full story," Foolishness said.

"What are you talking about?" I asked.

"Lady Time and all her allies, even the Prince, are just using you," Folly explained. "You will never be free of them."

"You will never be your own person, so long as they tell you who you are and what you need to do." Foolishness shook her rocky head. "They blame us for their troubles."

"They are the *real* power-hungry ones," Folly added. "Why else would they want to punish us for speaking up?"

"They're on the side of good," I said, my tone too weak for my own taste.

"Good?" Folly laughed. "Then why didn't they tell you the truth? That Lady Justice was the one who sent you flying down to Earth, along with Orpheus and the Sinisters?"

"I deserved to fall," I declared, ashamed to admit it, but seeing no other choice. "It was only right."

"Oh, you poor, poor soul," Foolishness murmured delicately. "It sounds like they've indoctrinated you already."

Folly laughed as my fists clenched.

There was no good that would come of them, I thought. Their very names were indicative of their natures. I could not believe anything they had to say.

They had probably been expecting that from me. I shook my head and turned toward the portal. There was nothing to gain, and I was getting tired. I did want to go home.

"If you don't believe us," Folly began, "all you have to do is check the memory."

I hesitated. After a moment of indecision, I turned around. "What are you talking about?"

"The memories of this realm and the one encompassing it are all available to you here," Foolishness said. "All you have to do is summon your power and put your hands in the stream. It will come to you, once it recognizes your power."

Once more, I faltered. Then I decided to do it. After all, if it wasn't true that Starry Knight had sent me to Earth, then

Alora and Aleia hadn't withheld any information from me. And if it was true … I was going to have some difficult conversations with Aleia when I arrived back on Earth.

Moving further away from Folly and Foolishness' rocky figures, I called forth my power. Energy drippled out slowly into my palm before I dipped my hands into the water. For a moment, I allowed myself to close my eyes and settle in, cradling the comforting stream; the river's water was cool and fresh, stimulating me, even as I realized it was brimming with the essence of life.

"This is amazing," I whispered to myself. The water ran purely translucent, in shades and stripes of pure water and pure blood. It was distinctive enough from blood that I did not wince.

But before I could give into my childish urge to splash around and play, or fall victim to an inner desire to drink the water, a crystal-like bubble slid into my hands. I plucked it out and looked into it.

Nothing happened. Maybe I needed Aleia to read it? I wondered. Recalling I had my own power, I pressed into the aura encircling the small bauble.

Instantly, a new world opened up. "Hey," I called out, suddenly wondering if had been a trick.

I saw my daydream world, where I could see nothing but the Celestial Kingdom. I heard the music of Starry Knight, and I allowed myself to relax.

Heading toward the music, anticipation tickled through me. Maybe I would get to see her, hear her. Maybe hold her, or have her reach out for me.

It had happened before, I rationalized.

Her star was close, close to my own. I was surprised to realize it, but I turned to see my own star had been burning just as brightly as hers. I'd never seen it before.

"Wow," I murmured. "I wonder—"

The music stopped.

I could hear shouting and weeping. I could feel pain singeing into my flesh and bones. Fire erupted inside of me. My wings beat against the tides of the universal ocean.

And then silence. Silence as the star before me, home to my love, crumpled, leaving gravity's shadowed rainbow to bend around and choke it. I felt myself being pulled in, unable to avoid it.

I cried out words I could not hear as I felt drawn into the implosion.

Like my baptism earlier, death was choking me and darkness was surrounding me before even it left. And then I was hollow—more hollow than I had ever felt or been. Pain slashed through my heart, and my body, though crushed and squashed and pushed down, resisted as nothingness settled inside of me and surrounded me.

Sharp, bright blackness cut through me, collided with me, and suddenly, with the rage of a supernova, I was cast down

207

even harder against the rock bottom of my life. I was pushed again, and again, and again.

Only to find the rock bottom breaking.

I *whoosed* through, breaking into a new ocean of stars and people and souls.

Not knowing when it would end, I finally closed my eyes.

Only to find myself back on the riverbank, my fist clenched around the marbled memory.

"Augh!" I gasped and took deep breaths. "What … what was that!?" I cried, my voice hoarse.

Folly and Foolishness laughed. "You see? Your Lady Justice was the one who sent you to Earth. She wooed you, and then destroyed you, as was her duty as the Star of Justice. You didn't fall of your own accord. They lied to you."

My eyelids fluttered as I shot up. I was weak, and lonely, and defeated.

I barely realized it as I dropped the crystal and stumbled back, tripping and falling headfirst down into the Rabbit Hole.

☼18☼
Confusion

I didn't allow myself to fall completely unconscious until I knew I was out of sight of the marina. Rage settled into me, keeping me safe until I was well-hidden and tucked into the woods behind the Lakeview Observatory.

There was no sign of Elysian or Aleia as I came back. I was fine with that. They could wait on me, I decided. They'd lied to me and hidden the truth from me. I could no longer allow them to do that. I could no longer forgive them for betraying me.

"That's right," I grumbled to myself. "I can't let them hurt me anymore."

My foot caught on a tree root, and I stumbled. My arms moved to push me up and keep going, but I slipped.

The sweet smell of the grass overcame me, and the earthy scent of the woods engulfed me. My fingers laced through the dirt as I finally gave up and collapsed.

Humming. Someone was humming. Someone was humming in the rain.

I could feel my nose twitch as scattered raindrops sprinkled down from the sky. My sleepy eyes pressed together with

THE STARLIGHT CHRONICLES

fatigue's unique form of gravity, glossed over with dew and the full weight of fresh air.

The humming continued.

The feeling of heat under my head and the pressure of hardness behind my wings—all of it collectively kept me in a lull, half-weary with sleep and half-awake with discomfort.

And completely fed up with the humming.

"Would you stop?" I murmured, my speech slurred. "That's annoying."

"Sorry."

At Starry Knight's voice, my eyes flickered open. And there she was.

She was sitting beside me, her wings folded behind her as she sat gracefully. Her arms were wrapped around her knees as she hugged herself for warmth. The rain pitter-pattered against her skin, giving her eyes a glossy, violet sheen as she watched me.

"Go back to sleep," she whispered. She reached up to my head; I felt the whisper of her fingers against my skin, and her healing caress flowed throughout my whole body.

Anger bubbled up under the thick layer of sleepiness. I was too tired to decide if I hated her. My eyes closed again, unable to do anything but heed the call to slumber.

I grabbed her arm and slid her hand into mine. She jerked back, but I didn't let go. "Stay," I whispered.

Starry Knight stopped fighting me. It was the closest I was going to get to "Yes," from her, I assumed.

But as I was crawling away from the last reaches of consciousness, heading back into sleep, I heard her whisper a response. "I will save you," she promised, "no matter the cost. You must trust me."

I think I muttered something back. The warmth of her hand stayed in mine as the darkness of empty dreams took me.

It was hours later, I assumed, when sunlight flickered across my face and the dancing light managed to wake me up once more. Long moments passed before I could hear the birds twittering, where I could smell the rain-soaked woods raising up a protest at the disappearance of morning's cooling comfort.

Groggily, I sat up. I groaned as the memory of the night flashed across my mind, with all of its complications. Starry Knight had sent me to Earth, to punish me. The same Starry Knight who kissed me and pushed me away, the one who kept her secrets even if it hurt me, and the one who didn't want anything to do with me, even as I wanted nothing more than to be with her.

Maybe I had a dream last night, I thought. That was why she wasn't here now. After all, I just discovered she betrayed me. Maybe I dreamed she was watching out for me. I knew it was going to be hard to hate her. Why wouldn't I make it more difficult to do so? "That's reasonable," I muttered, picking myself off the small forest floor.

THE STARLIGHT CHRONICLES

It was only her words, too familiar for comfort and too distinctive to be mistaken, that allowed me to believe she'd ever really been there at all.

I went home. I went home, briefly amused to find myself sneaking into the house once more, and settled into my bed, curling the covers around me as I desperately tried to protect my heart.

☀

"Kid. Psst. Kid. Wake up." Elysian started walking on my head, trying to get me to move out of the bed.

"Ugh, not now, Elysian."

"We've got a problem."

There's always a problem when you're involved. "What is it? Do you want to talk about your behavior during our trip?"

"No, that's not it," Elysian grumbled, his tone easily warning me I was pushing it.

The thought I was getting on his nerves amused me, but I still wanted to sleep. The world was just easier to deal with when I could sleep through it. "Can it wait till tomorrow?"

"First of all, it is 'tomorrow,' and you need to get up. Your friend is here."

"Friend?"

"That kid with the blog and the camera. Mikey, right?"

"Oh, *why?*" I didn't want to talk to him. All the sleep shot out of me as I realized the absolute last thing I wanted to do was tell Mikey that I was in love with Starry Knight, too. Not after all the teasing I'd put him through about it.

Rationality resumed as soon as I sat up. I wouldn't tell him about *that*. After all, was there any real need to tell him? I didn't even have all the answers when it came to Starry Knight. I didn't want him pestering me about it.

Yes, it was much better and much safer not to tell him or Gwen.

"Ugh." *This just keeps getting worse.* I didn't want to tell Gwen, either, even though I knew I would eventually have to. I glanced over at the small calendar on my desk. How long until graduation? I wondered.

I silently decided being seventeen was harder than being sixteen. (At least before I could blame my age if something went wrong; being seventeen meant I had to try harder not to do that, if I wanted to be taken seriously.)

"What's Mikey doing here?" I asked, moving around and beginning to sort through all my things. I needed to get ready. This was a battle I didn't want to go in blind and unprepared.

"I don't know, but he's been calling and texting you all morning." The door opened downstairs and I could hear Cheryl greeting him (by calling him "Max," no less).

"Ugh, I hope he's not here because he got in trouble," I muttered.

"I'm not the one in trouble. *You* are." Mikey came through the door with a grim look on his face, and I wondered all of a sudden if he had seen Dante as he walked Gwen home. "Nice hair."

"What? What's wrong with my hair?" My hands flew up and patted around, desperate to make sure it was all still there.

"Your hair's gotten lighter," Mikey said. "Like it's got golden highlights in it. Don't worry, I'm sure Gwen will like it. We've got bigger problems."

Nervousness hit me. Maybe I was in trouble with Mikey? "Did I do something wrong?" I asked, angry I had to tell myself not to squirm.

It was getting hard to keep so many secrets.

"No." Mikey looked confused. "Why would you ask that?"

"Uh, no reason," I said, laughing nervously.

"Okay, well, you're acting weird." Mikey shook his head before plopping down on my bed. "Did something happen last night when you were off on that ship?"

"Plenty," I assured him. "I'll tell you about it later. Why am I in trouble?"

"While you were gone, I stayed at the marina, waiting for you," Mikey said. "And I saw her."

"Her who?"

"Starry Knight, of course." His eyes went troubled for once, instead of dreamy. Instantly, my stomach churned and my eyes narrowed. That was not a good sign.

"What's wrong? Is she okay?" Fury bit at me for my concern instead of being completely apathetic to the matter. "Did something happen?"

"Yes. I saw her at the marina and decided to follow her."

"Did you find out who she is?" I asked, trying not to let my hopes get up or my excitement to show.

"No. She went to meet Orpheus."

"What?" Rage, anger, hate—all of it seemed to skit across my soul.

"Yeah. Really. I am not kidding," Mikey insisted. "She left the marina just after you left, and then she went over to the Time Tower, and that's where Orpheus came to her."

"So *he* came to *her*?" My brow furrowed. "He came to meet her, or she was looking for him?"

"Okay, I don't know, but she wasn't surprised to see him." Mikey sighed. "Now, stop interrupting me. It's important."

"Alright, I'll stop."

"They talked back and forth a bit, and I didn't get it, of course, but then she said she wanted to make a deal with him. She wanted to trade *you* for the rest of the Sinisters." Mikey sat back and folded his arms over his chest. "I'm not making this up."

THE STARLIGHT CHRONICLES

"She wanted to 'trade' me?" I repeated.

"Yes. You know, like a prisoner of war or something." He rubbed his head. "I guess you were right about her, Dinger. I'm sorry I didn't listen to you sooner."

That caught my attention. "What do you mean?"

"She can't be your ally if she's trying to get you killed or captured or whatever. I mean, I thought she was beautiful and everything, but I don't want to date her if she's like that."

"It would be hard to double-date," I agreed, unable to resist joking about it. It was too … it was too weird.

Mikey raised his eyebrows at me. I shrugged before a thought hit me. "When she did make this deal? Had I come back from my trip?"

"No, you were still gone. It was settled about half an hour after you left."

"Okay. I see … " So she had come to me in the woods after making the deal with Orpheus. She mentioned something about saving me, right? I wondered. Could this be part of her plan? The vision of her supernova—and my punishment, my descent to Earth, away from the Celestial Kingdom and all my friends and fun there—struck through me. Was Folly and/or Foolishness right? Was she "wooing" me again, in order to destroy me, as a matter of Justice?

I sighed. "I want to go back to bed," I muttered.

"How late were you out last night?" Mikey asked curiously. "I mean, I know it's a weekend, but it is past noon."

Elysian spoke up, surprising Mikey as much as me. "We'll have to see about finding Starry Knight," he mused. "I think this warrants some tough questions, don't you, finally?"

I knew what he was referencing. Elysian had held Starry Knight captive at the end of our last big battle with the Sinisters and Orpheus, and I'd been more interested in gaining her trust than in the answers to my questions. I told him to let her go, and he was upset with me for it. He was still upset with me for it.

I still believed, despite all my reasons and feelings to the contrary, that it was the right thing to do.

A small burst of hatred shot through my gaze as I looked at the small changeling dragon prancing around on my bed. Mikey had just told me there's a potential coup happening among Starry Knight and Orpheus, and Elysian is trying to make me feel stupid? For a decision I made weeks ago?

Yes, that would be Elysian. Especially since he still looked glum about the previous night. Remembering his despair and bitterness, I decided to let it go. For now. "We'll try to find her, I guess," I told Mikey, "but let me tell you about what I got to see while Aleia froze time for us."

"She froze time?" Mikey gaped. "That's so cool!"

"Yeah, it was pretty awesome." I smiled. "When we came back, it was midnight." Glancing out the window, I added, "And then I came home to sleep, and I've been sleeping ever since."

"You didn't come home right away," Elysian reminded me.

THE STARLIGHT CHRONICLES

"I fell asleep in the park," I explained easily enough. There was no need to tell him about Starry Knight. "And then I came home. I was really tired."

"What happened on the ship?" Mikey asked.

"You'd never believe me," I said.

"Try me," he challenged. "Maybe I can get a blog up about it." Before I could object, he added, "It would probably make for better reading than the meeting between Starry Knight and Orpheus."

I sighed, but indulged him anyway. It was good to have someone to filter through my thoughts as I recounted my adventures. There were some parts I left out, for a variety of reasons; they were embarrassing, they were too painful, they were too shameful, etc. I especially left out the last part, where Folly and Foolishness had revealed the truth about me falling to Earth because of Starry Knight.

When I finished, he just sat there with an awed look on his face. "Wow."

"Yeah, I know," I agreed. "It was pretty cool, but there was a lot to learn and a lot to sort through."

"It's still worth it," Mikey said. "You're a Star, not some ordinary human."

"I guess that explains all the good grades and skill set, huh?" I laughed, even though the voice of logic in the back of my mind said it was *not* the right time to joke about that, and that I was wrong about my Starlight Warrior skills helping me out, especially when it came to Martha's tests.

"I wish I was something special," Mikey admitted.

I said nothing to that. Mikey wanted to make this about him, and I didn't want to divert our topic to the hours of counseling he needed to feel better about himself. If I really was in danger, I needed to stay focused, so I could protect myself, and people like Mikey, too.

"Sounds like you've got a lot to think about," Mikey said. "Between the monsters and Starry Knight, there's still the matter of that organization that kidnapped you."

"Oh, yeah." I'd forgotten about SWORD. "I hope they don't start causing me problems too. I have enough to deal with."

Later, I would think that by then, I should be used to disappointment.

☼19☼
Surprises

As the school week began, I saw nothing of Starry Knight or Orpheus, or any of the Sinisters and their minions. To be honest, I didn't really want to look for them. I was still reeling a bit from the Celestial Kingdom and the Rabbit Hole, and I was content to spend a lot of time daydreaming about surfing the cosmos.

I still had plenty of work for Cheryl and Stefano, and for the final month of tenth grade, including making sure I argued with Raiya at least twice during every class. I also had to keep Gwen entertained, which I did while cheering on Central's track team. (It was my first year of not actually being on the team, since I had my job at the Mayor's office.)

It was an easy week, I thought, but nevertheless, I kept my usual Friday after-school routine, which included a sort-of date with Gwen (and since she was babysitting him, Adam) at Rachel's. I also lucked out, in that I avoided Elysian.

He'd mentioned to me, a long time ago, about needing time to mourn the loss of our perceptions on life, and I decided to give it to him. It wasn't like I really wanted to bother him anyway, so long as Apollo City remained safe.

"Ah, I needed this," I practically crooned, as I sipped the mocha from my cup. "I don't know how you do it, Rachel."

"Haven't you read *Jack and the Beanstalk*?" she asked. "Magic beans leading to a fabulous treasure from a giant?"

I laughed. "The giant demand of coffee from the peasants. That's brilliant. Worthy of your grandfather, even."

"Well, I'll admit I had his help in that one," she said with a chuckle.

"Still, you make some great coffee. Best in town, I swear. It does wonders."

"I suspect it has something to do with quality and practice," Rachel replied. She glanced out the windows and frowned. "There's a restlessness in the air today."

I'd felt it, too, ever since I came back to Earth. The Sinisters might have taken the week off, or their minions were on vacation, but there was no denying the reality I faced. And the reality was, as much as I liked not having to worry about skipping out on Gwen or leaving class unexpectedly or breaking curfew, they were planning something.

Part of me wondered if Starry Knight's alleged deal—and I said "alleged," because as much as I trusted Mikey, I didn't trust him nearly enough when it came to Starry Knight—had something to do with it.

"I don't know how to explain it," Rachel continued, seemingly lost in thought.

"Well, summer vacation is coming up."

Rachel cheered. "Yes, and my wedding along with it," she agreed. "Maybe that's it. Anticipation."

THE STARLIGHT CHRONICLES

I was just about to tease her about wedding jitters when the door to the café opened, and Rachel sighed as she looked over at who had just come in. "I'll be right back, Hamilton."

"What's wrong?" I asked her. I followed her gaze and immediately swung back around to hide my face. Dante Salyards had just come into the café.

Fear lashed through me, striking me immobile. Hundreds of questions leaped at me, only to be met with the same answer. *He's here for me.*

Obviously, right?

Rachel sighed, drawing my attention back to her. "He and his business partner have started coming here more often," she told me, shuddering a bit. "He likes to flirt with me, though I don't like it and he knows I'm getting married soon."

My shoulders relaxed in the smallest degree possible. "Why don't you just turn down his business?" I asked in a quiet voice, trying not to draw any attention to myself. Another thought hit me: *It was a good thing Mikey was not with me.*

Rachel pursed her lips. "I'll admit it's for the money."

Delicious taunting tempted its way through me. "The money?" I asked sweetly. "But he's interfering with true love. That's not like you, Rachel."

"I've found I can be quite mercenary about some things," Rachel admitted. "Especially when it comes to unpaid bills."

What bills would Rachel have to worry about? I wondered. Ever since she welcomed me, I'd made her café all the rage to visit by my peers. That had essentially doubled her business. Surely she wasn't worried about going under? I frowned, as I would not have been happy with that possibility.

The complexities of running a business held no interest for me. That's why I'm going into government work, I reminded myself silently. "Must be pretty important."

"Yeah, it is." She pulled out my bill and set it on the table. "Starting tomorrow, I'll be catering his partner's offices every day; we just finalized the paperwork earlier. They must be here to celebrate."

"Was it a big order?"

"I guess you could say it was a tall order."

I grinned at the coffee word play. For Mikey's sake, I was about to ask her how often Dante came in, and the times when he was likely to, when I heard the bell above the door chime. A rush of confusion swooshed through me as Stefano—my boss, the mayor of Apollo City, the man I was beginning to see as an entry-level mentor to my long-term political goals, and the same man I admired every day I went to work—sauntered in, catch sight of Dante, and eagerly shake his hand in greeting.

Fortunately, Rachel inhaled sharply as I gaped wordlessly at the exchange. She didn't see me fluster as she squared her shoulders and put on a smile. "There he is now. Be back soon, hopefully."

I thrust my face between the pages of my largest textbook and tried not to strain my ears while I hid my face. I could only hope Stefano wouldn't see me; then, at least, I might have had a chance at staying clear of Dante and the rest of SWORD's operatives—

"Well, hello there, Hamilton!"

Stefano was my boss, and as such, I suppose it was natural to think he would make my life miserable at some point. But right then and there in the coffee shop, it seemed a little much. As much as I suddenly became afraid, anger bit through me. Couldn't he have minded his own business?

A steely grin made its way onto my face as I slowly put my Chem book down. "Hello, Mayor Mills," I greeted. All the years of pretending to listen in class and care deeply about all the right and popular causes—every moment I'd spent honing my skills in acting the part of the good listener, the teacher's pet, the good son—all of it had led me to this critical moment. "What are you doing here?"

"Come, Hamilton, call me Stefano. We agreed on it, remember?"

"Sorry."

"No problem. I've come on business," he informed me. "We're finally going to have some good joe down at the office." He smiled. "I know you'll appreciate it. You always talk about this place, and I can see why. I've also managed to score a good deal with the owner here, so by hiring out we've saved money and have better coffee."

THE STARLIGHT CHRONICLES

My cheeks burned, still angry. "So because of my recommendation, you decided to come here?" I asked.

"Well, I had Dante, my associate, recommend it to me, too," he said, gesturing behind us, where Mikey's dad was clearly making Rachel uncomfortable.

Grateful once more for Mikey's absence, I mustered up the fortitude to ask, "Who is he?"

Stefano smiled. "He's the new consultant I hired for the city on security matters. Your mother suggested it to help with the court hearings. I need to make it look like I put every effort into preventative measure against those superheroes and their monsters." He leaned down close and whispered, "I don't really think it'll matter much, but this guy is good. He's come highly recommended from several agencies and governments."

Dante had mentioned they were a privatized company, I recalled, as Stefano continued to sing the man's praises. But a consultant agency cover was still unexpected. Although I suppose it couldn't *exactly* be like it was in the movies, I decided.

I considered it the highest providence when Gwen poked her head around Stefano's shoulders. "Hey, Hammy."

Adam came up beside her. "Hammy!" he squealed.

"Oh, that's so cute," Stefano said, offering his hand for a high-five for Adam. "This is your younger brother?"

THE STARLIGHT CHRONICLES

"Yeah," I said. "He's quite a handful for only three years old, but we like him." I tried not to laugh when Adam ducked behind Gwen as Stefano tried to get him to smile.

Gwen cleared her throat delicately and then smiled.

"Oh, and this is my girlfriend, Gwen Kessler." I quickly introduced them and scooted over in my seat.

"Well, it looks like you have a date," Stefano observed. "I'll leave you to yourselves then. It looks like my associate's finished putting in our orders. I'll see you at the office tomorrow, Hamilton."

"Sure," I agreed, allowing my gaze to stay on him as he sat down with Dante on the other side of the café.

"What's wrong?" Gwen asked.

Everything, I wanted to say. "Nothing."

"You have a strange look on your face."

Protruding pain marched into my wrist, where my mark burned in frustrated submission. For a long moment, I stared at my hands, unsure of whether or not to move.

"Now you really have a strange look on your face," Gwen said.

"Uh, be right back," I told her. "Bathroom." It was the oldest, most awkward excuse in the book. But there was nothing to be done about it; I hurried out of the room, heading toward the back door. I jerked open the door to the alleyway in the back.

Only to find Grandpa Odd standing directly in my intended path. I jumped back, stumbling to remain balanced.

"Ah, am I in your way, lad?" he asked.

"No ... no, I just thought I heard someone knocking on the door," I lied.

"Well, thank you for opening the door," Grandpa Odd said with a kindly wink. "You can help me carry the rest of these in."

I glanced down to see he was carrying a crate of milk jugs. Before a grimace could light up my face, he thrust the crate into my hands and said, "Take those to the kitchen. Rachel needs them."

I gaped, my mouth waving open and closed as he promptly turned around and grabbed another crate, intending to force my hand. Pain latched itself to my arm as I frowned.

I needed a new plan, I thought, entering the kitchen and placing the crate on an empty counter. I had to get out of there. Grandpa Odd might have been trying to help Rachel, but there were potentially lives at stake. I needed to get out of helping him.

"Only eight more out there," Grandpa Odd informed me cheerfully.

"I have to go," I said, shaking my head.

"Nonsense. How hard could it be for you to help an old man like me with his chores?"

"If they are *your* chores, I don't see why I should help," I grumbled. "I got to go. I, uh … forgot something at my house. For Gwen."

"Ah, well, then you must hurry. 'One can give without loving, but one cannot love without giving,' after all." His eyes twinkled at me, almost accusingly. "If one such as Amy Carmichael said it, it must be true."

Briefly stupefied, I just stared at him. "Er, yeah," I agreed, and then pushed past him and hurried away, not even bothering to make sure Gwen—or Dante, or the mayor, or anyone else potentially involved in the whole situation—saw me.

As I pushed into the mark on my wrist, unleashing my transformation, I felt the weight of my dilemma momentarily leave me; yes, I had a monster to go battle, but I was going to have help with that. Escaping from Gwen, protecting Adam, hiding from Dante, and slipping by Stefano were all things I was still largely doing alone. Once I was free from them, I could really be myself.

Doing my superhero duty is starting to feel like an escape, I warned myself.

A moment later, I decided it was hardly my fault for feeling that way. There were twists and turns and problems all over. How could get this get any more complicated? I mean, Mikey's dad had been hired by Stefano to protect the city. What would happen next? I wondered.

THE STARLIGHT CHRONICLES

I'm never going to get used to surprises. The thought was both an observation and a promise as I hurried toward the looming battlefield ahead.

☼ 20 ☼
Confrontation

"The demon's over there, by the observatory." I pointed forward. "There's an aura over it." Studying it, I noticed the aura had little wisps of blue emanating around it. "Weird. It's a little different than usual, but it shouldn't be a problem."

"What do you mean, different?" Elysian asked.

"I'm not sure how to explain it," I said. It seemed similar to the rogue demon from before. "We'll have to be careful."

"Alright, we'll get there," Elysian said. He swept through the air with me on his back. I knew it wouldn't be long before we arrived. I scanned the skies for signs of Starry Knight. "We're going to pick up Aleia really quickly, too."

"Okay. Just hurry."

"I know where she's staying," Elysian said with a huff. "It's on the way."

"Alright, alright."

Elysian glanced back at me, showing me the merest slip of a smirk as he asked, "So, who's watching Gwen?"

"Come on, Elysian," I grumbled, "don't make me hurt you."

"I was just curious."

"Shut up." I gave Elysian's horns a ferocious tug. "Just don't worry about it."

"Did you call Mikey?"

"I told you to stop it," I grumbled. "Come on, just get to the aura, would you?"

"I'm just trying to make you feel better, kid," Elysian said.

"I'm not going to feel better by feeling worse," I retorted. Gwen was going to have to wait; I had a feeling my "bathroom" excuse was going to be replaced. And while Mikey would have been helpful, on the off chance Dante didn't follow me to the battle scene, I didn't want them running into each other at Rachel's.

I wondered if Jason was at work. I could text him, I thought. See if he would tell Gwen that my uncle or something was just rushed to the hospital.

Elysian dived and wove his way through the buildings before slowing down in front of a tall cathedral. Before I could ask, he nodded up to the small bell tower, where Aleia's figure was waiting for us.

"Let's go," she called, jumping off her perch and landing behind me.

"Hang on," I said.

Elysian found refuge in the clouds again, heading over toward the lake.

"The aura's coming from Lakeview Observatory," I told her.

Aleia nodded. "I see it as well." She pulled out her crystal and considered it carefully, or as carefully as she could. Her

THE STARLIGHT CHRONICLES

blonde hair whipped back and forth across her face as she studied the small orb. "It looks like Starry Knight is already there," she said.

I didn't say anything; I knew anything I could say would only condemn me.

"What's going on with them?" Elysian called back. "It's been a good week since the last attack."

"Who knows?" I said, rolling my eyes. "It's not like they're on some kind of forty-hour work week."

"It might have to do with the deal Starry Knight arranged with Orpheus," Elysian pointed out.

"What deal?" Aleia asked.

"This could be a setup," Elysian warned.

"It's not," I muttered back, even though I had to admit he could have been right. Not that it was likely. "We don't—"

"What are you talking about?" Aleia interrupted. "What deal?"

Elysian responded while I fumed. "We heard Starry Knight had made a deal with Orpheus to trade the rest of the Sinisters for the kid."

"Kid?"

"Hamilton."

"Oh." She narrowed her gaze as she thought about it. "I don't think it's likely."

"Ha!" I scowled up at Elysian. "See? Even—"

"It's not likely," Aleia repeated. "But—"

"But what?"

"It's possible, but not likely."

Normally, I might have faltered, full of doubt and worry. But the memory of Starry Knight sitting next to me in the rain, watching over me as I slept, and holding my hand next to my heart, blazed into my mind.

I wanted answers. I wanted answers from her, and nothing would stop me this time, I vowed. "Let's hurry, Elysian."

He roared in response, and I felt the pressure of the wind increase drastically as we hurled toward the observatory.

As we approached, I could hear alarms going off, and the small staff and student workers were running out, heading for their cars or hurrying off in any direction.

Aleia jumped off Elysian's back in front of a student. I was shocked to see it was Logan. What was he doing here? I wondered. Then I recalled this was his new office now.

"Please, sir. Tell us what happened," Aleia implored.

Logan's eyes flickered nervously to Elysian. "Uh, well … "

"Logan," I called down from Elysian's back. "We need your help."

"Wingdinger." He took a deep breath. "I should have known you'd be here. Starry Knight is inside, fighting off one of those creatures—"

"The demons."

"Right." He took another steadying breath and then jolted as a loud explosion rang out from the building behind us. "Oh, no!" Logan jerked wildly in shock.

"Calm down," I yelled. "I know it's hard, but we need information. Can you tell us what happened?"

"Well, we were just working," Logan told me. "We were just working and then there was a loud noise like that one, coming from the research lab. When we hurried up to see it, it began to attack us. We ran, and Starry Knight came, and then … " He waved his hands wildly in the air, explaining how he and his coworkers managed to lock the research lab up, trapping the demon in with Starry Knight as they ran out the door.

" … I didn't think it was a bad idea," he added. Another loud jolt behind him made him cringe. "But now I have a feeling our lab is getting destroyed. And it was just recently finished, too."

"Can you take us inside?" I asked. "We could use your help to locate and destroy the monster more quickly."

Logan faltered and sputtered, and then finally took a deep breath. "If it will help," he decided. "I know you can protect me. I want to try to keep the lab together, too."

THE STARLIGHT CHRONICLES

"Okay," I agreed, thinking it really was a shame Logan was smart, but surprisingly careless when it came to his own life. As much as I appreciated his trust, I didn't think I would risk my life for a research lab. (But then again, I suppose I was doing that anyway to get to the demon monster.)

We rushed inside. Elysian transformed into his smaller self, and hopped up onto my shoulder.

"Here." Logan slid his access card into the top research lab. The door blinked and opened, revealing a large room. A giant telescope and computer board stood out like an island in the middle of the room. The observatory's rounded rooftop encased the machinery like a glass cover over a cake plate, and it was surrounded by a circular staircase leading to different doors.

Where was Starry Knight? There was no one in the room. I glanced over at Logan to see him pushing past Aleia on the other side of me. "Come this way," he instructed.

Around the room we went, descending down the winding staircase. Another loud *crash!* resounded from below us, louder than before.

Logan pulled out his card again. "I sealed off the research lab," he explained, "so it's right here. You guys go in first."

"Okay," Elysian grumbled. "Just open the door, would you?"

"Elysian," I hissed. "Be nice, won't you?"

Logan swiped his card and scooted out of our way. Aleia and Elysian hurried forward.

"Thanks." I offered my hand to Logan. "Go hide. We'll protect you."

"I will." He took it, and instantly I saw his emotions flash across his face. Fear was there, mixed with relief, and a smidgen of hope. Before I let go of his hand, fierce determination took hold of him, and he added, "And whatever you do, don't touch the meteorite in there."

The demon monster behind me cried out, distracting me from asking Logan why he would be worried about such a thing. "Thanks," I muttered, before hurrying into the strange room.

I didn't have long to look around, but a cursory inspection of the lab made me think of the movies. Instruments ranging from centrifuges to microscopes to bulky, box-shaped apparatuses littered the counters, while books were opened and computers flashed with calculations. Though it looked like a small tornado had blown through the room, no permanent damage seemed to have been done. Of course, that was to me. I was hardly a scientist.

Starry Knight had the demon pinned down in the corner of the room. Looking at it, I was worried Krono's brother had decided to make an appearance.

Rather than invisible, this demon monster was made of a ghost-like wispy sinew. Blackened eyes, hollow and horrifying, glared at Starry Knight, who had managed to pin it down between several arrows of light.

She stood over it with Aleia by her side, the two of them talking in hushed voices.

THE STARLIGHT CHRONICLES

"What's going on?" I asked.

"It's a *fenfleal* demon," Aleia explained.

"A rogue?" I frowned, my earlier suspicions confirmed. "What was the monster after in here? Was he after Logan again?"

Starry Knight narrowed her gaze at me, her suspicion clear. I belatedly recalled she didn't need to know I'd gone snooping after her, trying to get any information I could out of Logan.

"It doesn't seem like it," Aleia said, before either Starry Knight or myself could say anything else. She turned to Starry Knight. "What was he after?" she asked. "You were here faster than we were."

I grumbled under my breath. Aleia didn't need to remind her of that.

"You bound him with blood," Elysian noticed.

"Yes, I did," Starry Knight agreed.

"I thought you didn't like that," Aleia murmured.

"It's easier to bind them down," Starry Knight admitted, her lips pursed in irritation. "And that way I can question them."

"Well?" Aleia asked. "What did he say?"

"He has asserted he is a demon, serving the Master of the Void," Starry Knight said. "That's all I got so far."

"Alküzor," I murmured, more to myself than anyone else. I was surprised they actually heard me. The silence in their stares was deafening.

"Yes," Starry Knight finally confirmed.

"Let's see what he wanted," Aleia said. She turned to the *fenfleal* demon. "Tell us what you wanted."

The monster roared in frustration. I pulled out my sword and held it to his throat.

"Tell us now," I commanded.

The *fenfleal* demon seemed content to snarl. He raged against the arrows holding him down, but there was no evidence his effort made a difference.

Elysian growled. "Let me take care of him," he offered, snorting out a small stream of smoke. "I can get him to cooperate. "

"Wait," I said. "Maybe I can do something." I tucked my sword down into the scabbard at my side before reaching out a hand. With as little thinking as I could, I reached out and grabbed ahold of his arm.

The pain I had been trying to avoid contemplating raced through me; I pushed back against it, rationalizing that Starry Knight would be able to fix me up when we were done.

Emotions swirled around my hand at last. A mixture of pride, power, and determination all rushed past me. I grinned, pushing further up and further in with my power. "Tell me what you want," I said, my teeth gritted together in pain.

THE STARLIGHT CHRONICLES

Fire steadily burned more brightly around my arm.

"Kid, you're killing him," Elysian called out.

"Be careful!" Aleia added.

"I've got it," I insisted. My eyes closed as my power wrapped around his heart and entered in. Darkness settled in and around me, as I was able to see his heart in my hand. I felt my own soul jerk in response, trying to escape before it could attack.

The single-mindedness, settling on a black chunk of rock, entered into my mind before my own power surged; heat seared into the demon's body and burned through its heart.

I opened my eyes to see the demon's essence swirling into a pool of power in my outstretched hand, before collapsing in on itself. I gasped. "Wow."

"Are you okay?" Starry Knight's question was brusque and sharp, bringing me back into the moment.

I glanced over at my audience. "He was thinking about a black rock … I'm guessing he wanted the meteorite. It's here, isn't it?" I asked.

"The meteorite?" Aleia asked.

"The one that slammed into the town last year," I said. "Logan said it was being moved here from the college. It has to be here. The demon was thinking about it when my power … " My voice trailed off. *Did* I kill him? Was he banished to another realm? I wasn't sure how to phrase what had happened to the demon and *not* sound awkward.

"Yes," Starry Knight said. "The meteorite is here." She nodded to the glass case on the far side of the room, where the black rock from the demon's vision resided. "He was in front of it when I got down here," she said. "So that makes sense."

"Why would he want it, though? It's just a piece of rock," Elysian said.

"It did quite a bit of damage to Apollo City," I reminded him. "Construction wasn't finished up until recently."

"It was after the meteor came that the attacks began," Starry Knight said quietly. "It is possible he wanted it because of the people it killed."

"What do you mean?" I asked.

"Things that take life—things that draw blood—sometimes gain power through destruction."

Aleia spoke up. "That's possible. He could have wanted to use it for something of his own planning."

"The day they tried to move it from its landing spot," I recalled, "it caused an explosion." The green eyes from Alora's time pool came to the forefront of my mind. "And it held great evil."

"We'll have to keep tabs on it," Starry Knight asserted. "Even if the Sinisters haven't paid attention to it, it could only be a matter of time before they see it as a way to demoralize the public or cause further destruction."

"Agreed." Aleia nodded.

A moment of silence passed before Starry Knight swung around. "Well, if that's everything," she remarked, "I'll take my leave."

It was time to get my answers, I reminded myself. *Do not let her get away without answering your questions.* "How do you know Logan?" I asked. "You recognized him before, when the other demon attacked him. You knew he worked at the college and you know he's been studying the meteorite."

"Have you been watching the meteorite before this?" Aleia asked.

"No," Starry Knight said, just a little too quickly. I didn't have to touch her to see the hesitation and regret flutter off of her shoulders.

I remembered what Jason told me before, when I went to the college the first time. The mayor wanted updates about the meteorite. "Do you think SWORD knows about it?" I asked.

"I wouldn't presume to know what SWORD is thinking," Starry Knight assured me with a great deal of malice, "besides working toward their own benefit and power." Her violet eyes narrowed at me. "And how I know the scientist here is my own business; I don't intend on sharing it with you."

Before I could object and remind her she was my ally now, she turned, spread her wings, and leapt off into the night.

"I was hoping she'd heal me before she left," I muttered.

"We'll see her again," Aleia reminded me.

THE STARLIGHT CHRONICLES

"A little more suffering won't hurt you anyway," Elysian added, too gleefully for me to refrain from kicking him.

"That was brave of you to try to read that demon's heart," Aleia commended me, changing the subject as we headed upstairs.

"Thanks. I wasn't sure if it would work," I admitted. "And the pain was pretty intense for a few moments."

"Before you destroyed him, it would have been," Aleia agreed. "Your Starsoul is still alive, wrapped around your Soulfire. It would seek to protect you from evil's power."

I thought about the other *fenfleal* demon I'd managed to destroy, the one who tried to take me down in Logan's heart. That was what happened before, I realized.

The cool air outside Lakeview Observatory seemed foreign to me. For a long moment, the strangeness of the universe hit me. It was a moment where I looked at my life and my body, and all around the world where I was, and I saw it with unfamiliar eyes. What was this thing called life? How strange was it that I was me, and Aleia was herself, and Elysian, and that we all had destinies bigger and odder than we could imagine, all wrapped up in the bigger fabric of fate being woven, even as it was already made?

"Were you able to get anything else from him?"

Aleia's question broke my mystic meditation. "No." I sighed. "I wish, but evil hearts don't seem terribly complicated. At least, his didn't."

"The *fenfleal* demon is typically very focused on the task at hand."

I stilled at the new voice. We might need to make a quick escape, I thought. Especially since Dante Salyards had decided to make an appearance after all.

"What are you doing here?" I asked.

Dante's dark look sent chills down my spine. "I think it's time we had another chat," he said.

"I don't want to, thanks," I bit back. "We're busy at the moment."

"Kid, come on," Elysian hissed back. "Let's talk."

"It would be the first time we had a talk," Dante observed, not without some alacrity, and shifting his attention to the dragon on my shoulder. "Agent Salyards of SWORD," he introduced himself. "Pleased to make your acquaintance."

"The pleasure is nonexistent," Elysian assured him.

"Come now, why such hostility?" Dante nearly laughed. "We're on the same side."

"Are we?" Elysian shot back. "You have a funny way of showing it."

"By introducing myself?"

"By hiding your true intentions."

"I believe I told the 'kid' here, as you call him, that we were brought in to control the demon monster situation. Or should I say, 'situations?'"

"Did the mayor hire you?" I asked. "What are you planning with him?"

Dante's brown eyes—so like Mikey's, but without the warmth of shared friendship and brotherhood—narrowed as they looked at me, much as Starry Knight had only a few moments before. "At SWORD, we have a policy of confidentiality when it comes to the exact nature of the interests of our company and our customers," he replied easily enough.

"Confidentiality is convenient enough," I said. "But if you want us to trust you, you'll have to break a few rules."

"How do we know whose side you're really on?" Aleia asked.

"We're on your side," Dante insisted.

"Which side is that?" Elysian asked, as he began to transform. The long, scaly skin of his dragon form began to grow, and instantly I knew what he was planning.

"I'm on the side that's protecting Wingdinger, of course."

That was not the answer I had been expecting; nor was it what Elysian was expecting. I knew because he paused in mid-transformation.

"What do you mean?" he asked.

"I'm on the side that's protecting Wingdinger," Dante repeated, his voice straining under impatience.

"What do you mean?" I asked. "I'm not in any danger."

"Even though Starry Knight is out to trade you to Orpheus in exchange for the Sinisters?"

I had brushed off Mikey's warning easily enough before, especially after a week without action, but hearing it from Dante, a man I did not respect as a father or see as a true ally, made me wary enough to reconsider. "What do you mean?" I asked again.

"This is war, kid!" Dante snapped. "This is war, don't you see? There's a war going on, all around you, all the time. But now that you're here, with your power, you're in great danger. If we lose you, we lose all hope to make any difference in this world."

"What does that have to do with Starry Knight?" I asked.

"She's offering you to Orpheus in exchange for the Sinisters. Her *sisters*," Dante emphasized with disgust. "Orpheus wants you out of the way, and she wants the Sinisters returned. Seems like everyone else wins."

"But she's my ally," I insisted, remembering her sitting beside me in the woods. Remembering her healing power wiping away my wounds. Remembering her determination to protect me. Remembering her lips on mine.

"Don't be foolish. She's your enemy."

Folly and Foolishness' warning rang through me. *She wooed you, and then destroyed you.*

"If that's true," I said, slowly putting my words together, "then why didn't she capture me tonight?"

"Orpheus wasn't around. She wouldn't want you to get suspicious or fight her about it. It was a *fenfleal* demon, right? The Sinisters don't have connections to all demons, especially those."

"But—"

"Maybe you should ask yourself why she would make such a trade," Dante said. "You, for her sisters. Seems like a pretty likely swap, doesn't it?"

"I'm not one to trade my friends in for family who had abandoned me," I shot back. "Unlike you."

"But she did make the deal. I was there. I heard it," he insisted. "And you leave my son out of this, do you hear me?"

"I wouldn't have to keep him out of it if you hadn't come back," I argued.

"It's not something that's good for him," Dante insisted. "You shouldn't have allowed him to get mixed up in this; you probably shouldn't have gotten involved in it either."

His words, so similar to Starry Knight's, only made me angrier. I was ready to get into a full-fledged battle with Dante. It was one thing to make me doubt, but it was another to make me believe something else altogether.

246

But before I could unleash all my hard-learned logic and rhetoric skills on Dante's unwittingly tragic form, I belatedly heard another newcomer arrive behind me.

"Dad?"

I felt the world slip away as I turned to see Mikey's eyes. They were wide, and full of recognition and hurt as they moved from me to Dante.

"Mikey."

I wasn't sure at first if it had been my voice or Dante's who had said it, but as Mikey turned his gaze to me, I knew was me. Seeing the shock mixed in with hurt on my best friend's face as he saw his dad for the first time in nearly nine years had to be the most horrifying thing I'd ever seen.

After a long moment, probably the longest moment of my life, Mikey turned around and ran.

I didn't blame him, but I knew I wouldn't be able to follow him. At least not right away. I had to deal with his father first.

Dante's face was livid as he looked at me. "Did you tell my son about me?" he demanded to know.

"No," I sputtered back, trying to work through my shock at Mikey's arrival. *Why had he come here?* I hadn't called him. Surely the news people hadn't managed to come yet, had they? I glanced around. No one was in sight.

Dante was the only one, and he was looking at me curiously. "I thought I would give you the chance to tell him you were here," I said, deciding to hit back as much as I could. "I didn't want to disappoint him."

"Well, he was disappointed anyway," Dante retorted, suddenly cold. He sighed. "Never mind. We have business to discuss."

The coolness of his gaze, along with the apathy he cloaked himself in after he'd just seen Mikey, made me furiously angry. "I'm not going to work with you." I signaled to Elysian and nudged Aleia. "We're leaving."

Elysian transformed, saying nothing (for once), and Aleia and I hopped up onto his back. Before Elysian took off, I turned back to Dante and said, "Stay away from us—and Mikey, too, if you know what's good for you."

It was the most blatant and dangerous threat I'd ever muttered at that point in my life. But I meant it. I didn't want Mikey to keep paying for all the problems his dad had created, both between them, and between Mikey and the rest of his world.

In my anger, I allowed Elysian to fly through the city, staying on the topside of the city cloud cover, as I stewed. I hated Dante, I thought. I hated him, and I hated what he had done to his son, and what I'd let him do to Mikey and me because of my silence.

It was some time later when Aleia tapped me on the shoulder. "Can you put me down?" she asked.

"Huh?" I jolted out of my waking nightmare. "Oh, yeah. Where do you need?"

"Just down there," Aleia said, pointing to a quiet spot in the northern district.

A few moments later, I took her hand and helped her down from Elysian's back. The pavement felt cold to me, pushing through the protection of my boots.

"Thanks," she said. "I appreciate the ride."

I looked around. The place was familiar to me. Recognition burst through a moment later. We were in front of the church where, a few months ago at Christmastime, I saw Lady Hope dancing with some of her children over a manger scene.

"I've been staying here," Aleia explained.

"As a nun?" I asked, incredulous.

She laughed. "More or less," she confessed. "I've found the company to be very pleasing."

"Well, I guess that's good," I muttered, silently cringing. It would not have been my first choice.

"Why don't you pay me a visit tomorrow?" Aleia asked.

"I have work in the morning," I recalled. "But we can do later on in the day."

"Alright," Aleia agreed. "We'll work out a plan tomorrow. Try to go home and get some sleep, Hamilton."

"I'll try." *No promises.*

☼21☼
Conflicted

Aleia's words had echoed through me as the night passed, and my own attempt to get some rest proved to be an exercise in futility. I tried, but I did not succeed until the latest hours of the night, where the darkness covering the world was ready to release it.

Fortunately, two things saved me from falling asleep at work. Rachel's Café began catering the mayor's office, as Stefano had mentioned, so I had plenty of her coffee. I also managed to stay awake because Gwen texted me a lot, heralding in a new source of trouble for the day.

I'd forgotten I left her, along with Adam, at Rachel's to go to the observatory and fight off the demon, so we were not having much of a good conversation. But it was one conversation from which I was unable to excuse myself.

Which was only fair. Well, probably still less than fair to Gwen, after all the times I'd skipped out on her.

It was fair enough, I decided, after reading a rather lengthy, tearful-sounding plea to meet with her in Shoreside Park after I was done at work.

And while I was pretty sure she was angry, I was determined to reason with her. At least about our friendship, so our break-up story wouldn't be so damaging to my reputation.

I studied her as I came close, trying to read her emotions carefully.

"Before we say anything else, I want to say I'm sorry."

The words coming out of my mouth sounded fake to my ears, but I reasoned it was only because I was not used to apologizing, and I largely didn't believe in it. But there are exceptions to every rule, and if a woman is upset with you, that's usually the exception. And seeing Gwen's face as she turned to look at me through her sad, beautiful, honey-brown eyes, I had been pretty sure it was time for the exception to prove the rule.

"Let me buy you dinner," I suggested, scooting closer to her on the small park bench, and hoping I didn't look as tired as I felt. "Rachel's is right over there, right? We can get some coffee, too, or something else? You had a lot of fun the time we ... uh, we went ... "

I paused here, trying to recall the last full date we had. "You liked going to the track meets, right?" I asked. "We can find something like that to do."

"Hammy—"

"I was thinking of seeing if you wanted to maybe have dinner at my parents' house, too, sometime, if you would even want to meet them. They're not exactly the—"

"Hamilton—"

"Please, Gwen, don't be mad at me. I just totally forgot to get something at my house the other night, and then I had to go somewhere for the mayor—"

"Please stop," Gwen interjected. "As I told you in my messages, I'm fine. I don't need to be bribed or cajoled into being your girlfriend, you know." She sniffed. "It's actually a bit insulting when you try, too."

"I wasn't trying to bribe you," I muttered back.

"I wanted to talk to you about something."

"What is it?" I asked, feeling a trickle of dread descending into my stomach. *Was she going to ask for a "break?" Was there an "anniversary" thing coming up I needed to make a big deal out of?*

She sighed. "Do you still *want* to be my boyfriend?" she asked. Before I could ask why she would even say such a thing, she said, "Let me explain. You're busy. I know that. And I'm just asking because I can handle working around your schedule if you need it. I didn't realize when we started dating that you wouldn't have a lot of free time, but that's not your fault."

This was not going the way I'd expected, especially after ditching her, and then forgetting I'd ditched her. I had fully expected a letdown and a breakup; I was prepared for it, even.

She looked up at me with big eyes. "A few months ago, I wasn't sure about giving you a chance. I was upset with my parents for liking you better than Tim, and I was afraid of all the stuff going on, you know, because of the city's troubles, and … well, I thought about what you said before, about committing to something. And it was right. Hearing it from you was just what I think I needed to see you'd changed."

She has no idea how much has changed, I thought.

"And I've realized this past week especially, how much you're trying to do such a good job with everything that it's stretching you a bit thin." Gwen continued, "So I was worried you might feel like you're too busy for me, but I really want to be your girlfriend still."

"You do?" I asked, surprised. "But what about all the times I've run out on you or forgotten stuff or been called away on business?"

"Well, you told me why you had to go, right?" Gwen sighed. "I mean, most of the time."

"And what about the times I've called you and had to hang up suddenly? Doesn't that annoy you?"

"I can text you from now on," she assured me.

This was strange, I thought. "What about all the times you've been upset with me?"

"I've forgiven you, haven't I?"

"I guess, but—"

"Hamilton, are you *trying* to dissuade me from continuing our relationship?"

No. Yes. Maybe. "No, it's just … I mean—"

"I don't feel like I am good enough for you."

Her admission floored me. "Of course you're good enough for me, Gwen," I insisted, immediately backtracking. "I mean, who else is this patient with my schedule,

THE STARLIGHT CHRONICLES

unpredictable as it is? And you help me out tons by keeping Adam out of my hair."

She laughed. "Well, good to see I'm useful."

I took her hand. "Gwen, you're so pretty," I said. "And smart, and funny, and you get along well with my friends. There's no way there is anyone better out there to date than you."

"I love you, you know."

"What—huh? Uh … " If her previous admission had floored me, this one managed to push me through the floor of reality and into a hole.

Gwen gave me a small smile. "I know you have a problem with love," she said. "I mean, look at how your parents treat you, and how you don't really have anyone to turn to in your life with your problems. So don't worry about it right now. But I wanted you to know I'm here for you."

Her comments were unsettling, and not for the reason I thought they were. "That's … well, thank you." I kissed her cheek and smiled (awkwardly, no doubt) before hugging her.

"Do you think you could love me back one day?" she asked.

The old Hamilton Dinger would not have hesitated in the least to say "yes." He might have even managed to zealously declare he was already madly, passionately in love with her, even if he wasn't.

THE STARLIGHT CHRONICLES

The new one screamed at me to say absolutely nothing, because it was better than lying to her or misleading her.

Some kind of a compromise resulted from the internal standoff inside. "Of course," I muttered into her hair. In the split second after, I shoved the guilt and shame down by telling myself Gwen would always be one of the loveliest people I knew, and I loved her as a friend if nothing else.

I took a long moment to hold onto her, to imagine how pretty she looked, and how pretty and perfect we looked together.

Then the moment passed, and I was somewhat relieved.

I glanced at the time. Aleia had asked me to meet with her today, I recalled. She hadn't said a time, but I could probably head over, I decided.

But after looking at Gwen's face, I changed my mind. Like my guilt before, I shoved the instinct to run away down. I had to give her some time. I had to do *something* for her.

So we talked, and we walked, hand in hand, all the way around Shoreside Park. I listened to her tell me about schoolwork and Adam's latest antics, how her parents were going on vacation this summer, and other stuff like that.

I talked about nothing in particular. It's very easy to talk about nothing like it's something.

All I could think about was how Gwen was perfect. She was perfect. She was gorgeous and popular, but not snooty. She helped me out and she was very forgiving, but she didn't give away her self-respect by clinging to me all the time.

THE STARLIGHT CHRONICLES

Everything I'd said earlier was truth. She was the best person I could have dated.

Even in my most cynical of days, I knew she was the perfect girlfriend for me, the one I'd been dreaming of … at least, the one I'd dreamed of having before.

But now I didn't want her. I didn't love her back. Not in that soul-rushing, warped-thinking, heart-grabbing, all-consuming manner, anyway.

I didn't want to hurt her.

I didn't know what to do.

"This would be a great time for a demon attack," I murmured to myself, half-hoping that in my desperation Adonaias would allow something to stir up unexpectedly.

"What did you say?" Gwen asked.

"I have to go," I said, finally unable to take it anymore. I have to fix this, I thought. Aleia would know what to do, and if I could make myself feel better about all this, it was worth skipping out on Gwen. "I, uh, forgot I have to meet with Cheryl this afternoon. She's got some work for me to do on her big case."

"Oh. Well, that's okay." Gwen gave me a big, approving smile. "You go and take care of your mother. I'll call you later, okay?"

"Okay." I was secretly a little surprised at Gwen's easy acceptance. I reached over and squeezed her hand; instantly, I felt better, because there was a small underscore of irritation beneath a strong wave of admiration. "Sounds good."

"Good. I'll probably need to talk to you," she said playfully. "I'm working through studying for the finals coming up."

"Martha's got it out for us in APUSH," I agreed.

"Me especially, I'm sure!" Gwen laughed. "After scoring you as a boyfriend, I'm expected to get up to number two in the class."

"You can do it," I assured her, waving. "See you."

"Bye!"

I watched as she went down the block, and I thought about how Gwen didn't deserve me. She wasn't just good enough for me, she was too good for me. There I was, pushing her away even as she was determined to love me.

I waited until Gwen was just a shadow on the sidewalk before disappearing to the other end. My steps quickened as I headed out to find Aleia, deciding I would make her tell me where to find Starry Knight.

I was going to settle this between us, once and for all. The longer this went on, I knew, the more complicated it was.

As I ran, part of me thought about whether or not I should try to get a hold of Elysian.

I shrugged it off a moment later; Elysian's counsel would only make me mad. He would tell me, as he had with Starry Knight, that love would only make things more difficult—as they indeed did. He would tell me to back away from Gwen, possibly entirely. And I didn't want to do that, and for more reasons than the impending social disaster my reputation would suffer, or because I would probably need to find a new babysitter.

I mean, it *was* possible I could still grow to love her, right?

But even I knew that meant nothing to me while I was still unsure about Starry Knight.

It infuriated me. I had the perfect girlfriend, and I couldn't enjoy the fact she'd just admitted she was in love with me, and all because I had some interdimensional crush on an arrogant, self-righteous, overprotective, obsessive, secretive, maddening, and beautiful woman with wings and a bow and arrow.

I burst through the doors of Aleia's church, not stopping to hesitate or prepare myself for the rush of conflict I knew undoubtedly awaited me on the other side. I knew it would catch up to me shortly.

And it did, as soon as I heard the organ music.

I'd never liked the organ. It always made me think of a haunting lull, a stream of music designed to lure an unsuspecting person into danger or into the heart of terror. The eeriness of its music embittered me, making me dread death all the more, since there was nothing there but fear in the end.

But when I saw that it was Aleia playing—in her human form, no less, with no armor and no daggers at her side—I sighed.

She looked up at my arrival. "I was wondering when you would show up," she said in greeting.

"I might have come sooner." I glanced around. "I've never felt comfortable in places like this."

She laughed, surprising me. "I can assure you this church was built to protect people, to be a place of refuge for the lost and hungry, as well as the lonely and those who are hiding. It is not something you should fear. I imagine most of the discomfort is from some of the people here."

"I doubt we have much in common."

"I disagree, but I won't argue with you over the matter," Aleia promised. "Tell me what's wrong. You seem tired."

"I am tired," I confessed. "But I'm also tired of."

"Because of a lack of sleep?" she asked. "Or is it because of Starry Knight?"

"How did you guess?" I snorted.

She came and took my arm, patting it sympathetically. "She has always been a bit of a thorn in your side."

"Is that what your crystal ball told you?" I asked bitterly.

"A memory bubble is hardly the same thing as a crystal ball." Aleia sniffed prudently.

"Gwen told me she loves me."

Aleia raised her eyebrows. "That's quite a surprise."

"It's surprising that someone would love me?" I shot back.

259

"No, it's just unexpected." She frowned. "You don't have to take your frustration out on me."

"Sorry." I held out my hands. "I'm confused. And angry."

"About what?"

"About this whole situation."

"What situation?"

"You know what situation. Stop asking stupid questions," I bellowed, my patience snapping. "I know you lied to me, and I know the truth. I know Starry Knight is the one who made me fall. And despite this, I can't seem to stop thinking about her. Which is horribly inconvenient, because I just had the nicest girl in the whole world tell me she loves me!"

Aleia frowned. "What do you mean, you know the truth? Starry Knight didn't make you fall."

"She did, too." I stuffed my hands in my pockets, suddenly guilty. "I saw the memory of it from your time pool."

Aleia pulled out her small orb. "Put your hands on this," she instructed. "Let me see what you saw."

I glared at her, but I listened. If I was going to show her that I knew the truth, I should be willing to prove it.

The memory I'd seen from before blossomed up in the misty smog inside of the orb as my power reacted to Aleia's. This time, I didn't feel grabbed into the memory itself, but I saw it, like it was a movie or something.

I waited until Starry Knight's star exploded before pulling back some. "See?" I said. "That's where I fell. She pulled me down with her, punishing me."

Aleia said nothing for a moment. "Who told you that?" she asked.

"Well, it's not like it was an accident, right?" I bit back. Guilt twisted another knot in my stomach, and I tried to resume a normal tone. "Folly and Foolishness were there. They told me what happened. They said that they'd heard about it, they'd seen it. They knew she'd 'wooed me' in order to destroy me."

"They tricked you into using the memory pool."

"Well, sorry about that," I muttered quickly. "But it's not fair to me if you and Alora had something to hide."

"We didn't lie to you, Hamilton."

"I know you did!" I snapped back. "I saw it. There's proof."

She sighed. "I can explain that. When you were recreated as the Star of Mercy," Aleia began, "you were placed beside Starry Knight's star. You were friends."

"You don't have to lie. I know I was in love with her, and she only tolerated me. I must have been pretty stupid before she sent me to Earth." I slumped down on a nearby pew. "But it doesn't matter. She doesn't want anything to do with me."

"That's not true, either."

"Oh, yeah, I suppose she'll need some help with her Sinister sisters," I muttered, recalling Orpheus' deal.

"You need to listen. This is a complicated situation. She loved them very much. She has always been more concerned with her duty than her own heart, and that hasn't changed," Aleia said defensively. "But please let me—"

"If she hasn't changed, then is history going to repeat itself?" I asked. "A few months ago, she tried to supernova, and now she's made a deal with Orpheus."

"Well, okay. There's that. But that's not like her. We can trust her."

"*You* can trust her."

"Calm down, please," Aleia admonished, her own voice starting to raise as I pushed on. "You're—"

Fury snaked along my insides once more. "And *that's* why I need to know the truth about what is going on," I added for good measure. "If she's betrayed me before, she might do it again. I need to know so I can, first of all, get over her, so I can have a good, happy, *normal* relationship, and second of all, so I can protect myself."

I didn't add the third thing I would want to do—get revenge. I was not going to play the fool to anyone, not even Starry Knight.

Aleia cleared her throat. "Right now, she's back at Lakeview Observatory," Aleia told me, "but Hamilton, there's something you should—"

I hurried off before she could say anything else. I hadn't been able to keep my schedule open for track, and it was really a shame, I thought. Regret hit me again as I sped away, cutting through the back alleyways and hidden streets.

I heard her call after me, but without Elysian, Aleia was unable to keep pace with me. I soon left her behind, along with any illusion that I had any true allies.

☼22☼
Accusations

Lakeview Observatory came over the horizon easily, almost like the ground decided to move it closer to me, rather than letting me approach it. A strange eagerness took hold of me, as though I was nervous. It didn't happen often enough for me to recognize it immediately.

It was only as I entered the building that I paused; it was close to closing time, and I didn't know where Starry Knight was in the observatory. I had to be careful as I searched; it wasn't like a lot of people were just allowed to come in at their leisure.

I would fervently swear on my grandmother's grave Logan had invited me, I decided.

If you say something loudly enough and passionately enough, people are unlikely to contradict you. If you say it enough, people even tend to believe you.

It was this calming thought that pushed me onward. I tiptoed past Logan's office, where I could see a small beam of light under the door.

A renewed spark of anticipation bound me. *What if Starry Knight is here in her regular self, too?*

My skin tingled as I turned the corner; I was back in the observation room, where the large telescope, with its lights off and only the bluescreen of the computers surrounding it, looked just a bit frightening.

I slinked around the stairs, moving up quietly. I glanced and saw an open door, and headed for it. Awareness fluttered through me.

And there she was, standing in front of the meteorite display. It had been taken out of its glass case with care, and arranged on a sterile platform.

For a long moment, I watched her as she studied the object, slightly disappointed she was her usual, Starlight Warrior self. Part of me was curious as to why *she* was curious about the meteorite, but the other part of me—the part I was uncomfortable with—was just happy to see her.

The discomfort unraveling in my gut at Gwen's selfless loyalty, even after weeks of being snubbed as she tried to keep me in line, forced my common sense and my hand.

I pressed the mark on my wrist and transformed into Wingdinger. There was no need to let her see me in my regular self, I reasoned. She had enough of an upper hand.

One I didn't know the extent of, I reminded myself, as I stepped into the room quietly.

She instantly straightened her shoulders; she knew I was there.

"You shouldn't be here," she said, with no particular tone.

"I was under the impression the observatory was about to close."

"So you're here to usher me out?" Starry Knight's eyebrows rose in speculation. "No thanks."

"That's not why I'm here," I muttered back. "I want some answers."

"Is Elysian here, too?" she asked. "Shouldn't you call him, so he can bind me up again?"

"I don't want things to be like that. You know that."

She pursed her lips, no doubt upset I hadn't taken the bait, and said nothing.

Frustration began to snip at my patience. "Come on," I demanded. "I need to know things in order to work with you. Haven't I earned it?"

I moved in closer to her and stood on the opposite side of the meteorite.

Wariness filled her gaze, but she remained silent.

"You told me before I didn't know much about our enemies. Now I do. I know how to control my powers now. I know about the Celestial Kingdom, and the Prince of Stars."

Inches away from her, I continued, "I promised you I would keep fighting. Why can't you trust me?"

"It is my job to recapture the Sinisters," Starry Knight said. "Not yours."

"You can't stop me. And you were the one who lost them in the first place," I scoffed. "I saw what happened when I went to see Lady Time."

"Yes, how is Alora?" Starry Knight retorted. "Probably still angry about the hole in her Space-Time fabric."

THE STARLIGHT CHRONICLES

I frowned. "How did you know about that?" Then I shook my head. She was just trying to distract me, I realized. "Never mind. I know what happened when you made me fall, and I know you've been the cause of my problems ever since."

Finally, sentiment flickered in her eyes, before her stubborn obstinacy replaced it. "I won't deny that I am responsible for your suffering," she said quietly.

The last threads of my self-control snapped. "What were you thinking, sending me to Earth?" I asked bitterly. "Was it to punish me? Adonaias had forgiven me, and we were supposed to be friends!"

Before she could respond, I felt all my hurt, anger, and confusion fall out of me. "And now, we're supposed to work together here. *We* are supposed to capture the Sinisters, and *you* are not supposed to leave me behind. You betrayed me."

She said nothing again; she just looked down to the floor. Her silence was enough of an admission of guilt.

I marched closer to her, demanding to see her eyes as I accused her. "You betrayed me, and lied to me—"

"I didn't lie to you."

I frowned, confused. Realizing I was getting off topic, I switched tactics. "Tell me about the deal you made with Orpheus." Not wanting to betray Mikey, I added, "Dante's back from SWORD. He told me about it."

"Did he? And you trust him?" she asked.

"He told me that he's on the side that's protecting me," I told her.

"Well, that's a laugh," she muttered.

"What's that supposed to mean?" I snapped. "Or can't you tell me that, either?"

"SWORD is not our enemy," Starry Knight said. "At least, not when it comes to the Sinisters. But it is not our ally, either."

"There is no 'us.'"

She ignored me. "They only want power. If SWORD is after protecting you, it is likely only because of your power."

"At least they aren't averse to working with me."

"Agent Salyards is not," Starry Knight corrected me. "But the rest of SWORD is conveniently absent, isn't it?"

"So? He is probably the only one assigned to our case."

"He might just be doing this because of his son. Your friend with the blog."

I decided to ignore her this time. "How much do you know about me?"

"Plenty, thanks to your friend's blog."

I suddenly wondered just *what* Mikey was writing. I didn't proofread anything he'd written, and I didn't really read it, either. I made a mental note to check on it later.

THE STARLIGHT CHRONICLES

Starry Knight folded her arms across her chest. "I also know SWORD should not be trusted."

"Why not?" I asked.

"You mean besides the fact they imprisoned us?" She shook her head. "They're targeting us. Haven't you noticed they're following us around?"

"Have you talked to Dante at all?"

"Not much," she said, surprising me with a smirk. "But then, I wasn't looking for an opportunity, either."

"I can understand," I bantered back. "He doesn't seem like an easy person to get along with."

"Especially on his terms." Starry Knight wrinkled her nose. "He seemed to like playing the spy a bit too much."

I almost laughed, before I realized it was too easy to be her enemy and then her ally. I'd slipped back into the friend zone without noticing.

What is wrong with me? Why couldn't I sufficiently hate this woman? Anytime I was around her, anger somehow turned into madness, and madness into magic.

"They also have Taygetay," Starry Knight reminded me. "I would know if she had been sealed away. She is still alive, but she has been restrained."

"How?" I asked.

"I have a couple of guesses," Starry Knight said hesitantly, "but nothing is certain. I am waiting to see if Orpheus can summon her."

"You're the one who wants to trade me to off to Orpheus for the Sinisters," I accused. "Is that when you were going to check?"

Her mouth opened to respond, and in that second, time seemed to stall. I saw her lips and couldn't stop myself from wanting them under my own. I took another step closer and locked eyes with her as the tension around us morphed. She faltered and sank into silence once more.

"I can't trust you, can I?" I asked.

Fear sharpened the soft violet into hard crystals. Her hands came up and forced me back. "Maybe you shouldn't, then."

"That's not what you told me before."

At my words, she backed up away from me, as though I'd slapped her.

Reaching out, I caught her face between my hands and felt her lean in close as I pulled her toward me, resting the wingdings of my feather-crown against her forehead. She stilled, her breath caught in her throat.

For a moment, neither of us said anything, as I allowed the rush of longing to run over me.

"I don't trust you, even though I want to," I admitted, finding the courage to look into her eyes again. I was unable to move, even as I decided not to. She could decide what she wanted, I thought.

Starry Knight clenched her shaking hands into fists. "I should go," she said, stepping back.

I said nothing, silently mourning the lost moment.

She paused a moment, before glancing back at me. I watched as her emotions changed; there was more firmness, bordering in on desperation. "If you want to be free of me," she said, "all you have to do is fall in love with a human."

"What?"

"That's what you wanted to know, isn't it?" Starry Knight asked, her smile suddenly cold and brutal. "I am the reason you fell. I am the cause of your suffering. You were right; we were once friends, but there's no way we can be friends now. So, if you want to be free of me, free of your past self, all you have to do is fall in love with a human."

"That won't work," I objected. "Alora and Aleia told me I've already used my wish."

"Love is the most transforming power in all creation," she said, turning away from me and pushing past me as she headed toward the exit. "It offers second chances. It brings new life where there was none. If you want to be free, all you need to do is embrace it."

"But—"

"Don't be a fool." She turned and narrowed her gaze on me, before adding, "Again."

As she glowered at me, her eyes mocking me, her face cold and resolute, I only felt hatred blooming inside. My fists clenched together, and I was too stunned at the hardening of my heart to say anything I really wanted to say.

"I've had enough of this conversation," Starry Knight announced. "I'm leaving. Let me go."

"Oh, it would be my pleasure," I grumbled, hurrying after her. "But I'm not done—"

She swiveled around with a sneer on her face, making me stumble. "Don't you have a girlfriend or something you need to go and take care of?"

At her comment, rage momentarily immobilized me. I watched as she left, wondering if it was possible she was just taunting me. Even while I assured myself she was bluffing, the attack had been too personal and too close to the truth for comfort.

My fingers curled into a fist. "Wait!" I called back, and hurried after her.

☼23☼
Treachery

I rushed outside, and, for a moment, I thought Starry Knight had managed to elude me once more.

Briefly, I thought about trying to fly, before dismissing it. My wings, while they were now a darker red, were still on the stubby, useless side. Part of me wondered if I ever would fly.

But that was a mystery for another day.

Movement caught my eye. Starry Knight was just about to take off.

"Stop!" I cried. I pulled out my sword. "We aren't finished here."

She stilled and then turned around. "You're going to fight me?" Her disdainful tone made me tightened my grip.

"Yes," I said.

Starry Knight glared at me. Despite the distance, I heard her murmur as though she'd whispered it in my ear. "Fine. Let's do this your way."

Her bow appeared in a flash of light. I gripped the hilt of my sword and hurried forward. I knew I wasn't going to have a chance if she decided to use her arrows. I had to get her off balance and defeat her on her own ground.

"Augh!" I cried out as I attacked, thrusting down. Her bow slammed into my sword, and energy crackled around us as we met each other, blow for blow.

It was almost like a dance. A brief feeling of déjà vu struck me as we sparred and parried weapons.

As I managed to hold down her weapon, a flare of worry crossed her expression.

"What's the matter?" I asked. "Afraid I'll win for once?"

Her eyes narrowed as she sideswiped my sword, allowing her to retreat.

But rather than letting her escape, I pushed forward. She stumbled, and I saw my opening. My sword pressed forward, ready to trip her, and then trap her.

Her bow came up; with a cry of her own, she managed to push back.

Our weapons met and locked, and after a moment of deadlock, I felt another wave of resolve push through her.

"This has to end," she muttered.

"It will, when you surrender," I shot back.

"That's not going to happen." She twisted her bow, and suddenly my grip was lost. Both our weapons went flying to the side; I heard them clatter onto the ground beside us.

"Impressive," I muttered.

Weaponless, I momentarily faltered. And I paid for it. She lashed out her own stream of power, her Soulfire's energy reaching out and bruising me.

The pain in my torso stung, as her power razored through my tunic and under my armor. "You'll pay for that," I said through gritted teeth, rubbing my hand over the small wound in my torso. I felt the warmth of blood and wondered at it for a small second. How could she do this to me?

Did she really hate me that much?

I remembered her eyes as she'd looked at me through the rain. *I will save you, no matter the cost. You must trust me.*

Was I that stupid? I wondered.

As my confusion and hurt and anger all rolled together inside of me, Starry Knight took the time to regain her breath. Her smile grew haughty as she looked down at me. "Eris was right," she taunted. "You are my greatest weakness. It's time to get rid of you."

She lashed out a power-packed punch, grazing my shoulder as I ducked and rolled. As I tumbled, I kicked up a leg and caught her on her hip. I heard her gasp in surprise as she stumbled, delaying her enough for me to recover.

We stood up and glared at each other. She was turning out to be a harder opponent than I thought.

Starry Knight reached up and pulled an arrow out of nothing. The light blazed before me, and I realized I was at a distinct disadvantage.

Before I could think it through, I raced toward where my sword had fallen.

Starry Knight took flight behind me and tackled me.

THE STARLIGHT CHRONICLES

"No!" I yelled, as the cement of the sidewalk caved in some as we fell, and I shoved her off of my back. My elbow hit her hard in the side as she toppled forward.

Her arrow slammed into the sidewalk in front of us, and I squeezed my eyes shut at the bright intensity.

"Ugh." I faltered backward. Blindly, I groped for the sidewalk. I hurriedly stood up and ran, my eyes blinking back their sight just in time to stop myself from running headlong into a tree.

"I've got you now."

I turned at her malicious words, only to see four arrows racing toward me. My eyes squeezed shut again, unable to do anything to stop them.

No pain came as they *whooshed* past me.

Tentatively, I opened my eyes. "Whew." I breathed a sigh of relief, glad to see she'd missed. I was about to taunt her on her poor aim, before I realized her arrows had pierced through my tunic and half-gloves, effectively binding me to the tree. "Hey!" I called out. "Let me go!"

Chilling laughter answered me. "Now, why would she do that?" Orpheus called out.

My wound, still burning, splintered as I sucked in my breath. Turning to Starry Knight, who was trying to compose herself, I frowned. "So this is how you wanted it."

She came up beside me, just near enough that she was out of my reach. "I thought it would be better this way," she said, the hard tone in her voice heavy with spite.

Orpheus laughed. "I appreciate it," he said, "that you were able to drain him of his power, too."

Realizing he was talking about me, I growled. "I still have plenty!" I assured him.

I turned back to Starry Knight. "I hate you!" I screamed. Power fueled itself inside of me, as I burned with the desire to show her just how much I did hate her. "You weren't supposed to do this."

"Quiet," she barked back at me. "I'd hate to have to exert any more energy in dealing with you."

"Augh!" I cried out again, fighting with everything in me to make her arrows loosen, to let me be free once more. Energy shot out around me, sparking the arrows, but nothing diminished their steady light.

I fought back against the effort as Starry Knight turned her attention to Orpheus.

"Where are my sisters?" she asked. "We had a deal." She narrowed her gaze down at me, as I groaned in response.

"You'll get them," Orpheus promised. "I've already called them. They'll be here shortly. Assuming they listen, of course."

"Yes, I've noticed your rather poor skills in managing them," Starry Knight retorted.

"Now, now, my darling, no need to insult me," Orpheus chided her gently, shocking me enough to get me to stop fighting against Starry Knight's arrows. I watched as he reached out and pulled back his hood, fully revealing his missing eye socket and crude features.

Even though I couldn't stop myself from shuddering at his terribly ugly face, one thing was clear: Orpheus was still in love with Starry Knight. His twisted, lovesick smile said it all.

I slumped against the tree behind me, breathing deeply as I tried to process it all. It was hard.

Orpheus was still infatuated with her. He didn't just want her power; he wanted her love.

"Save the sweet talk," Starry Knight snapped. "There's no need for it."

I almost cheered at her rebuke, before I remembered I was supposed to hate her.

"I'll save it for later." Orpheus complied, giving her a mocking bow. "Assuming you actually keep your side of the deal."

"What's that supposed to mean?" Starry Knight frowned. "I brought you Wingdinger. We're waiting on you to uphold *your* end of the bargain."

As if on a cue, several voices, of which I was too familiar, came rushing out of the night sky, mixed in with an array of colors.

Elektra was back, I saw. I'd wondered how she faired since the incident at City Hall. Celaena, the fat, purple one, came in next to her, while Asteropy, in her bright yellow tone, managed to set herself apart from the rest of them.

I almost laughed to see Maia. She settled down into a tree branch and yawned.

"What's this all about, Orpheus?" Asteropy sniped. "I was in the middle of important business."

"No you weren't," Celaena countered. "You were playing with your hair."

"Better than stuffing my face with earthly sweets," Asteropy shot back.

They fought some more, Elektra willingly jumping in, while Maia looked like she went back to sleep.

Orpheus fumed, before he turned back to Starry Knight. "Well, there you are."

"I have to seal them away first," Starry Knight insisted. I watched as she pulled out another arrow. Her bow jumped to her hand as she called it, and for a moment I wondered.

Why didn't she do that earlier? She could have won more easily against me ...

Her first arrow blazed out, heading straight for Maia.

Not a breath passed through my lips as I watched. Everything seemed to happen in slow motion, until the very end.

THE STARLIGHT CHRONICLES

Maia peeked out of her one eye as the light exploded into her vision. "Whoa!" Maia flinched at the last possible second, falling out of the tree and into a bed of bushes. "Hey! You almost shot me."

I nearly laughed, but I caught myself; there was no need to draw attention to myself.

Maia hurriedly got up, just as Starry Knight began her offensive. I watched her arrows slice through the darkened woods, as Maia and the other Sinisters began to fight back.

"Come back here," Orpheus commanded, trying to call them back as they sunk deeper and deeper into the woods. I watched him as he furiously paced and ranted, cursing his charges and throwing a small tantrum.

But when everyone else seemed too caught up in everything, he grinned.

He grinned, and then he looked at me.

Oh, great, I thought sarcastically. This is going to be fun.

"Well, Wingdinger, I'd say now's as good a time as any to deal with you."

"Starry Knight needs the Sinisters sealed away first," I argued. "If you don't wait, you won't get your end of the bargain."

"I'm getting to destroy you. That's enough," he said.

"I thought you wanted her power," I taunted, nodding toward Starry Knight. "Weren't you in love with her on the other side of Time? Didn't you want her, before you fell?"

Orpheus stalled.

I kept talking. It was the only sure way I had of surviving. "Lady Time told me all about you. She said you fell prey to Alküzor because you didn't think the Prince was right in denying you Starry Knight."

"She was the only one I wanted," he grumbled, remembering. "It was the only thing I ever asked of the Prince." He spat on the ground as he came closer. "The Prince is so high and mighty," he said. "What could he really know of my love for Lady Justice?"

"Enough that he said no," I blurted out. "You weren't good enough for her then, and you aren't good enough for her now."

"Since when is love about being good enough?" Orpheus growled. "For someone who knows a lot about the dealings of the other side, you sure don't know what love is."

"At least I was smart enough to turn back from Alküzor," I shot back. "I was recreated."

"You were a fool." Orpheus' voice grew as he turned his full hatred onto me. "You were easy to convince to leave the Prince's side, you know. All it took was talk of power, of being free to do as you please."

Orpheus glared at me, glared *into* me. "Your Soulfire was weak to begin with."

He stood in front of me now, reaching toward me. I pushed back against Starry Knight's arrows. Surely, I thought and prayed, with her distracted, their power would fade?

I had nothing to do but stall and hope Elysian and Aleia would come looking for me. "Yours was weaker," I argued back. "Starry Knight was able to reject you before. She'll be able to reject you again, just you watch. I'd wait for her to capture the other Sinisters if I were you."

Orpheus stilled.

Finally, I thought. Finally, a sore spot. "It would be a pity and a waste if you were to ruin your chance now by making her mad. She'll never love you if you don't uphold your bargain."

"She never will love me," he griped, "so long as you are around."

Shock hit me harder than any blow could have. "What?"

He didn't answer me. His hand, grayish-colored, with skin tightly drawn, clawed through me.

I choked at first, before screaming out in pain. Heat seared through my chest as I felt my heart squeezed.

"You will be destroyed!" Orpheus yelled at me.

Through my pain, I looked to see his eye burning with rage and anger, as his own power pushed into me, reaching into the heart of my being and searching for my Soulfire.

As abruptly as the pain had started, it ended.

I looked to see Starry Knight had pushed herself between me and Orpheus.

"Orpheus!" she roared. "You must stop. We had a deal."

"You were going to reject me," he raged. "That's what he told me," he said, pointing his finger at me.

"I wouldn't believe a word of what he says," Starry Knight said in a strangely calm voice. "He's probably just trying to save himself."

Orpheus' power receded, and she turned to face me. "You thought you could talk your way out of this?" she asked. "You're a fool." And then she struck me, hitting me across the jaw.

"Ouch!" I managed, before slouching over in pain. The wound at my side was still bleeding freely. "You'll pay for this!" I cried back.

Starry Knight turned back to Orpheus. "See? He's only upset that I bested him, and that I will pledge myself to you once he and my sisters are taken care of."

That burned me more than anything else.

"Now," Starry Knight said, "get your charges back here so I can seal them away."

He seemed to calm down some as he nodded.

Starry Knight grabbed my tunic and pulled me closer to her face. "And you," she yelled, "don't say anything that will make me hit you again. You're weak enough."

I was going to say something back, but as she released me, I felt her healing power wash over me. My eyes flashed to hers, only to see the warning in them.

Understanding dawned.

THE STARLIGHT CHRONICLES

It was time I started playing the game myself.

☼24☼
Truth

A smirk came slowly to my face. "Orpheus is still weaker than I am," I called out.

Orpheus turned back to me, his eye penetrating into me. "You're the one who has been captured," he retorted.

"But you can't even call the Sinisters to you," I pointed out. "You have those four running around in the woods at night, and Taygetay is still not here."

"What's Taygetay got to do with it?" Orpheus fumed. "She's been captured by your people."

"SWORD is not an ally of ours," Starry Knight corrected. "As such, I will need her sealed away before I give you Wingdinger here."

"The four out there are surely enough," Orpheus objected.

"That wasn't our deal."

"It's four of them for one of yours," Orpheus argued. "That's more than fair."

"This isn't about fair," Starry Knight shot back. "It's about honor and power. If you want power, you'll give me what I want. And I want my sisters back."

Orpheus huffed. "This is outrageous."

"We agreed to it."

Orpheus groaned and resumed his earlier pacing. After a moment of frustration, he stopped and stared at her.

The longing on his face was as sickening as ever, I thought.

"If it's the Sinisters you want, my dear," Orpheus crooned, "then I'll give them to you." He reached out, caught a wayward lock of her hair, and caressed it through his fingers.

I shook in fury. My own fingers tingled as I recalled the softness of her silken tresses. "Don't touch her!" I cried out before I could stop myself. The thought spurred power through me, and I was determined to break free.

Orpheus chuckled at me. "She's mine, you fool," he hissed. He moved his hands to cup her chin. "She belongs to me now."

"The Prince told you no before," Starry Knight reminded him, trying to step back.

"What does the Prince have to do with this? You are free of him, and so I am. He means nothing to me. My new master says I can have your power, but I want your heart as well." He pulled her close to him, even as she pushed him away.

"I've waded through both sides of Time for a taste of you," Orpheus purred. "And I'm so close … "

Agony lanced through me as I once more fought off Starry Knight's arrows. "Stop!" I cried.

A dragon's roar rang throughout the night. I looked up just in time to see Elysian slice through the night sky, severing Starry Knight from Orpheus' hold.

"I've never been so happy to see Elysian," I muttered to myself. I heard Orpheus rage as he scrambled around, trying to fight off Elysian.

Aleia jumped off, landing in front of me. "Are you hurt?" she asked. She pulled out a dagger and sliced through an arrow, breaking and its power over me.

Before I could answer her, Celaena and Elektra appeared, no longer fighting with each other, but united in battle against Aleia.

"Watch out!" I exclaimed, using my free arm to push her out of the way.

Celaena and Elektra, deprived of their target, found another one in Starry Knight.

They jostled together in air, fighting with each other. Lightning and power collided, lacing through the night sky in patterns of destruction.

Aleia slashed through another arrow. "Thank goodness we found you in time," she said.

"I couldn't agree more," I murmured. "Thank you." She cut through the last arrow, and I slumped downward.

Aleia ducked down beside me. "Are you hurt?" she asked.

"I'm not bleeding anymore, and Starry Knight healed me," I confessed. "But I might need a moment here."

"Okay." Aleia nodded. "I understand. I'm going to go help them fight, okay?"

THE STARLIGHT CHRONICLES

"Okay. I'll be there shortly."

"Don't forget your sword," Aleia reminded me before she sped off to help Starry Knight.

I placed my hand over my heart, where Orpheus had used his power to grab onto my own. After making sure I felt more or less like myself, I stood up.

My sword was not far away, and grabbing it would be smart, so I decided to do that.

No sooner had I picked it up than Elektra barreled into me from behind.

"It's about time I had my revenge," she declared. "And while I'm at it, I can grab your power, too."

"Orpheus wants to destroy me," I told her. "You're supposed to be under his charge."

"As long as the curse on me remains," Elektra said, "Orpheus is not my rightful master."

"What curse?" I asked her. I picked myself up, with my sword ready.

She ran her fingers along her neck, and for a moment I thought she was trying to trick me. But a glimmer of reflected light caught my attention. "We are restrained by a curse," she explained, pointing to the shard. "And we will be, as long as your power pushes back on us."

I frowned. "I didn't place you under a curse," I said, hating myself for getting more distracted. Upon closer examination, I saw that the shard looked a lot like a fragment of Aleia's memory bubbles. I'd have to worry about it later, I decided, as Elektra, tired of focusing on her flaws, reverted to demonstrating her power.

Her nails shrieked across my vision, the power grazing my forehead. My sword countered, hacking a good inch into her skin.

As she screamed in fury and her silvery-colored blood leaked down her side, I glanced around; Starry Knight was tangled up with Celaena, who, despite her size, was pretty quick with her cat-fighting skills; Aleia was preoccupied with Asteropy and Maia, who managed to come out of her stupor long enough to play; and Elysian was still after Orpheus.

"Orpheus!" Elektra cried. "I need more power!" She scuttled over before I could stop her.

She ended up blocking Orpheus' escape, as Elysian roared and breathed down a shot of celestial fire. Orpheus managed to push Elektra into his way, allowing her to be burned by the dragon flames.

Orpheus ducked to the side and ran into me. Had Elektra's fire bath not been so surprising, I might have caught him before he caught me.

His wispy hands, so small and tight, grappled around my throat. "It's time to finish you," Orpheus said. "Your power might be bright, but it's time to extinguish it."

"You wouldn't be able—Augh!" I choked on my scream as his one hand around my neck tightened, while the other once more pressed into my heart, looking for the power it hid.

THE STARLIGHT CHRONICLES

Just as before, I felt his own power slip into my mind, muddled up against mine.

My heart lurched forward as my Soulfire burned against Orpheus' power, as it had with Elektra's. I wriggled around, trying to escape. My feet lashed out, weak without oxygen. My hands curled up around his in a brittle grasp.

And then I found everything going dark and empty, as my body limped over and my Soulfire was free.

The Blood Flame burned my vision back, and I saw my spirit was once more outside of my physical body. Orpheus eagerly dropped my body onto the ground, and, at the flopping *crunch*, I decided I would take him out myself as soon as I could.

I hadn't noticed it as much last time, I thought, how there were such beautiful overtones and sinister undertones, complementing the realities of the natural world with the surrounding supernatural realities.

I could see emotions written all over everyone's faces, all at once. There was the tired sadness on Elysian's, the worried distraction on Aleia's; I could see the differences in the focused determination and hatred on Orpheus', and the horror and distress on Starry Knight's.

Something else caught my attention as I looked at her—the red feather in her hair.

Recognition finally hit me. The Blood Flame's heartbeat and the feather's inner, spiritual fire were the same.

It's mine.

My body twitched in accordance with my thoughts: I must get the feather.

The Sinisters turned away from the brightness of my power. I felt Orpheus' hands clasp around the heart of my power, crying as it burned him. But as he watched Starry Knight race over, he laughed.

"Let him go!" Starry Knight yelled, grabbing his arms and trying to force him back.

Orpheus threw her off, easily slamming her onto the ground next to my body.

"This is the end of your love, Lady Justice," he cried.

"No!" She jumped up, pushing through his defense. My Soulfire leaked back beside me, resting on my chest as she fought to destroy him.

"Stop this at once, you miserable witch!" Orpheus hollered, slamming her down beside me.

She placed her hand over my heart, and her hair spilled out over my tunic.

The feather in her hair burned all the more brightly as it beckoned to me.

Concentrating hard, I felt my Soulfire squelch in welcome pain as it moved through me mildly, allowing my fingers to twitch.

"Augh!" Starry Knight turned, just as I was about to grab it. She unleashed a strong blast of her power at Orpheus, sending him flying backward.

THE STARLIGHT CHRONICLES

She slumped over me when she was done, breathing deeply. I felt her drained power reserves as she peeled off her glove and placed her hand on my chest.

"Please," she whispered softly, shaking badly. "Come back to me."

She was doing it again, as she'd done before. She was calling my soul back to into my body, asking my heart to find a way back to hers.

My Soulfire was settling nicely inside of my heart when I noticed the fear in her eyes. She was worried for me. Blistering, wounded pride and heartache rushed in as I recalled our battle earlier.

As if she could sense my confliction, she embraced me, pushing my heart closer to hers. Her hair drifted over enough for me to grab onto the feather.

Starry Knight jolted when she saw me move, and she watched as I gripped the warm softness between in my fist. "I suppose it is yours," she admitted, her voice barely a whisper.

Before I could open my eyes and confront her about her treachery to me, Orpheus was suddenly back.

"You fool," he muttered, bringing her face close to his as he berated her. He grabbed her hair and neck, choking her against him. "We could have had everything—*everything*—if you had only loved me!"

I groggily opened my eyes to find myself back inside my body, feeling as though the natural world was intent on increasing gravity's power over me.

My hands reached up and wiped away the tiredness on my face. The feather brushed against me and its flame lit up in a burst of power.

I almost screamed before realizing it wasn't burning me. The warmth settled around me as I held it.

Starry Knight finally managed to free herself from Orpheus' grip. She fell right on top of me.

"Umph," I muttered, as her elbow dug into my side.

"Come back here!" Orpheus cried.

She scrambled back, trying to dodge Orpheus as he reached for her again. I twisted away from her, crawling up onto my knees. "Stay away from us!" I yelled, latching onto Orpheus' hands with my own.

In less than a second, fire pulsated through me and around me, unleashing its energy as a weapon.

I felt my wings widen and burn, transforming from their blackened roots to their blood-colored tips into wings of pure fire.

Orpheus shrieked in anguish, gnashing his teeth together in pain and weeping for relief. I don't know how long I held onto him, screaming in shock and pain and retaliation, before I realized I didn't know how to stop.

Power radiated from the fire in my heart and soul. Orpheus' cries were no longer heard, as all the emptiness of his skin and robe were burned off. He disappeared into my power, forced out from the shelter of my fiery wings, while I was left to be consumed inside of it.

Help me, I whimpered to myself. I didn't know how to stop.

I felt Starry Knight move from below me. She reached up and tugged at my arm. I felt the cooling rush of her healing powers, I saw her own power wrap around her as she leaned into me, and I heard the whisper of her voice against my ear.

"Come back to me."

The fire burned down from my hands and I felt myself let go of the rest of the world as I clung only to her.

"Come back to me … " There was more urgency now, even as there was more tenderness.

"Please, Almeisan."

My eyes flew open wide, and my heart opened up, drawing in all my fire as my power fully awakened inside of me. I didn't know whole worlds could be wrapped up in a single name, but as I heard my own name, the one from the other side of Time, I heard the strange music of feeling and life and power sing through me—body, heart, mind, soul, and spirit.

"I love you, Almeisan. I'm in love with you."

No greater proclamation, incantation, or manifestation had ever come to me before in all my life than in that moment. Suddenly, there was no fear, no pain, and no hesitation. I felt the joyful realities of truth love for the first time as Starry Knight lean in to kiss me, willingly, passionately, and persistently.

THE STARLIGHT CHRONICLES

My heart throbbed with pleasure so much it was almost painful, as I kissed her again and again, until the fire outside and around me only burned within me.

The heat became a warmth, and as the warmth gently met the misty night, I pulled back from her.

I felt her own name in my heart and on my tongue, but when I opened my mouth, nothing came out. I frowned, swearing inside of myself that I'd just had it, that I'd known it, that I needed to say it.

But it wasn't coming. It was as if instead of a name, I'd found a hole in my memory that was etched in the size and shape of her name. I could trace around them and write them, but never read them or decipher its meaning.

"Are you alright?"

Starry Knight's violet eyes ripped through the flames of my surreality. I felt myself inhale air and nearly choke in response. My fire had lit quite a bit of the woods on fire.

I could hear sirens in the distance, getting closer.

Finally, I gazed down at Starry Knight's face once more, and I felt the lingering wholeness of my identity grind against the fallen nature of conflict inside of me. *She loved me.* Her hands were resting on my tunic, still clenched in terror, as though they were trying to hold onto the moment as much as the magic.

My own arms had wrapped around her and, as my confusion, even in clarity, grew, I dropped them and stepped back.

"No." I breathed.

She stilled. Before she could reply, I shook my head. "What is love without trust?" I asked. "I can't trust you." I can't trust myself, either, apparently, I added silently to myself, as my own heart began to ache.

"If you can't forgive me for tonight—"

"Forgive you?" I nearly shouted. "For just tonight?" I suddenly wanted to shake her. "You sent me to Earth, after I'd been forgiven. You've kept secrets from me, and endangered my life. How could I ever forgive you for all of that? For all of this?" I waved my hand around, gesturing to the broken tree branches and the burning grass, the remnants of my own star power.

Starry Knight stepped back, taking all the warmth in the world with her. She nodded. "I understand."

"Well, I'm glad someone does, because I sure don't," I bit back. I only wanted to be angry at her, and be angry at her for possibly forever.

"If it helps, I release you from your promise," Starry Knight spoke up.

"What?"

"I said, I release you from your promise," she snapped, more embarrassed than angry.

"What promise?" I asked.

"Your promise to be a defender. You needn't worry about having me hold you accountable."

She was trying to get rid of me altogether, I thought. Well, it wasn't going to happen. "I didn't make a promise to be Starlight Warrior just to you," I snapped back. "I also made one to the Prince, and I'll keep my word on it, thanks."

She bit her lip, saying nothing, even though I knew she wanted to.

An ache rushed to my head, as the pressure behind my eyes exponentially increased. I felt the same compulsion to leave as I had earlier, when I was talking with Gwen. The moon seemed to be in solidarity with me, as it ducked behind the clouds and hid.

I intended to do just that, too, until I heard the familiar voice coming from the ground.

"I told you she would never love me so long as you were around."

I swiveled around to give Orpheus, or what was left of him, a piece of my mind. Until I saw him.

Gone was the creepy-looking man in the black robe. His hair remained a shade of ebony slightly darker than the shadows in his remaining eye. But his skin burned pure and white, almost shimmering against the darkness of the absent moonlight.

I saw Aleia come over. "What happened to Orpheus?" Her voice had a strangled quality to it as she looked on Orpheus' transformation.

His robe had burned away, leaving a princely, ornate outfit, shining white with delicate, golden stitching. There was not a speck of evil clinging to him.

"I don't know," I admitted.

"You purified him." The sheer awe in Elysian's deep, big dragon voice almost made me jump.

Starry Knight's voice, strangely scraggled, spoke up. She pointed to my side. "You had blood on your side from earlier. It got caught up in the blaze of your full power and purified him when he grabbed you."

"When *I* grabbed *him*," I corrected.

She rolled her eyes, but nodded. I decided I could almost stay mad at her, despite that.

Orpheus just looked down at himself. "I'm ... myself again," he said. "Well, almost," he added, touching the brim of his empty eye socket. "I've been freed of Alküzor's power."

Aleia came up beside him and touched his arm. "Yes, you have been. It's a miracle." She smiled brightly. "This is an absolute miracle!"

"Where are the other Sinisters?" I asked.

"They left when they saw Orpheus burning," Elysian said. "They no doubt felt his power disappear, and that is what caused them to retreat for now."

"So, you have nothing to show for betraying me to them," I informed Starry Knight.

"I wasn't going to let them hurt you," she muttered.

"Yes, thank you so much for that," I replied. "Imagine, hurting me so they didn't have to. What a great idea."

"I understand you're angry," Starry Knight began again, "but—"

"But what?" I hissed. "But it's all okay, because you say you love me?" My voice dropped so it could only be heard between the two of us. "I wanted so badly to have your approval," I admitted. "But I see it was not needed. You're not worthy of me."

She said nothing, staring at me with a clear gaze.

"I want to do what is right," I continued, feeling uncomfortable. "But I don't want to have anything to do with you anymore." My own voice was beginning to crack, as my headache pounded inside of my head.

I rubbed my temples and looked at her. She was as still as ever.

"I'm leaving," I said. "Tell Elysian to give me the full report later. It's been a long day."

"Fine."

There was no emotion in her words, but as I turned and began to walk away, and the moon was painted black and the stars went to sleep, I had to fight with myself to forget the sound of her teardrops—just two—as they slipped down her face and fell onto the sidewalk.

THE STARLIGHT CHRONICLES

☼25☼
Gifted

I wasn't sure how I lived through the rest of the weekend. Maybe I was on autopilot. That was probably it. I was on autopilot because I didn't want to sleep afterward. Maybe I couldn't sleep. I don't know, because I didn't sleep. That's supposed to affect your memory.

I didn't want to go to sleep, because I was worried I would wake up and find that the whole thing had been a dream.

I'd wanted to find out the truth, and the truth was, I couldn't handle it.

I was in love with someone I couldn't trust, someone who had deliberately put me in danger. Someone who was in love with me, someone who knew me, and just didn't care to tell me anything. Or work with me. Or be there for me.

It was maddening.

Before I knew it, it was Monday again.

I moved through the day like a zombie. I got up late, after a fitful sleep. Since I was running late, I didn't make it to Rachel's for coffee.

Gwen chattered with me throughout the day during our classes.

I tried—tried so, so, so, so much—to pay attention and care. I tried to make myself like her more, think more of her, and care more about her.

But you can't just choose to love someone. Love both happens to you and you allow it to happen to you.

My heart was upset with me for loving Starry Knight, and my head was upset with me for not loving Gwen.

Finals were coming up. Martha was on a tirade about that. And Raiya was absent from class, so I didn't even have her to distract me from my quiet suffering.

Sure, I was all smiles on the outside, all high-fives and Game Pac championships and Tetris King. You fake it until you make it, when you're as concerned with success and looking successful as I have to be.

I called out from work, for the first (official) time. There was no monster to battle, and no evil to fight. I was just unable to do anything ... normal. My life could never be normal again.

Could it?

It was only when I caught sight of Mikey, leaning against Rachel's Café, that I felt some of my numbness leave me.

But that was, of course, only so more pain could come rushing in.

How was I going to tell him about Starry Knight? I wondered.

Fortunately, as he looked at me, I didn't think that was the topic he wanted to discuss.

"Hey, Dinger," he greeted me.

"Hey, Mikey." I waved back. "What's up?"

"Nothing. You?"

"Nothing."

We exchanged glances, and I sighed to myself. I didn't want to comfort him, but it was better than wallowing around in the filth of my self-pity party. It was the antithesis of my birthday party in my head, and I didn't like it. But either way, any party should be catered by Rachel, I reasoned with myself. "Gwen's coming soon," I said. "You want to join us?"

"You have little enough time for her," he rebuffed.

"Come on." I gestured inside. "You can help me fend off Letty and Grandpa Odd."

Nothing.

"My treat."

"Okay."

Well, that figures, I thought.

"I guess it's the least you could do, since you thought I was lying to you about Starry Knight, too." He came up beside me. "Didn't you?"

I'd wondered if he had noticed before. "I do owe you an apology for that," I agreed. "Boy, do I owe you one for that."

"You also owe me for not telling me about Dante."

"Dante? You're seriously calling him that?" I asked.

THE STARLIGHT CHRONICLES

"You call your parents by their first names," he argued.

"I know, but my parents have normal-sounding names. They aren't named after people who go through the Underworld."

"Huh?"

"You've never heard of *The Divine Comedy*?" I asked.

"No."

"It's a book we're going to have to read in AP Lit next year, if my sources are correct."

"I'm not taking AP Lit," Mikey reminded me.

I laughed. "Okay."

Normal started to creep back in after we started talking more. I didn't mention Starry Knight.

Mikey told me the few things he knew about his dad. None of them were surprising. He'd lived in Apollo City since marrying Mikey's mother, and then up and moved one day. Mikey didn't know why, other than it was because of his job.

I filled him in on what mostly had happened before. I didn't mention a few things about what happened the week Mikey had been transformed into a hideous monster by one of the Sinisters.

I did mention how the mayor had hired SWORD as "security consultants," and Mikey even laughed at my Mafia comparison.

We didn't talk about Starry Knight.

Gwen came, and while she was surprised and not entirely pleased with Mikey's company, she recognized that he needed us.

It worked out well anyway, since Gwen got another text from Laura, asking for some help with the cheer camp Via had planned for the summer. We graciously excused her as she ran off to save her friend.

I kissed her as she left, and even managed to make myself think I enjoyed it.

It was only when I looked up to see Aleia tapping on the windows outside that I suggested Mikey go and study for his finals, since he didn't want to fail.

Once he agreed and left, I hurried out.

Elysian was wrapped around Aleia's shoulders like a scarf, with a lazy snarl on his face.

"You're up," I said in greeting.

If I had had trouble sleeping for the past few days, Elysian had it worse. Although, I recalled, I wasn't sure if he needed it as much as I did.

"Hello, Hamilton," Aleia said with a small smile. "How are you feeling today?"

"Fine." I lied.

"I can come back a little later," she said. "If you feel it would be best."

"No, it's fine. I'm just tired. Still."

She nodded. "Walk with me, okay?"

We headed toward Shoreside Park. I wasn't sure I wanted to head for the woods, but we eventually sat down on some grass, letting Elysian roll around in it like some kind of scaly snake-dog.

"I'm going to be blunt," she warned.

"Okay."

"You made a mistake."

"A mistake? About what?" I asked.

"Starry Knight."

"What are you talking about now?" I grumbled. "I didn't think it was a problem. I don't care about her, and she doesn't care about me."

Aleia sighed. "I tried to tell you the other day," she said, pulling out her memory bubble. "She didn't make you fall."

"She admitted to me that it was all her fault."

"Well, that's how she would have seen it," Aleia said. "Look."

I pushed the small crystal ball away. "No thanks."

"You used your wish to come to Earth."

Shock slapped me out of my apathetic stupor. "What?!"

Aleia nodded. "You were in love with Starry Knight. The Sinisters were under her power, but something happened and her power was unable to stop them from escaping."

I remembered the vision of the crumbling star from my dream before. "So she decided to supernova?" I asked.

Aleia nodded. "You didn't want to leave her."

"I was in love with her." The pieces of the puzzle fit in together with blistering clarity. "She destroyed herself because of her duty, and I wished to go with her."

"You did more than that, and that's part of the reason she can't trust you anymore than you can trust her."

"What did I do?" I asked.

"You wished for them to go to Earth." She gazed out into the horizon. "Instead of going into the void, into the fires of Alküzor's Realm, she was saved by your wish." Aleia took hold of my hand. "You wanted to be with her, to the point where you risked everything to do so, even if it meant damnation."

"Well, that was stupid," I blurted, and she laughed. Probably more at my face than the actual situation, though. "But my wish is also what brought the Sinisters here."

"Yes."

"So it's my fault that I'm here?"

"Yes."

"But it's her fault …."

THE STARLIGHT CHRONICLES

For being the kind of person I would fall in love with.

The story managed to wrap itself around me more as Aleia continued. "You were reborn as a human, with no memory of your previous life, because of your wish."

"But I managed to bring everything here."

"Yes."

"You like saying that a lot."

"I know," she said, this time with a giggle.

"So what now?" I asked.

"That's up to you."

"Well, I broke it. I broke what was left between us," I said. Suddenly, the abyss of regret and loss came rushing up to me, and I felt my toes skim over the edge.

"You have both been broken," Aleia agreed. "But sometimes, because something has been broken, it becomes more precious as it is rebuilt."

"I don't think she'll want to rebuild it," I said, wondering if I really wanted to try myself. "Besides, I have Gwen now. And Starry Knight even told me herself, if I wanted to be free of her, all I had to do was fall in love with a human."

"It's not so easy to do that."

"It's got to be easier than making up with her," I insisted, standing up. "After everything that's happened, everything she's hidden from me, and everything before and after everything … I don't know if I can do it, let alone if I want to."

She shook her head.

"Besides," I added, "Gwen's perfect for me. She's good, constant, and helpful. Simple. She knows me."

"No, she doesn't," Elysian spoke up. "She doesn't know about you as Wingdinger."

"So what?" I bit back. "I don't know who Starry Knight is."

"We cannot choose for you, Hamilton," Aleia said. "But I wanted to give you the facts I had about what happened to you before."

"You could have told me this before," I accused.

Aleia sighed. "I am a fallen Star myself," she said. "And I am among the forgiven. But there are some things that we do not speak of. Some of us have taken vows, and we must keep them."

"Like Starry Knight?"

"Yes, for one."

I snorted. "That's the best thing about Gwen," I said. "She can be trusted, and she can trust me. She doesn't have to hide behind some sacred code or vow."

"There's more to it than that."

"I don't really want to hear it," I said. "Are we done? I want to be left alone for a bit."

THE STARLIGHT CHRONICLES

"I'll leave you to your thoughts," Aleia agreed. "Come, Elysian. Let's give him some space."

The tiny dragon flared his nostrils. "See you at the house, I guess."

I nodded. "I suppose."

I waited until they were out of sight before heading in the opposite direction.

I wandered through the city, aimlessly at first. The lost moonlight from previous days seemed to return as the day slipped away into the night.

The truth was, I admitted to myself, that I was afraid. I'd been afraid (and more than a bit) when Starry Knight called my bluff and attacked me.

She had already proven that she could hurt me, again and again, but there was something inside of me that kept looking for her, kept calling out for her.

I was afraid I would lose myself in her, and even if it worked out, it would be more than everything I could have ever hoped for. Many people who live through life hoping for the best and actually getting the best aren't that lucky, in my opinion. There had to be something more than even the best out there, and as much as I wanted it, I was also afraid of it.

There was also the terrifying idea that I just didn't want anyone to have that much power over me.

She understood what kept me from trusting her, and loving her without that—that was just impossible. Love without trust was a recipe for disaster. And I had enough disaster to worry about. We both did, I corrected myself. We had a mission, and it needed to get done.

But there was something even more important underneath all my objections; something that went to the core of my being, and as much as I knew I should be honest about it, I didn't want to be honest about it. I didn't want to look too closely because I knew looking at it would make me reconsider my stance.

In the meantime, finding myself once more at Rachel's, I had Gwen. I could love Gwen. I could trust Gwen.

I could even trust her with the secret identity of Wingdinger.

A small nudge inside my heart went off, but it was buried behind all the hurt and pain and restlessness. I would worry about it later, I decided. It wasn't like I was going to tell her now, anyway. It was hardly the time, I thought.

Trust was a tricky thing. I leaned against the brick of Rachel's, thinking about Adonaias. Even he had been hard to trust, I thought, remembering how I'd tried so desperately to run away from him before.

The door opened; I didn't see the slim, scrawny figure make her way over to me until she was beside me.

"You should go home," Raiya said in greeting.

"Nice to see you, too," I muttered back.

"Here." Raiya held out the cup in her hand.

THE STARLIGHT CHRONICLES

"What is it?" I asked.

"It's a mocha. Your favorite." She gave me a small smile before pressing the cup into my hand. "There's no use making Rachel wait to lock up, is there?"

I sighed, giving in. I reached out and took it.

And then I almost dropped it, as a slight whisper of a touch grazed against her hand. Instinctively, I felt her emotions, and I nearly flinched.

I felt a rush of concern and care, a gentle tenderness that radiated from her. It was strong enough that I didn't need to double-check it, even though I did. I stared at her back as she turned and headed back toward the door.

It was then that, for the first time, I realized how much she cared about me, and how just wrong it was that she should. In the blink of an eye, my relationship with Raiya—all her arguing, all her irritating habits, and all her teasing and prodding—was colored with new tones of friendship and hues of grace, contrasting sharply with the unfairness of my perception of her intent and unknown insecurity.

Pain kicked into my gut, and shame twisted around inside of me.

I'd been such a jerk to Raiya before. Maybe Rachel had had a point earlier, when she said I should be nicer to Raiya. "I'm sorry," I said. The words were out of my mouth before my pride could object. (Not that it mattered that much; there was too little of it left.)

Raiya paused, and then looked back at me. "For what?" she asked, her voice strangely hushed, like it was caught in her throat.

I suppose she would be surprised, I thought grimly. It wasn't often I said those words, let alone meant them. Still, my nerves were slightly grated. After all, did she really *not* realize how terrible I'd been to her?

It was probably annoyance that caused me to shift my focus. "For not inviting you to my birthday party," I told her. "You were right about the cake. The chocolate was my favorite."

She reached up, running a hand through the loosened locks of her hair as she avoided my gaze. I watched as her hand left her hair to reach down and grip the bracelet she wore around her wrist.

While I like to think she was still in a bit of shock at my apology, much went unsaid between us. Even from a distance, I could see trace amounts of her emotions wisp around her, but it was her thoughts that went completely undiscerned. And I was more interested in those.

Finally, she spoke again. "I forgive you."

I remembered how she'd responded to my teasing before; it spurned me how I'd been so proud and haughty, and she'd been so uncharacteristically vulnerable and hurt, yet she'd still been kind enough to think of my cake.

Anger at injustice burned inside of me. How could she just forgive me after I'd done so much to hurt her? *How does that happen at all?* There was a pause of silence before I felt my patience break and the question slipped out. "How can you forgive me, just like that?" I snapped, unintentionally appalled; after all, I'd intentionally hurt her, and I knew it.

"Well, it's just a party, for one thing, Hamilton," she said quietly, surprising me as much as I'd no doubt surprised her. "And for another, I know I have not exactly made life easy for you. If anything, I should be the one asking for forgiveness."

There was a strong, confusing amount of conviction in her statement; I didn't know what to say.

The clouds moved past the moon outside, and everything dimmed; but I felt her look at me, and *really* look at me. There was a moment where I knew she saw me, and had no illusions about who I was. I felt a mix of dread and shame, and hope; and in the next moment, I felt the world change as the moonlight reemerged.

I could almost see the cold darkness of her gaze, and I realized for the first time how she carried moonbeams in her eyes. I felt a rush of warmth and shame as I looked down at her mouth, shocked to wonder if it would surprise me as much as her eyes had.

"We open tomorrow at six. You can come back then."

I straightened, keeping a hold of the coffee she'd given me and putting myself to rights. As I headed out, I turned and said, "I hope you realize, this doesn't change anything. I'm still going to argue with you."

"Oh, I had a feeling that was the case," Raiya assured me with a small smile. "I would have been disappointed otherwise … Humdinger."

I walked out into the darkness, in some ways able to see my darkness much more clearly. I didn't think Raiya knew it at the time, but she'd given me a precious gift, even if it was a painful one. And it was excruciatingly painful—she'd allowed me to realize I could forgive Starry Knight for hurting me.

It would take time. It would not be easy. But I would do it. I didn't deserve forgiveness, not from Raiya or from Adonaias, and Starry Knight didn't deserve it from me.

I love you, Almeisan. I'm in love with you.

But I loved her. I loved being with her and fighting with her. I loved the dreams I had of her. I'd fallen in love with her on the other side of Time. I'd chosen to use my wish, the forbidden power of a Star, to be with her. There was a side of me that realized how foolish life had been before without her, and how there was no way I could go back to a life without her now.

And if I couldn't trust her, I would just have to trust in what I could for the moment: Adonaias' word, truth, and the everlasting.

THE STARLIGHT CHRONICLES

AUTHOR'S NOTE

Dear Reader,

If you're like me, you know there's something magical about beginnings. That's when we realize the deep, mystic movements of life, and understand how they are real, more real than anything else we can see or think or dream.

Of course, the middle part is just awful. (Most of the time.)

At least, I think the middle is the hardest part of the journey. Writing *Submerging* was just as important as *Slumbering* and *Calling*, but it was not as much fun. And I know why: Hard work has come, and it is time to dig deep, working through the responsibilities commitment brings.

And work is just awful. (Most of the time.)

But we need it. Case and point, the first thing God really did for man was to give him a job. We need work to grow, even as it is work.

In the believer's journey, belief and commitment are complemented by trust, love, and learning. This is where baptism is often brought up, to symbolize solidarity with the soul of Christ in his death and resurrection. To be submerged in the realities of our faith—the acknowledgement and disparity over the sin nature and its consequences, the death of the self, and the recreation only available through the Holy Spirt—is to be inspired to work toward a Christ-centered world, a world that often includes things like love and friendship alongside work, stress, and, much to Hamilton's dismay, even tests.

That is part of the reason this book's focus is on the idea of consecration and sanctification, symbolized through baptism and trial. Not only is his experience with Lady Time a symbol of his commitment, but it also becomes the source of truth. Later, his commitment to this truth is tested by Starry Knight's seeming betrayal.

Hamilton's experiences in this book are deeply rooted in my own shortcomings; in all my life, I doubt I've ever found anything as difficult as forgiving the people who have wronged me. And that's a strong tell about me, and my pride.

But Hamilton and I will go on, of course. Not easily, not painlessly, not quickly, not without rest. We'll keep on keeping on, until the very end.

These are the things you see when you no longer see the shore of your old home, where the emotions have worn off, and something deeper has grown. This is an ongoing cycle in the believer's life, though as unpleasant as it can be, it shows growth and maturity.

Thank you for making your way through another chapter in Hamilton's life and adventures. We hope to see you again soon in Book 4!

Until We Meet Again,

C. S. Johnson

AUTHOR'S ACKNOWLEDGEMENTS

EDITOR

Jennifer C. Sell

Jennifer Clark Sell is a professional book editor and proofreader. She works from her home in Southern California. With her years of professional and personal experience, she offers several quality packages for authors. Find her at https://www.facebook.com/JenniferSellEditingService.

Photo Credit: Savannah Sell

AUTHOR'S ACKNOWLEDGEMENTS

COVER ILLUSTRATOR

Amalia Chitulescu

 Amalia Iuliana Chitulescu is a digital artist from Campina, Romania. Raised in a small town, this self-taught artist has a technique which is delineated by the contrast between obscurity and enlightenment, using dark elements in a dreamy world. Her areas of expertise include the use of theatrical concepts to create a macabre and surrealistic world that still maintains a highly recognizable attachment to reality. Bridging a diaphanous environment with light elements, an eerie view, she creates a dream world of dark beauty, done with a blend of photography and digital painting. Find her at
https://www.facebook.com/Amalia.Chitulescu.Digital.Art

Photo Credit: Amalia Chitulescu

THE STARLIGHT CHRONICLES

SAMPLE READING

Chapter 1 *from*

REMEMBERING

BOOK FOUR of *THE STARLIGHT CHRONICLES*

C. S. Johnson

THE STARLIGHT CHRONICLES

☼1☼
Habits

In the chill of the early morning air, I was no longer my ordinary self.

I had transformed; I was ready to fight. Power flowed through my veins, purging all weakness from me, and giving me a rush similar to consuming twelve cups of coffee after being asleep for twenty years like Rip Van Winkle.

Energy inside of me twisted, building up and trickling the warmth of my supernatural energy down toward my fists. I lashed out punches, the heat of my power scorching the dew-covered grass.

"I have to be stronger!" A kick lashed out next, breaking hard against the trunk of a tree. I used it to propel myself up the trunk and duck around the branches.

It's perfect. "Okay, Hamilton," I murmured to myself. "Time to fly."

I glanced down just in time to regret it. The ground was a good eighteen to twenty feet away. A lump coagulated in my throat; I had severe doubt my wings would hold me. They were, nearly a year after accepting my destiny as an *Astroneshama*, or Starlight Warrior, still rather flimsy and small. Especially when I compared them to Starry Knight's.

My so-called co-defender might've had a zero personality, but she sure had nice wings. Starry Knight's wings were like angel wings—white, long, graceful, and strong.

Meanwhile, mine were stubby and dark, with a blood-red base and fiery red tips.

If I didn't hate Starry Knight, I might've admired her.

There was a loud *snap*, and quickly I was called back to reality. Holding my breath, my eyes squeezed shut as I jumped, just as the tree began to tilt.

And then I hit the ground, simultaneously moments and seconds later.

I tried to keep my yelp in, but an awkward "Ow … " escaped as I landed hard; first on my feet, and then on my butt.

"Look at the bright side. No dog poo or demon blood this time."

I groaned at the sound of that voice. If it weren't for the pain screaming at me from my legs, I would've screamed in frustration at the unwelcome interruption of my training session.

But then Elysian—my changeling dragon/part-time mentor/roommate—never did seem to listen to me, screaming or not.

"You'll never learn how to fly like that, kid," Elysian asserted as he appeared by my side.

"What're you doing here?" I was slightly surprised to see Elysian transformed into his life-size dragon self.

"I can tell when you transform, idiot." Elysian frowned. "I'm your mentor, and we are connected by a bond not easily broken."

"Uh-huh, right." I rolled my eyes. "You could tell I transformed, but not that it was for practice? That bond we have ... it's not by chance a government savings bond, is it?"

"No, but I didn't sense any trouble, either, so I thought you might be trying to show off." He narrowed his gaze. "Or maybe you were telling that girlfriend of yours about your secret."

I sighed. "I wasn't going to tell Gwen."

"You've thought about it."

"Of course I've thought about it," I snapped. "But I haven't done it. And every time I think of it ... I don't know, I just don't want to." Gwen Kessler was a woman worthy enough to keep a secret like my superhero identity. But somehow the timing never seemed quite right.

After nearly eight months of dating her, I was beginning to wonder if there ever really *was* a right time.

Elysian's *hurmph* brought me back to our conversation. "Good. We don't need her being a liability."

Seeing him too happy with my decision made me argue against it. "Hey, don't be like that. Mikey's been doing okay with keeping the secret."

"Yeah, sure. You say that while he's writing a blog about it."

"He doesn't mention *Hamilton Dinger*. Just *Wingdinger*," I argued. "There's a big difference between my real name and my superhero name."

That was true on many levels. Hamilton likely wouldn't have acknowledged Wingdinger at all, unless it was to make fun of him. Especially if it had been a year ago, when the meteorite struck Apollo City and unleashed a whirlwind of evil.

"You're sure your friend wouldn't accidentally let it slip?"

"Not intentionally." I shrugged and sighed, tired of this argument with Elysian. It wasn't the first time he'd brought it up, and it wasn't the last time I would fall for it. "This is so hard sometimes."

"It doesn't help that you haven't been sleeping well. And how the last few attacks have been … complicated."

"You don't need to remind me."

The last several attacks—including one at Rachel's wedding this past summer—were easy, but my abhorrence for Starry Knight's presence left me angry and tasting bile by the end of our battles. More than once, Elysian had caught me working out my frustrations by training harder. Or yelling out tirades when my parents and brother were conveniently out of the house. Or something else satisfyingly destructive.

Elysian slinked back into his smaller dragon self. "I know you're frustrated by this whole situation. But you have to realize, this is not just about *physical* force. Waking up this early is not helping you work through your heart issues."

I snorted disdainfully. "I happen to like practicing at this time of day."

"I'd laugh if I was sure I'd be able to stop."

"Shut up," I growled. "I like the colder morning air. And practically no one is up yet."

"I guess you must, because you've been getting up early for weeks now."

"You say that like it's a bad thing. I have a lot on my plate right now, with Gwen and the SATs coming up this year."

"I don't think those are the reasons you've been unable to sleep well," Elysian said. "And it's not the reason you haven't been fighting well, either."

"What do you mean? I've been just fine when it comes to fighting off evil," I snapped.

"There will still be battles of the heart you must face, not just the ones you can dress up as Wingdinger and go around shooting energy beams or waving your sword around."

For a long moment, I said nothing. I knew all too well of the "battles of the heart" Elysian was talking about.

The very last thing I wanted to do, however, was talk about it. Especially with Elysian. Especially when he was right. "So … I'm not going to get stronger by practicing like this?" I asked, deciding to play the fool.

He sighed, snarling out a small puff of smoke. "You still don't get what I mean, do you?"

"Does it really matter?" I muttered back.

Elysian huffed and crossed his small dragon arms. "You'll see progress in how you act and in what you say. You won't find a very good view of the complete picture this side of the River Veil, but you need to be aware of what is really happening before you can do anything."

I used to never care about the stuff he talked about. It'd largely been like that ever since we met. When I didn't want to hear anything about his other worldly realm, he would more or less blackmail me into doing this superhero stuff anyway, by saying if I didn't protect the world or whatever, Gwen and all my friends would die or get their souls stolen.

But even though I laughed it off at first, I finally came around to see it was true. I'd seen the monsters attack, and how the demons ravenously devoured the souls of their victims and forced them into a coma-like state. And I'd even seen the power of Time and all the beauty and ugly it carried inside of it.

Dubbed the "sleeping sickness" by the delusionary media, the demon epidemic in the city had been dismissed by most of the mainstream outlets as hardly "newsworthy." Since the attacks were also casually linked to foreign and domestic bioterrorism at one time, I was willing to bet they'd been paid off. Although SWORD, the Special World Operations and Research Division, also seemed to be a likely candidate for providing the right kind of incentive for their silence.

The rest of the world thought it just miraculously cured itself. But I knew the only known cure for the "sleeping sickness" was to kill the demon, which really only me and my

THE STARLIGHT CHRONICLES

comrades—Elysian, Aleia, and Starry Knight—knew how to do.

Thinking of Starry Knight burned pure pain into my already raw heart. I knocked out another punch, hitting a nearby tree hard enough to leave significant damage. The forestry service would think Smokey went postal.

"Hey!" Elysian flinched. "Watch what you're doing. You almost hit me."

"Sorry. Trying to work out some of my extra energy," I murmured back, only somewhat apologetic. In truth, I felt worse for the tree than I did for Elysian, but I also felt sorrier for myself than anything.

I had accepted the truth about my destiny, and I had even joined in the fight to stop evil, save the world, and sacrifice for the good. But it didn't seem to offer much in return.

"I doubt that," Elysian countered. "You haven't slept well in weeks now, remember? You just admitted that not five minutes ago."

Another reason for me to hate him. He loved to remind me of everything I wanted to forget.

"Aren't you supposed to wear lipstick if you're going to act like my mother?" I retorted. I caught sight of the Apollo Time Tower, the only building visible from practically anywhere in the city, in the distance. It was getting close to six in the morning. "I'm going to Rachel's for coffee."

Elysian folded back his wings and curled up in the hood of my winter jacket. "Do you really think it's a good idea if you can't sleep? Maybe you should take the day off."

"I'll need energy to get through the day, Elysian. School started again last month, remember?" I rolled my eyes. "And it's not like I'm actually going to sleep if I take the day off."

"I think you should."

"*I* don't. The last thing I want to do is to be left alone with my thoughts all day long."

"Are you still afraid of thinking about Starry Knight?"

Murderous thoughts and various vile threats instantly consumed me. I choked him around his small, scaly neck and spat out, "*Don't* say her name in front of me."

Elysian spit out a flame in response, singeing my arm. I allowed it to hit me, even though it stung. The fire on my wrist felt better than the ache in my chest. "You know, you've always needed to watch your emotions," he told me. "But I think, in this case, ignoring them isn't working any better."

"I'll work on thinking of another plan, then," I shot back. "Until then, this is the best one I've got. Deal with it before I have to choke you again. Or before I decide to use my sword on you."

"That's part of the reason you're having issues, you know."

"What?"

"Your sword."

"Nothing's wrong with my sword," I muttered.

"No, there's something wrong with *you*."

"What's wrong with me?" I had to watch the volume of my voice, as I almost found myself hollering loud enough to wake the dead.

"You see your sword as a weapon."

"Swords *are* weapons."

"They can be used to protect people."

"They are used to harm the enemy," I argued.

"You're too keen on revenge and causing the Sinisters pain. You haven't been doing that good of a job lately because of that." Elysian's tail wrapped around my arm, almost comfortingly. "Hurt people hurt people," he told me, "and you are hurting people with your pain."

"Just stuff it." I bristled at his compassion. I'd take his rebuke over his pity any day. "I guess you would know," I finally replied. "Since you're a hypocrite who couldn't get past his own pain at being tricked into committing crimes for his brother."

Elysian frowned at me. "Alright, alright. Fine, I don't want to talk about that, either. Let's just go, okay?" He sighed wearily before curling around my neck. I didn't say anything, and I never would, but I was grateful he didn't get too upset at me for my temper. It was a strange way of being loyal, and I needed it.

As we walked in preferable silence, I glanced at the moon, the small crescent still out and blazing in the late October sky like a warped sword.

The bubbling swirl of colors just hinting at the horizon made me recall another time when a blazing light had scratched up the sky.

It was little over a year, I thought, since the meteorite came crashing into Apollo City. The meteorite that carried the Seven Deadly Sinisters and their leader, Orpheus, right into my hometown.

A grim smile formed on my face. If only that was all it had done, I thought.

It wasn't the first time I'd thought that. I was with Gwen when the meteorite hit, and as the city reeled from its blow, and I found out—albeit gradually—I had supernatural powers.

In addition, there was the matter of everything else that came right along with it: A super-irritating, familiar-like dragon, who could morph into different reptiles; dangerous enemies, who were often just as focused on fighting with each other as they were on attacking the humans of Apollo City; and an eternal overlord, too powerful and humble for me to properly contemplate, who called me out of my reluctance to face a destiny greater than I could ever imagine.

And a maddening, yet stunning, archer-girl who pushed me away even as she pulled me in, the girl I loved with a depth that made me wonder how life could go on without her—

even though I'd yet to recall her name—even as she was the girl who resided right next to the hatred in my heart.

The one who had betrayed me in order to save me.

My fist clenched as I un-transformed from my superhero self.

I just had to become stronger, I decided. I could get rid of the Sinisters, and I would never have to worry about Starry Knight again. I could focus on work and school and Gwen and going to college and getting my law degree and getting a job and then traveling the world and running for president.

I didn't need to fall in love.

Just like any normal kid.

333

THE STARLIGHT CHRONICLES

Thank you for reading! Please leave a review for this book and check out C. S. Johnson on Amazon for other books and updates!

Made in the USA
Columbia, SC
22 September 2017